MW00897014

The World of Imagination

The Hifdh Students of MCC Academy

TABLE OF CONTENTS

FOREWORD

A NOTE FROM THE TEACHER

In the name of Allah, the Most Gracious, the Most Merciful

Dear Reader,

This book is the culmination of the creativity, imagination, and dedication of an exceptional group of highly talented young authors.

As their teacher, I have been honored with the opportunity to work very closely with these unique individuals. The most incredible thing about this particularly hardworking group of authors is that every single one of them has undertaken the noble task of becoming guardians of the Holy Qur'an. *Hifdh-ul-Qur'an* refers to the memorization of the Qur'an, the final book sent by Allah (the Most Exalted) to guide humanity towards the truth of Islam. The mind and heart of a *hifdh* student are extremely unique, as they absorb the *noor* (spiritual light) and blessings of Allah's words day in and day out.

Can you imagine the extraordinary potential of such an individual?

Writing is a remarkably powerful skill and tool. It allows us to express ourselves in unique ways; it helps us effectively spread knowledge and communicate amazing ideas; and it enables us to journey deep into the caverns of our hearts and minds. Writing truly has the ability to change the world. And indeed, we have seen countless examples throughout history in which a single word written by the pen has been enough to move mountains.

Each of these young authors has now completed a journey that was both arduous and highly rewarding. However, I have high hopes that this is only the beginning of their journeys, not only as writers, but also as Muslims who strive towards excellence and beauty in everything they do. Each of these precious children will always have a very special place in my heart, and I have no doubt that they will go on to do great things and make a positive impact on the world, Insha'Allah.

Sincerely,

Safa S.

August 2024 / Safar 1446 A.H.

ABOUT THE AUTHOR
AISHA HUSENI

Aisha Huseni is in 6th grade at MCC Academy. She wrote this story for those who think that they can't do big things and change the world. Her most favorite sports are badminton and soccer. Her hobbies are sleeping and sketching.

For A.S, my very cool classmate who inspired me to make this story.

— A.H

The Midnight Mission: Saving Home

By Aisha Huseni

E lara and her friends were sent on adventure to find a way to save their hometown, a land filled with courageous warriors and heroes. Millions and millions of heroes were willing to save their beautiful hometown. Since there were so many others willing to do this, why was it them who had to go on this quest?

***

Chapter 1: A Normal Beginning

The day had started just like any other, the sun was shining brightly and the birds were chirping. This was the land of important heroes who had saved their land or done the impossible. Elara was just a kid—a normal, ordinary kid.

The crowds of people in the village were followed with the chatter of their daily lives. People were walking to shops and others were hanging around the lake.

Elara was set for the day, with her backpack on and her mind set on what she planned on doing today. She made her way to school and looked around, there was Lyla and Finn.

"Greetings to you..." Elara said pointing to Finn then Lyla "and you."

This was an inside joke; it was made to mock the professor's voice. He would always say it when he thought they would get into trouble soon, and he was almost always right.

"What? Do you think we're going to get into trouble today?" Finn chuckled, "You could be right, y'know?"

"I think Finn's the one who plans on doing that." Lyla jested.

Finn replied shortly after realizing what Lyla said "No, not me!"

Lyla was staring at Finn with the "You sure?" face and Finn was looking at Lyla with the "Yes, I'm sure." face.

Elara finally decided to break the silence and interrupted their staring contest: "Whatever, we're going to be late for class!" then ran away from them to get to class on time.

The first bell had rung and they all rushed to class, hoping they would be on time.

They made it.

***

Chapter 2: The Start of Something Big

The day was going great—almost too great. Normally, Elara would have gotten in trouble for talking or being late; today wasn't like that. But why focus on that? Today was terrific, and Elara wasn't going to make this day go to waste, even though it was weird.

Elara whispered to Lyla, "Today feels different...in a good way though."

Lyla nodded, "Yeah, I know, almost too good to be true. Am I right?"

Finn was too busy talking to his other friend, Aric, to notice the other two girls talking. Lyla and Elara didn't really talk to Aric; he wasn't bad, annoying, or anything; he just didn't talk much and looked serious most of the time. Finn did look quite happy talking to a boy his age that he could relate to. I mean, who wouldn't?

The lesson had continued with the whispering of the students in the background, almost no one was paying attention. Either everybody was feeling the way Lyla and Elara were feeling, or the lesson was just plain boring.

After the lesson was over, the students made their way to each of their classes and had eventually made it to lunch, still feeling a bit of unease. Elara had bought lunch and so did Lyla and Finn. Finn had decided to call Aric over since he would normally sit by himself, he had also bought lunch.

"Are you guys feeling weird or is it just me?" Elara finally blurted out to Finn and Aric since Lyla had said she felt the same way.

Finn had replied, "Nah, I feel great." looking at Aric, waiting for his answer.

"I feel alright." Aric had said, hoping that his answer would be enough.

Elara looked at both of them and finally added, "Guess it's just me and Lyla then."

***

Chapter 3: A Questioning Day

Lyla was oddly quiet the whole time. That wasn't like her; she would normally be the one talking and starting the conversation. Today was most definitely weird and different.

Elara had decided to change the conversation since no one else wanted to.

"So, what's up? Do you guys have any plans for the weekend?" Elara said, sounding enthusiastic.

"Well, no, not really." Lyla finally decided to reply.

"Yeah, no, I don't have any plans either." Finn added

Aric had just nodded in agreement, which meant that he probably didn't have any plans either.

Elara sighed, "Today just feels weird... and boring. None of you guys are saying anything."

"Yeah, I just noticed how weird today is." Finn replied.

"Told you." Lyla responded.

"Yeah, yeah, whatever." Finn retorted.

Elara and her friends all felt the same way; at least she knew they all noticed that today was strange and she wasn't alone.

"Well, what do we do now?" Lyla questioned.

"Sit in silence for the rest of the day? I don't know." Finn answered.

Aric, Lyla, and Elara looked at each other and looked back at Finn.

"I want to get to the bottom of this. Why is today like this? It feels strange. and I feel like whatever is coming is not good." Elara finally decided to say.

"And how are we going to do that?" Lyla continued.

After a long pause, Elara finally answered, "I don't know... any ideas?"

Nobody had answered; what were they supposed to do? They had no idea how they would "find out what's going on.".

"Hey, isn't that the principal?" Aric pointed at the principal, who was walking in the hallways.

This was the only time Aric had spoken in the conversation. They all turned their heads and looked the principal straight in the eye. What is he doing here?

***

Chapter 4: Strange Things

Today was getting stranger and stranger. First, they didn't get in trouble; it's like the teachers were too busy doing something to notice what they were doing. The principal had come here to do something too; it had to be something serious.

"Let's go do some questioning." Lyla said.

Elara turned her head back to look at Lyla and said, "I agree, let's go." She got up and looked at Finn and Aric, hoping they would come too.

"You guys are seriously going.?" Finn questioned.

"What does it look like?" Elara asked sarcastically.

Finn and Aric got up, and then Finn spoke up, "Looks like we're going to interrogate the principal."

Elara, Lyla, and Aric had never talked to the principal before, so they don't exactly know how he is.

Except for Finn.

Finn had been in the principal's office lots of times before. Why? Because he would joke around a bit too much sometimes.

"Listen, the principal is a serious guy, but he wouldn't stress over something small." Finn explained, "So, that means that whatever is going on is something bad. Considering how stressed he looks right now."

"That doesn't sound too good." Lyla added.

Elara finally spoke: "Does he get mad easily when he's stressed?"

"This is not looking too good for us right now, but yes, he sort of does." Finn admitted.

This wasn't good; all of them wanted to know what was going on but didn't want to upset the principal either. What were they going to say and do?

***

Chapter 5: Disaster Strikes

"Well, I think we should just take it slow, like..." Lyla decided and paused for a moment, then continued, "Like, ask him how his day is going.?"

"That's the best idea we've got so far, so I guess we just go with that?" Finn stated this and looked at Elara for approval of it.

"I agree; let's do the idea Lyla said." Aric added.

Elara nodded. "Okay, since that's the best idea we have and you all agree with it, it's good."

They all walked up to the scary, not-so-good-looking principal. The three of them were nervous and felt their tongues getting twisted up, like they were forgetting how to speak. Finn was the only one who was not worried about this. He was completely care-free.

Elara nudged Finn to get his attention while walking up to the principal. "You talking?" Elara managed to say it after finding the right words.

"Heck no! You talk!" Finn exclaimed in a whisper.

"You're the only one who can talk right now! None of us have ever talked to the principal before." Elara whispered back.

"Fine," Finn muttered.

They all walked to the principal until they were face-to-face with him.

Finn decided to speak first: "Well, Mr. Principal, we have met again." Finn said with a mocking grin on his face.

"Not now, Finn; I'm busy." The principal already sounded irritated.

"With what..?" Finn questioned.

The principal sighed then said, "Look, something is going on, but it's not something you should worry about."

Finn looked at Elara and the others, wondering if he should keep going with this. Elara nodded, so he kept going.

"C'mon, we need to know!" Finn begged the principal.

When the principal was just about to answer, something happened—something unexpected.

The lights had gone out.

Complete.

Total.

Darkness.

***

Chapter 6: Chaos

The lights were out, no sound of anything but breathing.

The principal yelled so everyone could hear, "Everyone come by the lockers!" hoping everyone would be able to hear him, he took out a flashlight from his bag.

Elara and her friends all had the same thoughts, "What? Was this planned? There's no way the principal keeps a flashlight in his pockets 24\7." The principal had turned on the flashlight so they could see.

Elara checked out the window. It wasn't only the school with the lights gone...it was..the world.

"Is this something universal!? Why didn't anyone tell us about this!? We deserve to know!" Elara spoke up.

"We were not sure if it was true..and we didn't want to worry the students." The principal replied.

"Well now we know. But what're we going to do now?" Lyla asked, she was trying her best to be calm but she was really frightened.

Aric decided to talk, "Not only that but if you told us we would all have flashlights and be more safe than we are now. But guess what? You decided not to tell us because of a reason that doesn't even make sense!"

Elara, Finn, and Lyla were surprised that Aric spoke up like that but there were bigger things to worry about right now.

The principal answered, "There is nothing we can do now, but we have the heroes still here, they'll figure it out."

"If they could figure it out, they would've done it by now!" Finn stated.

All the other students and teachers gathered together, making sure no one got left behind.

Everyone knew what Finn said was right, even the principal but he wasn't going to admit it.

"Anyone got a flashlight?" Aric asked the crowd hoping some of them would have it.

A couple of students had it, so Aric decided to be the leader and make them into groups while the principal was just standing there clueless.

None of them noticed Aric's leadership qualities, but now they did, it was great.

"Wow, Aric! Nice job, you really know what you're doing, huh?" Finn chuckled, he was really looking at the bright side of things, and it was helping.

"Yeah, good job Aric!" Elara smiled, Finn's "bright side" was honestly making everyone feel calmer and better, and so did Aric's leadership.

"Didn't know you had it in you, but good job." Lyla managed to sneak in a smile.

Aric just smiled at the compliments but the others knew he meant it as a thank you.

The principal was helping Aric with the grouping and getting all of them to safe areas since they didn't know what could happen in the dark.

What exactly was going on? They still wanted to know the whole story. What was the principal hiding? They wanted to know everything, not a single detail was supposed to be missed.

***

Chapter 7: Questions Answered

"Explain." Aric demanded the principal.

"Right, right." The principal took a deep breath then continued, "Well, to start off with, we have been threatened, or not exactly us..the heroes."

"By who?" Lyla interrogated.

"Not sure, but i think that it's the villains they have already defeated coming together, creating a strong force that we are not so sure the heroes can defeat."

Aric continued, "That means that the villains already know who they're dealing with, which also means that they know their weaknesses."

Aric looked like the one with his brain working, the rest of them were either terrified or didn't know what to say.

Elara tried to calm herself down and spoke, "Then we need new heroes, heroes who have not been noticed yet."

"Good thinking Elara, we need heroes they aren't expecting." Lyla got on.

"And that is...?" The principal asked.

All of them were silent knowing they all were thinking the same thing.

Elara spoke with a determined voice,

"Us."

***

Chapter 8: New Heroes

The principal stared at them with no reason to think they could be heroes.

"You're just kids." The principal stated.

"Yeah we need kids so that they don't expect it at all." Lyla answered.

"Plus, we have everything we need to be a good team. Aric's leadership, Elara's bravery and courage, Lyla's calmness and strategies, and my...?" Finn proclaimed.

Lyla was the only one who noticed that Finn didn't think he was important for them to save the world so she gave a reason.

"Finn, your brightside is very useful when we're going through something, you're just as important as any of us." Lyla added.

Finn just smiled at the compliment which he didn't think was true.

The principal interrupted and replied, "You guys could be put in danger! We should let the professional's deal with it."

"And how far have they gone with it? If we don't do it then there's no hope!" Finn argued.

The principal was actually somewhat considering what the kids said.

"It's dangerous." The principal added hoping they would look into it as well.

"We know. But we also know that we can do it." Aric figured.

And so, he agreed. These kids would be put in danger but they were determined and had the courage to do it.

"Are you sure you can do it?" The principal asked for the last time.

"When do we leave?" Elara said, her voice filled with determination.

The other three stood next to her, staring at the principal with the same look on their faces, their bravery showing.

The principal decided,

"First thing tomorrow."

***

Chapter 9: A New Journey

The kids had packed up the essentials, snacks, flashlights, first aid kits, sweaters, and a bunch of more things since they all had a backpack of their own.

The principal had a thought come to his head: "Would your parents be okay with this?"

"We won't be gone for long, and I don't think they'll notice in the dark anyway." Elara guessed.

"Yeah, what we really need to know is where to start." Aric presumed.

"I think I know... an artifact has been stolen." The principal mentioned but got cut off.

"Wait, we've learned of an artifact that brings eternal darkness when out of its cage." Lyla noticed.

"We have?" Finn asked, clueless about the things they've learned.

"Yes, we have. I think it was called something like "The Moonlight Sword," right?" Elara realized, looking at Lyla.

"Yeah, that!" Lyla approved.

The principal added, "And I thought you kids didn't pay attention!" with a chuckle.

"Well, I sure don't." Finn replied.

"Yeah, we can tell." Lyla snorted.

"Well, then it looks like you kids know what you're doing." The principal questioned.

"Well, no. Not yet; we need to know what artifact can bring light back so we can look for that." Elara answered.

The principal nodded. "I think I know; there is a book for it, "The Book of Wisdom." It will be located in the artifact museum where all of the prized possessions of the heroes are."

"So we just have to go there?" Finn asked, finding it to be easy.

"Yes, a heavily guarded museum." Aric added.

"It would be heavily guarded, considering they're the artifacts the heroes worked hard to get." Lyla replied, not thinking of this as easy at all.

"But what about the guards? Would they still think of us as thieves?" Finn questioned.

"Yes, they most definitely would. You guys can still back out of this if-" The principal got cut off by Elara.

"We will do and succeed on this quest." Elara declared.

The principal nodded and discussed the plan with them. Then off they went to become the new heroes of their village.

***

Chapter 10: The Museum

All of them had flashlights in their hands and walked through the darkness. It was very quiet, and the only sounds there were the sounds of their footsteps and the branches on the grass cracking.

"So how long until we get there?" Finn asked for the fifth time on this trip.

"We don't know Finn; we just have to keep walking on this path until we see the sign." Lyla disclosed.

"How does this "sign" look exactly?" Finn quizzed.

"Well, we will know it when we see it." Lyla clarified.

Finn then stopped where he was standing. "And does this sign maybe look like that?" he said, pointing to a sign that was pointing towards a large building, typically a museum.

"This is it." Aric recognized.

"We're here." Lyla added.

Elara whispered to them, "Keep your voices low; we don't want the security to hear or see us."

"Considering villains are on the loose, this place will be guarded completely." Lyla figured.

"How will we get in then?" Finn adjured.

"The windows," Aric decided, "that's the only way."

"So we break the windows or..." Finn asked, trying not to sound stupid.

"Yes, we break the windows." Elara conceded.

Elara went and grabbed a stone from the path they were walking on and threw it at the window; the others followed.

A loud smash was heard, and the glass cracked. The four jumped in and hid in a spot with their flashlights off for a couple of minutes just to make sure no one heard it.

"What now?" Lyla asked.

"We have to find the book." Aric revealed.

"Cmon, I think it's safe for us to go." Elara said, turning her flashlight back on. The rest of them turned them back on as well.

They continued the quest and left to go find where the book was being kept.

***

Chapter 11: Seek

They made their way to a giant hall with white walls and was shaped sort-of like an octagon. It was lit up with not lights but something more powerful, which wasn't affected by the darkness. There was shattered glass on the floor from someone who had broken in.

"Someone's been here," Elara noted.

All four of them agreed and nodded.

"Should we split up?" Lyla asked, thinking it was a good idea.

Aric decided, "Yeah, that will make us find the book faster."

So the four of them split up. Elara was going straight towards the ancient artifact section but didn't know since she had not seen the sign. Aric was going towards the Greek statues, and Finn was going towards the food court. Lyla decided to follow where Elara was going since she had seen the sign.

Finn was going straight to the food court; there wasn't anyone there because of the darkness. Also, this place was guarded since the heroes were threatened by the villains. It wasn't normally like this; the place was normally very crowded. I guess they had to fully shut it down because of the villains.

Aric had bumped into a statue first and quickly found out that he was by the Greek statues; he had bumped into a statue of Dionysis.

Lyla and Elara had found each other and were trying to find the book together.

"Elara?" Lyla whispered to Elara.

"Yeah?" Elara whispered back.

"I think we should hide, like right now." Lyla mumbled worriedly.

"Yeah, let's go." Elara motioned for Lyla to come behind one of the podiums.

One of the guards walked past them, trying to find out who broke the glass. They had found out.

"It looks like we've got company." Elara said it in the faintest whisper.

Lyla nodded. "This isn't looking good."

Elara was panicking. "It most definitely isn't; I hope Finn and Aric are okay."

Meanwhile, Finn had found a vending machine and was trying to get something out of it. Although it was not working at all, Finn was hungry and wanted to have a snack. Aric, on the other hand, was trying to find the others because he had seen the security come in.

"Where are they?" Aric mumbled to himself, checking every hallway.

Finn heard footsteps and did the dumbest thing ever: he spoke.

"Who's there?" Finn tensed.

Nobody had spoken, but the footsteps had gotten louder, meaning that whoever was coming was super close.

"Finn, is that you?" Aric said hesitantly.

Finn calmed down. "Yeah, it's me." Then added, "Surprise?"

Aric gave a quick smile and then said, "I heard the guards; I think they are going towards Elara and Lyla."

"Do you think they have bumped into each other?" Finn asked.

Aric shrugged. "I hope so. I think we shouldn't split up. It'll make it harder to find each other."

"Agreed. Let's go that way; I saw Elara going there."
Finn pointed.

Aric nodded.

So the two of them went to find Elara and Lyla being
the quietest they could be.

***

Chapter 12: Finding the Book

They had made it to the podiums with artifacts and
hid behind one of them just to make sure no one was
there.

Finn turned his head around just to see Elara and Lyla
on the podium next to them.

Finn nudged Aric's shoulder and pointed to Elara and
Lyla.

"What?" Aric asked, then looked towards Finn and
saw Elara and Lyla behind him.

Elara broke the silence. "Well, the book has to be
somewhere over here, right?"

"Yeah, it looks like most artifacts are here." Aric
agreed.

"What are we waiting for then?" Finn questioned.

"Didn't you see the security? Do you know which way
they went?" Lyla added.

"I say we go that way. Since all the powerful artifacts are there, Elara advised.

The three of them nodded, and so they went that way. The hallways were empty, so the four of them looked at all the artifacts to see where this book was, basically splitting up.

Elara's eyes widened at the sight; there was the book.

It was a purple book with a sparkling golden design. The book was thick and had hundreds of pages.

Elara smiled. "Guys, we found it."

The other three of them walked to Elara.

"It's beautiful." Lyla was loving the beautiful, sparkling book.

"Cool." Finn said, trying to sound as if he didn't care but was actually full of excitement to finally have the book in their sight.

Aric praised, "I have no words to describe this. It's amazing, and we did it."

"Yeah, us. A group of 14-year-olds." Finn boasted.

"Well, take it, Elara." Lyla finally said, not wanting to wait longer.

Elara reached for the book and grabbed it.

Wrong move.

***

Chapter 13: Close to Saving the World

A bell had rung, and security was rushing towards them. The four of them stood there, not being able to move because of the shock and how loud the beeping was.

"There they are!" One of the security guards said as he ran towards them.

"We don't mean any harm! We're here to save the world, or at least bring the light back." Finn had managed to get out.

"We're not going to believe a lie like that; that book is very powerful; it can lead to something horrible if in the wrong hands!" Another guard said.

"We aren't the wrong hands, though! We only want the light to return, and we will return the book right after." Aric insisted.

The guard sighed. "How did you kids get here in the first place?"

"You need to hire better guards," Finn blurted, but stopped himself from saying anything else.

"We'll see." The guard replied.

"Well? Can we save the world now?" Finn asked for the last time.

"I can't believe anything like that unless the heroes say it." The guard told them, 'It's an order."

"We aren't lying," Elara said, not being able to hide her resentment.

"This is it? Do you expect us to leave after coming such a long way?" Aric said, looking directly at the guards.

"Yeah, there is no way we're leaving now." Lyla agreed, looking at Finn to see what he would say.

Finn questioned, "Guess we'll be stuck in this darkness forever then?"

"You kids probably have no idea what you're doing anyway." The guard told them.

"We traveled all the way from our village to this museum on foot in the darkness, and you still think we don't know what we're doing?" Finn inquired.

"We can't trust you guys." The guard spoke.

Elara decided, "Who's your boss? Is there anyone we could speak to about this?"

The guard moved aside for their boss to come into sight. He looked like a serious guy with a face that basically said, "Don't mess with me.".

"What are your plans for the book, and why did you kids get sent to get it?" The boss said in a demanding tone.

"Well, you should know that the heroes aren't doing too well right now." Finn stated.

The boss nodded.

Elara then added, "So, we decided that we needed new heroes,"

"and that those heroes would be us." Lyla spoke.

"We need the book for that, so if you don't mind, could you hand us it?" Aric said in an almost threatening tone.

The boss decided, "You will have to return this artifact by tomorrow, no longer."

"Yeah, we will." Finn agreed.

"I'm not giving you a choice; if this book isn't back, I'll have a whole army sent looking for you kids." The boss said strictly.

The 14-year-olds nodded.

Now going back to the school felt amazing, they had basically won the titles of being heroes. Elara had the book in her hands, the heavy book bringing light to them with its gold decorated cover.

***

Chapter 14: An Almost Perfect Ending

Going back to the school took very long, but it was so worth it. Everyone was surprised when they saw the kids with the book, they were probably doubting them.

It was quite hard to ignore them since the book had such a strong light that you would think the darkness had gone.

"You kids got it?!" The principal was amazed.

"Obviously, did you think we wouldn't?" Finn asked with a laugh.

The four of them and the principal had a quick laugh.

"Well, we've got ourselves a new group of heroes, then?" The principal smiled.

The four of them looked at each other and then nodded.

"The darkness isn't gone yet, so how-?" The principal was going to ask but realized they had not thought of how the darkness would leave.

"I think there should be a page in the book with how to do that." Lyla said certainly.

"I already checked... We need the "Moonlight Sword"." Elara told Lyla.

"Then we have a new quest; let's go get this "Moonlight Sword"." Finn declared.

"I'm fine with that." Aric replied, looking at the others, ready to face anything.

The four of them had a new quest to take care of. They were going to defeat the villains and were ready to face anything and everything to save their homeland.

About the Author
Hafidh Aariz Rangoonwala

Aariz Rangoonwala is a 6th grader at MCC Academy. He has an achievement of being a Hafidh of the Quran and has four siblings including himself, and he also has both his parents. One of his favorite sports is basketball, and he likes soccer a little. Some hobbies Aariz enjoys are bicycle riding, and taking a jog. He is quite interested in how the universe works and how small we are compared to other planets, asteroids, black holes, etc. Aariz wants to help people who are suffering around the world, especially the people in Gaza.

Dedicated to Ms. Safa. Ms. Safa is the reason that I was able to create this story. She helped me with making the story and all the other problems that were coming my way. May Allah (SWT) bless her and her family.

—A.R.

THE WORLD THAT LOST LAND

BY HAFIDH AARIZ RANGOONWALA

Once upon a time, I was living with my family in Norway. Right now, it is the year 2050. My name is Hans Fredrik, and I am 12 years old. I live with my 2 siblings, Erik and Nora, along with my parents. My brother and I were out collecting food for our family when suddenly we heard a rumble from the ground. It wasn't the usual sound we heard during earthquakes. When I saw what was happening, my jaw fell. The ground was literally disappearing from the Earth, sinking in. My brother quickly took my hand, and sprinted back to our house. As we got back home, we saw our Dad, who had the rest of the family outside the house. "Run to the emergency boat, then we'll figure something out!" Dad yelled. He was running really quickly. So we ran as fast as we could, and we saw the ground behind us sink into the ocean. We were panicking, but my Dad didn't panic. He had Nora on his back, and I was on Erik's back. My mom was a little behind, but she was following us. Eventually, we all made it to the boat. A few minutes later, Norway had vanished. Everyone in Norway had boats, so we were all safe in our boats, above the water. We didn't have much food or water at all.

"How are we supposed to get food?" I asked.

"We'll just ask our neighbors," Mom answered. We went off sailing on our boat and set off.

Dad was sailing on the boat with Erik next to him, Nora was with mom, and I was by myself on the other side. This was going to be the longest cruise I've ever been on. Just when I thought I was going to explode because of my impatience, I saw a boat that wasn't too far.

"Wait, there's something in the distance." It was the Redrikaans who were our neighbors.

When we saw our neighbors, we raced over to them and at last, we finally reached the Redrikaans. Dad saw their boat, so he parked our boat next to theirs.

"Hello Mr. Fredrik, it is so nice to see you again, so what do you need?" Mr. Redrikaan asked.

"Can we have some resources because we don't have a lot of food or water?" My Dad asked.

"Sure, how much do you need?"

"How much do you have?"

"We have 200 coconuts, 15 gallons of water, and at least 300 bananas."

"We'll take 3 gallons of water, 50 coconuts, and 75 bananas."

"You got it, Mr. Fredrik; anything for you and your family."

"Thank you, Mr. Redrikaan, for your food and water, I really appreciate it." We got the resources, put them on the boat, and sailed back across the ocean where there is nothing but water, clouds, the sky, and thousands of boats.

"What are we going to do in our boat for who knows how long!?" I exclaimed, annoyed.

"We could play a game," Erik suggested.

"I have an idea!," I exclaimed. "What if we go down and see if we could find the land that disappeared?"

"What! Are you insane, Hans"? My mom asked, shocked.

"Erik, Dad, and I could go under the water and see what is down there," I said.

"Oh no, mister, you are staying here." Said my Dad.

"Why?" I asked.

"It is too dangerous for you to go down there," Dad said worried, "And you could possibly drown, and I don't want to lose you, Hans."

"Ok fine!" I exclaimed, annoyed. So Dad and Erik went deep into the water to see if the land was there. There were a lot of creatures down there like sharks, fish, eels, stingrays, and more. Some of the animals were gentle like fish, while others were rough like eels. Dad saw many types of fish down there, but he saw no trace of land at all. Even Erik didn't see a single piece of land, not the land that was supposed to be above the water, or what was supposed to be underwater. Once they came up, both of them were a little puzzled.

"I didn't see a single piece of land down there, and I could barely hold my breath." Dad said while panting.

"Same here; all I saw were just fish and sharks just surrounding me, which was weird." Erik replied. Then, everyone started to get worried and were panicking a little.

"What are we going to do now?" Mom said worried.

"Are we stuck here forever"? Nora cried. But then, Dad stated,

"No, we are not; we will find a way to save the world so we can go back to normal."

"I think I know where we can go next." I uttered.

"Where is that, Hans?" Erik asked.

"It's all the way in Iceland."

"So let's go to Iceland." Mom responded excitedly.

We started our journey through Iceland and it was a very long journey. There were many obstacles on the journey, like eels, some big waves, and more, but we eventually made it to Iceland after 3 days.

"What are we looking for, Hans?" Dad questioned.

"According to some books I read, there is a wizard that lives somewhere here in Iceland."

"What?" Erik said, confused, "Are you sure, Hans? Are you joking or are you telling the truth, because that just sounds like something I've never heard."

"I'm serious, guys. He lives in a tower, so if you see a floating tower, then that's where we're heading."

"Ok, you heard the young man; find that floating tower." Dad commanded. So we were all looking for a floating tower, but then, after a while of searching, Nora saw something out of the ordinary.

"What is that tower over there, guys?"

"The place we're going to see," I replied.

When we got to the island, we didn't know how to get up. There wasn't anything at all, but then when we were about to leave, a ladder just fell for us to climb. I climbed the ladder and got to the top, and what my eyes saw was glorious. It was a humongous tower, with it being small on the outside but huge on the inside.

"Wow!" "I've never seen anything like this," Mom said, astonishingly.

Suddenly, a man in a black and white robe came outside to see what we wanted. He looked quite old, but he seemed to not have any problems and was healthy. "Hello, it's a pleasure to meet you." The man said.

" It's a pleasure to meet you too, sir." Dad replied, amazed.

"Are you the wizard that lives here?" I asked.

"Indeed I am."

"We need your help to save the world and return the land." I exclaimed.

"I know, I've been looking at the ocean and seeing so many people in boats, planes, and cruise ships lately."

"We never saw or heard any planes or cruise ships." I said, confused. "Ok, back to the saving the world thing, what do you want me to do?"

"Well, can you make a potion to bring all the land in the world back?"

" Not the land that has already been in the water, but the land that just disappeared. " I asked.

"I feared a day like this would come, but I'll see what I can do.

"Ok, thank you for helping us." I said. While the wizard was making the potion, we were exploring his tower which had so much stuff inside like floating chairs, floating tables, floating stairs, and more. Pretty much everything in his house was floating. Then, after a few hours, the potion was complete.

"Here is the potion. You must throw it into the ocean after 10 minutes." The wizard said, "But be careful with it, though, because if you use it wrong, something bad could happen."

"We'll be as careful as possible with it." I said to the wizard. So we said goodbye to the wizard, got on our boat, and sailed into the ocean. A few minutes went by, and suddenly, a massive wave hit us. We were injured pretty badly and now the potion was gone, but somehow, the boat was still on the water and didn't have any broken pieces. Now we had to get to the boat which took a while to get to, so we got to the boat and had to figure out what happened.

"Did anything happen?" Mom asked.

"I'm not sure." I said with confusion. Suddenly, the waves started to get bigger, the water was rising, and people's boats were going insanely crazy in the water. "WHAT IS HAPPENING!" I shouted. "SOMETHING TERRIBLE!" Mom screamed. The wizard saw this, so he quickly made another potion with all his power, came outside, and threw it into the water. Something crazy then happened, and then within a few seconds, the water was gone. No one was injured except for us and the wizard who had a lot of bruises on him but eventually, he was fine. The only problem was that everyone's boats were stuck on the land and needed to be pushed into the water, so we all helped everyone push their boats back into the water, and everyone was good to go. After a few days, we got back home to Norway, and everything was back to normal.

"Finally, we're back home safe and sound." I said happily.

"I know." Erik responded. "I can finally relax and go back to how my life was." We were noticed by lots of people, including the government, who gave us a bigger house, more food, and whatever we wanted. The wizard also got whatever he wanted, but he is a wizard, so he could just make whatever he wanted. Now the land is back, and everyone is happy again. If I go play with my friends now, they always let me choose the game, which I think is super cool. I'm able to play a lot more now since my Dad now has an amazing job. So everything was fixed and hopefully, nothing bad like the land incident ever happens again.

The End.

About the Author
Fadilah M. Syed

Fadilah M. Syed is a fourth grader at MCC Academy who is doing hifz, and she loves to make books. Fadilah loves to paint, draw, and crochet. One more hobby of Fadilah is to make books, of course! She loves to make her readers proud of her work. She also created a business recently, called F.M.S Boutique. She has an older brother who is in high school. She hopes you will enjoy her story!

For my whole class because this is a lesson for all of us. Helping others is something everyone should do and it will always make you happy!

—F.M.S

Fadilah's Adventurous Day Out

By Fadilah M. Syed

Once upon a time, Fadilah woke up on a gloomy autumn morning around six a.m. Fadilah loved nature, especially in the Autumn. She would often go on long walks in the forest, but today she wanted to ride her bike along the biking trail.

"I wanted to go bicycle riding," thought Fadilah, but her brother was sleeping. Fadilah's brother was in eleventh grade, and he often went bicycle riding with his sister, who was only nine years old. Fadilah didn't want to be alone in the middle of the Black Forest, because she was a bit scared. She went to wake up her brother.

"I don't want to go. I'm too sleepy," her brother groaned.

That left her with no option but to go alone.

Fadilah started biking to the Black Forest. The sun was rising, covering the street with warm yellow light, and the birds were chirping. As she biked down the trail, leaves fell from the sky. There was a cold breeze that blew on Fadilah's face, and she shivered, but she loved it. Eventually, she got tired and stopped under a big tree that was home to a bird's nest when she saw some blackberries on the ground falling from the tree. Fadilah wanted to take some home to show her family, so she picked some up and put them in the bicycle basket when she saw some of the colorful leaves moving. Fadilah was curious to see why they were moving; she wanted to investigate and found a small, cute bunny trapped in a net. The poor bunny was bleeding, so she went to help the bunny.

Fadilah placed the bunny in the bicycle basket and then rode around to find help.

Fadilah rode along the trail until she saw a house, which turned out to be a small hospital. Fadilah went inside and found a nurse. The nurse wore a white coat, had glasses and also had a stethoscope on her. The nurse had volunteered to help the bunny. When Fadilah went back to get the bunny, it had disappeared; she couldn't find the bunny. The injured bunny had run away. Before Fadilah could tell the nurse, a kidnapper came, blindfolded her and the nurse, and took them to an abandoned mansion.

She remembered a legend about a haunted mansion. In the legend, it is said that whoever enters the haunted mansion will face the witch's wrath!

Then she noticed that this was the same mansion and told the nurse. Once she realized that the kidnapper had disappeared, Fadilah and the nurse were wondering where the kidnapper went. When they looked up, he was hanging from the ceiling and a few seconds later, the kidnapper fell from the ceiling. They both screamed.

The mansion was dusty, and the floors creaked. The furniture was covered with dusty sheets, and cobwebs were hanging from the ceiling. Fadilah needed to escape the mansion, but they were tied up. So, Fadilah tried untying herself with her bracelet, and it worked. She quickly untied the nurse.

When she tried to unlock the door, it wouldn't open. Then Fadilah heard her brother's voice calling her name.

She was about to call her brother's name when all the lights went out. She remembered the rumors of a witch that lived in the abandoned mansion and was terrified!

Furthermore, she gathered the courage to call her brother.

He shouted back, "Where are you?"

Fadilah said, "We are in this mansion, all the doors are locked."

He replied, "Oh no! Let me find a way to get you out."

Fadilah's brother was going to use a giant log to open the door, and he told us to back up. He started hitting the door with the log. Suddenly, Fadilah heard a noise coming from another room. When they looked, there was water everywhere, and it started to flood the whole mansion.

She screamed for her brother to hurry because the mansion was flooding.

Her brother replied, "The door isn't opening."

Fadilah thought about what they could do to get out of the mansion. She had the idea that there might be a key to the door hidden somewhere.

She told her brother, who yelled back that he was going to try to find it.

Fadilah yelled, "Whatever you're doing, do it fast because the water level is getting higher and higher!"

The water level was rising, but all she could think about was the poor bunny that was hurt. Then she heard a cackling voice yell, "You will never get out!" Fadilah still had hope that her brother would find the key and free them from the haunted mansion, since

Fadilah believed that helping those in need would always lead to good things.

After a few minutes, she heard her brother yell, "I found the key!"Fadilah felt so relieved.

He quickly opened the door, and all the water drained out into the forest.

Fadilah hugged him, and screamed, "You saved us!" Then she introduced her brother to the nurse, and she thanked him. She told my brother about the injured bunny and that it needed help, so we looked for the medical center because that's where we last saw the bunny.

After a little while of searching, we found the bunny limping down a trail and started the procedure to save it. First, they took an X-ray from the medical center to see why its leg was bleeding and if it was broken. The X-ray revealed that its leg was broken, so the nurse wrapped it in a cast.

Everyone was happy, including the bunny. It was getting dark, so Fadilah and her brother left the Black Forest and went home, saying bye to the nurse.

But every day after school, Fadilah went back to the forest to play with the bunny, who became her best friend for life.

ABOUT THE AUTHOR
ZAINAB OMER

Zainab Omer is 10 years old and is in 4th grade. She has two brothers, and she goes to MCC Academy. She loves to play basketball. Zainab loves to color, draw, and bake. Her favorite food is pizza. Zainab loves to read books. Recently, she started a business named ZGS (Zainab's Gift Shop). She loves to make stories. She hopes that you like the story!

For my older brother who helped me and inspired me to create this story.

- Z.O.

The Mysterious Underwater Creature

By Zainab Omer

O nce upon a time, in the beautiful Parker Hills, two young children, Ali and Jennah, were sound asleep in their cozy beds as the sun began to rise and the birds chirped melodiously.

Jennah had a vivid dream where she swam underwater to search for an ancient creature. In her dream, she heard a whisper that said, "Find this creature, and you will get a pot of gold." She was unsure who had spoken those words. Excitedly, she shared her dream with her brother, Ali, over breakfast. The two youngsters quickly changed into their diving clothes that their dad had bought them a few years ago.

As they explored the ocean, Ali and Jennah searched under the sand while Ali went through a cave. The underwater world was entirely new to them, and they were mesmerized by the beautiful fish and coral. It didn't take long for Jennah to feel something touch her.

She felt something smooth and cold gliding over her skin. It sent a shiver down her spine. She looked behind and saw a fish swimming by her. They searched everywhere, but couldn't find any clues about the mysterious creature.

"There's nothing down here, Jennah," said Ali.

"Let's keep looking," said Jennah.

As the day progressed, Ali and Jennah dived for hours and hours, but they were exhausted, and their oxygen levels were running low. Jennah saw a shadow behind her, and her hair stood up on her arms, neck, and head. She slowly looked behind and saw a great white shark ready to eat them.

Jennah screamed.

Ali screamed.

"Swim as fast as you can," Ali said.

Despite swimming as fast as they could, the shark was still chasing them. They went through obstacles like caves and passed tall mountains underwater. Once Jennah looked behind, the shark was gone.

"I think we lost it!" exclaimed Ali.

Jennah and Ali checked their air tanks and realized they were losing lots of oxygen. They only had two minutes of air left in their tanks. They reached the surface on their last breath, panting heavily, and their whole body was aching.

Ali and Jennah went home and got some rest. After resting and recuperating, Ali and Jennah woke up refreshed and eager to try again.

"We have to go back and find that creature," said Jennah.

"We already searched the whole ocean. Maybe next time Jennah," said Ali.

"Please," pleaded Jennah.

"Okay," sighed Ali.

They dived again, looking for the mysterious creature. They went deeper into the ocean and saw sharks swimming while stingrays were camouflaged in the sand. Suddenly, they saw many dolphins leading them to a gold treasure box.

"Amazing! How could dolphins lead us straight to a whole box of treasure full of gold coins?" exclaimed Ali.

"Subhanallah, these creatures are beautiful," said Jennah.

Jennah and Ali thought of taking the gold box home or keeping it here for other people to see. They finally decided to keep it there for others to see.

"We have to continue searching for that creature," said Jennah.

"Alright, let's keep looking," said Ali.

Jennah searched under the sand, while Ali looked inside the caves. Suddenly, Jennah saw the creature from her dream.

"Ali, come here! I found the creature," said Jennah.

"Really?!" said Ali.

They were amazed by the creature they saw. It was a beautiful, majestic creature with magnificent colors and patterns.

"Alhamdulillah," whispered Jennah.

However, the creature quickly swam away, leaving them in awe of its beauty. Jennah and Ali also swam back up to the surface, feeling exhilarated by their adventure. They felt the wind pass their faces while they smelled the scent of the flowers spread in the air. Ali and Jennah went back home, happy that they found the creature, and they shared their story with their parents, who were proud of their adventurous and brave kids.

The next morning Ali woke up for fajr salah. He made wudu and prayed salah. He quietly went downstairs trying not to wake up his parents or his sister. Ali wanted to go underwater to find the mysterious creature that he and his sister found yesterday. But he knew not to go outside without anyone with him. Ali thought that he would stay safe underwater with the creatures. So Ali got his diving clothes and wore them to go outside.

It was almost 7:00 am, so Ali had to quickly. He went outside and went into the ocean. Ali swam and saw all the fish and sharks swimming around looking for food. Ali swam around rocks, but couldn't find the creature. The creature he and his sister found yesterday was unusual, so Ali kept looking for it. Ali saw a huge cave that was dark and looked creepy. Ali was scared and nervous to go inside, but he thought, "*What if the creature was in the dark creepy cave?*" Ali took deep breaths and thought about what his parents used to say whenever he got scared. They used to say that whenever you are scared, think about Allah (SWT) and say his name in your heart. Ali said Allah's (SWT) name in his heart.

Ali was anxious to enter the cave, but he did. When Ali entered the cave it was really dark. There were no fish, no sharks, and no people. Ali got really scared. The cave was an entire maze. Ali thought that he should go back, but he forgot the way he came from. Ali looked and looked and was tired and was really sad. He thought that he might never see his family again. Ali started to cry. He thought back at home what he had done wrong and that it was not a good idea to leave the house without anyone and with anyone's permission. Ali made dua from Allah (SWT) to keep him safe and someone finds him.

Jennah woke up. She realized that the time was 9:00 am. Usually, her brother wakes her up for fajr, but this time he didn't. Jennah got off her bead and went to go make wudu to pray late salah. Jennnah prayed salah and went to check on Ali, but Ali wasn't there. She thought Ali might be downstairs eating breakfast. Ali and Jennah's parents were not awake yet. Jennah went downstairs quietly. Jennah didn't see Ali anywhere. She checked the closet, but he wasn't there. She looked all around the house, but couldn't find him. She even looked outside. Jennah thought about what happened yesterday that when they found the creature Ali was amazed. Then she realized that he probably went into the ocean.

Jennah went and changed into her diving clothes and went into the ocean. Jennah looked and looked, but the only things she saw were fish and sharks, but not Ali. From far away Jennah saw a huge cave and it was really dark. Jennah thought Ali could not have gone in there because it was too dark. Then Jennah realized that she had looked all around the ocean but couldn't find Ali. Jennah made her decision and swam to the cave.

When Jennah reached the cave she went inside and saw a whole maze. She thought, "*How was she going to find Ali?*" She went through the maze and then kept swimming until she could find Ali. The lane she went through had a dead end. Then she saw someone sitting there on the corner crying. She realized it was Ali.

"Ali is that you?" said Jennah.

" Yes it is me!'' exclaimed Ali.

" Ali, where have you been, we have been looking for you," said Jennah.

Ali said, " I left home without anyone's permission".

"At least we have found you, I was so worried," said Jennah.

Both siblings embraced each other and went home. Their parents were already awake and asked them where they had been.

Ali said, " I left the home without anyone's permission, and I am sorry for what I did".

Their parents said, "Don't leave the house without anyone's permission again".

The whole family embraced each other and the kids decided not to leave the house without permission. Their parents were proud of the kids who were brave and strong, and who were always close to Allah (SWT).

The End

About the Author

Hafidh Saleh Akram

Saleh Akram is a 12-year-old writer who's currently in 7th grade and is Hafiz of the Qur'an. He lives with his parents, and four pet parakeets (birds). He enjoys reading books, playing basketball when he gets the chance, and likes studying history. He is also a student in MCC Academy.

For my parents, who are always there for me when I need them and always guide me when I need guidance.

—S.A

The Process of a Sword

By Hafidh Saleh Akram

S aleh Akram is a 12-year-old writer who's currently in 7th grade and is Hafiz of the Qur'an. He lives with his parents, and four pet parakeets (birds). He enjoys reading books, playing basketball when he gets the chance, and likes studying history. He is also a student in MCC Academy.

For my parents, who are always there for me when I need them and always guide me when I need guidance.

—S.A

ABOUT THE AUTHOR
IBRAHIM AADAM

Hi! My name is Ibrahim Aadam, and I am 11 years old. I am a hifz student, which means I am memorizing the holy book called The Quran. My passion is playing soccer, especially with my brothers. The inspiration for my story came from a piece of artwork in an old notebook of mine. I had sketched a flying house with a young boy and a time machine. This led to the story of "Max and his Adventures with the Flying House."

I would like to dedicate this story to my Mom, who inspired me to create the character for Max's Mom.

—I.A.

Max and His Adventures With a Flying House

By Ibrahim Aadam

Max is a ten-year-old boy who is in the fifth grade. He loves soccer and is homeschooled in Inglewood, California. Inglewood is a beautiful scenic town with palm trees, rivers, and lots of greenery. He loves living in Inglewood because he has many friends, and the weather is always perfectly warm. It is 2025, and this year he turns eleven. Today, he is learning about fractions in his lesson with his mom, who is his teacher. Max's mom is forty years old. He loves her so much because she is sweet, nice and can cook like a chef. She used to be a famous movie producer but became a teacher to follow her passion for teaching. Home-schooling Max allowed her them to spend more time together, having fun and exploring. Today, on another perfectly warm day, Max asks his mom what the date is.

His mom says, "January 29th."

Max responds with excitement, "Ooh, my birthday is in two days."

His mom says, "Yes, thats great but can we go back to the lesson now?"

Max begrudgingly agrees. Today they are working on Math. Max loves math, its one of his his strengths his mom always tells him.

"What's 5/10 x 6/10?" his mom asks.

Max replies quickly, " 3/10."

His mom happily shouts, "Yes! that is correct!"

The next two days feel like they are moving very slow for Max, as he eagerly waits for his birthday. Finally the day arrives, Max jumps out of bed quickly that morning, running to his mom to asks "what is my birthday present??". She says "Max, it's too early! we still have a whole morning of class, beginning with Math, get ready quickly and lets start our day" but before he runs back upstairs, she hands him a small blue box with a silver bow. Max opens the present with excitement and a huge smile. Inside is a set of shiny gold keys, he is confused, he looks up at his mom and asks, "what are these for?"

His mom cryptically responds, "You will find out later."

Since Max was young he always wanted to time travel. He was very curious about the future and how things would be different. He wondered would it have amazing flying cars? or giant flying houses?. He would sometimes have vivid dreams about the future and him exploring all the new and cool technology. Later that evening, at his birthday dinner, he caught a quick shooting star rush by. At that exact moment, Max wished he could time travel. He didn't quite believe wishing on a star would make his wish come true but deep down he hoped it would. He enjoyed his birthday dinner with his mom and forgot all about his wish. The next morning, Max woke up suddenly, he realized he didn't hear his alarm and his mom didnt wake him up. He turned to look at his alarm clock and screamed, "It is 2125!"he thought he might still be dreaming but just then the owners of the house in 2125 heard the scream and came rushing into the room. Everyone was scared, they hadn't seen Max before and he looked strange in his 2025 pajamas. They stared at each other for a few minutes before they quickly told Max to leave the house because he didn't live there anymore. Max rushed out of the house wondering where was his mom? Outside,

2125 looked different, there weren't the same palm trees or sounds of birds that he was used to, it was now gray and no trees in sight. Max remembered that yesterday in 2025 his Mom had given him a small set of keys for his birthday. He still had those keys and wondered what was he is supposed to do with them? He starts to walk through the new, unique neighborhood of 2125, he is amazed with the flying cars he sees whizzing by, he stares in awe watching them fly by. Hours go by and now Max is scared, lost, and worried because he has nowhere to stay, and it is almost dark. He has been trying his keys that he has in his pocket on every house in the neighborhood wondering if it will open a door for him to get in. Suddenly, he hears a strange sound and he looks up, he is surprised but amazed to see a flying house landing near by. He rushes to its front door by holding onto a colorful balloon which he found on a big tree, 2125 has flying balloons to get around faster, wow how cool Max thinks. He tries to open the flying house with the keys his mom gave him, and the key actually opens the door! He cries with tears of joy because inside the house is beautiful, he stares in amazement at all the cool things inside. He starts looking around the house, he sees a flying trampoline in one room, an indoor flying soccer field in another, and endless rooms with candy, marshmallows and all his favorite toys. Max has hours of fun, running from one to the next and finally goes to bed after playing with everything in the house.

Max wakes up the next morning and looks around at the house with all the fun things inside. Instead of feeling excited like he did yesterday, he feels lonely. He can't play with his awesome friends anymore, and he misses his mom and her delicious food. He was having so much fun yesterday that he forgot to eat. He remembers he had $20 in his pocket and decided to go out and buy some food. When he tries to pay, the shopkeeper says, "I don't know what this is, we only use digital money in 2125." Max frowns and says, "This is the only money I have." The shopkeeper felt bad for Max and didn't want him to be hungry, so he let him have the bland fried chicken and a pocket-size candy dispenser he wanted without paying.

When Max got back to the flying house, he ate his fried chicken, but it had very little flavor. He then thought about his mom's cooking, how flavorful it always was, and how much he missed her. He was bored and thought about playing with all the fun things in the house to make him happy, but instead he just became more lonely and walked around the house sad. While walking in the house, Max sees a mysterious black door.

He opens the door he sees a portal far away he sees 3 goblins asking why are you here? Max says I want to go home the goblin say "okay" max runs to the portal, he bumps into an invisible wall. He sees the second goblin, the goblin says "why are you here?", again Max says "I want to get home" the goblin says "ok I challenge you to a game of chess, if you win, I will show you how to get home". Max agrees to play the game, he was always good at chess.The game starts off strong, Max makes some strategic moves. The goblin scowels, "how are you winning? peasant!". Just then, Max shouts "Queen E7 checkmate".

" Good game human, I will raise the barrier, a promise is a promise". Max thanks the goblin and runs to the portal, but just then he sees the third goblin who asks "why are you here?" Max repeats, "please, I just want to go home, I won the game of chess so I can get home" . The goblin responds "okay fine but now you must play a game with me, beat me in rock paper scissors you get one chance only" . Max is confident he will win, but to his horror he looses! He begins to cry, so the goblin agrees to a rematch. This time max wins and he runs toward the portal quickly, he sees a lock on the button to press it he tries all his keys , he begins to panic, just then the first goblin appeared who opens the door for him.

Suddenly a trap door opens under him, he is trapped! The goblins laugh at him and says "you thought we would let you go home? You will stay here forever!". The goblins close the door, leaving Max in a small room that reminds him of a prison. Max remembers he still has the keys, maybe they will help. He reached into his pocket and uses the second key to unlock the door. He opened the door and was amazed, it was a portal back to his home in 2025. In the portal, he could see his house, friends, and mom. He looks around at the flying house and thinks about all the fun he can have in the flying house but realizes that he is actually sad and lonely to be away from his home in Inglewood where his mom and friends are. He then jumps through the door and into the portal as quickly as he can.

Max's alarm goes off, and he looks and sees that it reads 2025. He hears his mom call him, and he runs down the stairs and nearly trips on a toy on the stairs because he is running so fast. He gives his mom the biggest hug he has ever given her. She says to him, "Why are you so happy to see me?" He says "Mom, I went to the future, I saw flying cars and flying houses, it was 100 years in the future." She told him he has a wild imagination, and it was all just a dream. He says, "No, look, I used these keys you gave me in the future."

She replies, "No Max, go in the garage, those are the keys for the new car to take you to your new school." He sees the car and the wing doors, just like the ones from the future that could fly. He asks himself, "Was his time in 2125 really a dream, or was it real?" Just then he put his hand in his pocket and found the pocket candy dispenser and smiled. He realized in that moment, that even though the future was exciting and new, he was just very happy and grateful to be back home with his mom and friends. He couldn't wait to run outside and play soccer with them again.

He turned back into the house and asked his Mom "Hey Mom, whats for dinner today?" He couldn't wait to eat his mums delicious food again, is stomach growled like he hadn't eaten in 100 years! Well, since 2125 at least!

ABOUT THE AUTHOR
HAFIDHA SIDRAH ILYAS

Hafizah Sidrah K. Ilyas lives with her parents and three siblings. She did her Hifz and currently goes to MCC Academy. She likes to read, crochet, and learn new things about the world in her free time. When she grows up she would like to do many things and have a successful career.

THE INCREDIBLE GEM
BY HAFIDHA SIDRAH ILYAS

It all started with a big BOOM. I heard a loud "THUD!" coming from downstairs. What on Earth is going on?!?!?! But despite all this commotion going on in my house, I continued to watch my movie in my family house theater.

I was eating my popcorn when I heard a knock. A knock on my window? I checked to see what was happening when I saw a black figure. Oh my God! It was a robber! Wait, don't we have a Security Guard? What happened to him? I got up to close the blinds and lights, but in a split second, blood and glass were everywhere. I felt as though my breathing was low and I lost consciousness.

I woke up in my family house theater and found blood and glass all around me. It took me a few minutes to figure out what was happening. My cousins, aunt, and uncle weren't home yet, and my hand was bleeding badly. I wrapped my throw around my hand tightly to prevent it from bleeding. I helped myself to get up, and then my head was spinning.

Likewise, I walked to the kitchen, and when I looked around, everything was a mess: dishes everywhere, cups on the floor, and glass shattered everywhere. My head was still spinning, suddenly I heard a voice coming from upstairs...

The noise of my baby cousin crying. How could I be so absent-minded? My aunt and Uncle left me alone to take care of her. I started running and when I was halfway up the stairs, I noticed that my throw blanket was unraveling from my hand and fell on the first step. My hand was hurting so badly. I felt dizzy and fell to the ground, as my cousin's cries haunted me as I fell down the stairs.

When I woke up, someone was shaking me.

"Sarah!" someone yelled.

I then realized that it was my cousin Nova.

"What just happened?" I said.

"Thank God!" she said. "Are you okay? What happened while we were gone?"

That's when everything came back to me.

The robber. The glass shattering. My cousin was crying.

"Wait, where's Sirene?!?!?" I yelled.

I was lying on our couch with my hand in a cast. My cousin Nova was right next to me, and I saw my cousin Ehsaan running toward me.

"Oh my God, when did you wake up?!?" he yelled. "Everyone was so worried!"

"Mom! Dad! Sarah's awake!"

I helped myself sit up as Nova gave me a glass of water.

"Now you have to tell me everything that happened," Nova said as my aunt and uncle came running.

I explained what happened, and they patiently listened to everything I was saying. When I finished, my aunt and uncle's faces were blank. My cousins were confused. Everyone was asking me questions.

"What did the person look like?"

"Did you hear anything else?"

I answered all their questions, but now it was my turn to ask the questions.

"Khaal, do you know anything about this?" I asked my uncle.

But his face was blank. He was just staring at the ground with no expression.

"Khaal?" I asked again.

"I have to go," he said.

As he got up, everyone was looking at him as he got up and walked out the door. I looked at my aunt and my cousins, but everyone was so confused.

"Sarah, let's get you to your room," Khalto said. "The nurse should be here to check your arm."

"Ok," I said as Nova and my aunt helped me to our elevator.

That night I couldn't sleep. I lie there wide awake with the memory of the black figure and the glass shatter playing over and over again in my head. I had so many questions. Why did my uncle leave when I asked him if he knew anything about what happened? Why do I not know what is happening?

I decided to clear my mind and do something else since I couldn't sleep. I went to get a book. I couldn't focus. I tried listening to some music. I couldn't listen. I thought I should go and walk around the house until I got tired. I got out of bed and left my room to go downstairs and drink some water. But while I was walking downstairs, I saw a black figure. What in the world? I must be hallucinating. I went to get a closer look. But by the time I got there, the figure was gone. It must have been the new security guards Khaal hired. But I couldn't be sure, so I stayed and watched outside until I saw one of the security men. I knew it, I was hallucinating. I told myself as I went to the kitchen to get some water.

I checked the time. It was 10:07. My Best Friend, Amara, sleeps past midnight on school breaks. I decided I needed someone to talk to. I started to text her:

"Hey Amara," I texted her.

"Are you awake"

Not even 2 minutes later, I got a response.

"Yeah" she texted back

"What's up?"

"Something peculiar is happening," I say

" What is that supposed to mean?"

"Can I call you?" I say, but as I'm about to send it to her, I hear a knock on the door.

OMG. What in the world is happening? Who is at the door at 10 pm?

I stood still as a statue at the counter, not knowing what to do.

I slowly go to the door to check the peephole. I've watched and read way too many horrors and thrillers to know not to open the door at night and when you're scared.

Oh, thank God. It's the security guard.

I didn't want to open the door, and I didn't know what to do, so I just went upstairs to go and tell my uncle. I didn't want to wake up my cousins, so I tiptoed through the hall to get to my aunt and uncle's room. But as I was tiptoeing, I heard my aunt and uncle talking. Talking about me. I knew it was wrong to eavesdrop, but what are you supposed to do if someone is talking about you, and you need to talk to that someone? I don't care.

"So, what are we going to do?" I heard my aunt say.

"I don't know," my uncle said.

"She's 16," my aunt said. "She has the right to know"

"I know, but you think she's going to believe it?!" my uncle asked

"Yeah, you're right," my aunt said with a sigh.

What are they talking about? What do I not know? What are they hiding from me?

I had so many questions.

But first, I had to do what I came for.

I knocked on the door.

"Khala?" I said

"Oh, It's you," she said,

"Come inside"

"Um, I went downstairs to get um, some water and um, and someone's at the, um, door," I said. Oh God, I sound so weird.

"Did you open the door?" my uncle asked, looking like I just tased him.

"No, um, I only checked the peephole, it's um, one of the guards," I said,

"Oh, thank god," he said as he got up and left the room.

As he walked down the stairs, I tried to see if my aunt would tell me anything.

"Khala?" I asked

"Yeah? " she replied

"I feel like Khaal knows something about what's going on." I started,

"I wanted to ask if you know anything?"

"Sarah, trust me, nothing's going on," she replies with a scared look. "That was just a robber and the noises were just him breaking in, ok, everything is fine, ok, trust me."

But no matter what anyone says, I know something is happening. I know my aunt and uncle still think I'm too young to know. But I don't care.

When I went to my room, I called Amara.

"Hey, wait, you were saying something about something happening, and then you ditched me for like a whole 20 minutes," she started as soon as she picked up.

"Yeah, let me tell you......" I started to tell her everything that happened as she patiently listened. That's one of the good things about Amara, she listens to everything you say and doesn't ask questions until you finish. Unlike Aaliyah, Amara's cousin, she's a good friend, but sometimes she can be annoying.

"Wait, hold up," she started as soon as I finished.

"Yeah?"

"You're talking too fast, and I have no idea what you're saying. My mom is ranting and telling me to sleep, so how about you come to my house tomorrow and continue yapping about your tragic life?"

"ok, bye," I sighed as I hung up.

The next morning I woke up at 8:00; even though it was spring break, my body was used to getting up early. Anyway, I woke up and checked my phone; Amara hadn't texted me back yet. Of course, she's a lazy bird; how could I forget? I got up, got ready, and then went downstairs to get breakfast.

When I walked down the stairs, I saw my cousins Ehsaan and Nova talking in hushed voices, but when I came down, they looked at me and stopped. I wonder if they know what's happening or are just guessing.

Anyway, while I devoured my breakfast, I checked my phone every 2 minutes to see if Amara was awake.

When she didn't respond, I gave up and decided to go to her.

I quickly finished my breakfast and put my dishes in the sink, but I heard my Uncle shout as I was about to dart out the door.

"Sarah!" he said.

"Yes, Khaal?" I responded.

"I know you want to go out, but I'm afraid it's not safe for you," he said.

"Why am I not allowed?" I retorted. "Why isn't it safe for me?"

"Sarah, no one is allowed outside because of what occurred yesterday," my Khala said. I don't know where she came from or when she came here, but there she was.

"Ok, fine, then when are we allowed to?" I asked.

"When school starts," replies Khaal.

"But school starts in WHOLE TWO days!"

After a lot of bargaining, Khaal and Khala decided they would let me, but I have to be home by 2, and I have to have some specific annoying security guard, Chris, follow me wherever I go, which I DO NOT WANT, but hey, it's better than nothing.

As soon as I got to Amara's house, I darted inside while the useless security guard Chris stayed outside to ensure no one was intruding like anyone would. Anyway, I entered the kitchen to see Ms. Arden, the maid for Amara's House, making a late breakfast for Amelia. I said hi to her and Amara's mom, sitting in her office, and dashed upstairs to Amara's room.

"Amara!" I screamed as I entered her room and saw her bed wasn't made. "Get up! It's like 12-something!"

But then I realized she was already awake. LOL

"Wow," I said, embarrassed, "you're awake!"

"Yeah, I decided I needed to start getting up early before school starts," she responded tiredly. If she's trying to get up early to get her schedule right before school starts, she better start now.

Amelia was on her desk painting. She is an amazing artist!

"I was texting you, but you didn't respond, so I thought you were sleeping," I said

"Yeah, I would probably be sleeping right now," she said with a grin.

"Yeah, I guessed,"

"Ok, so what were you saying yesterday?" she said, changing the topic.

I told her everything that happened while she patiently waited.

"I asked my aunt and uncle, and they won't say any-thing, so I'm just going to not do anything," I finished off.

"Yeah, you're right; if you have no hopes of getting information from your uncle and aunt, then just wait until something weird happens"

After that, we just talked about school and stuff until her mom called her for lunch, and then I decided to go home.

"I'm home!" I shout when I enter my house. I'm probably the loudest person in the whole house.

"Hey Sarah, what did you do at Amara's house?" my cousin Nova asked,

Nova never really asked me questions like that, so I was kind of weirded out, but I still answered.

"Um, nothing much; we just talked, and then Ms. Arden made us lunch. Why?"

"Oh, um, I'm just asking"

"Ok..." I said as I went up the stairs,

I sat on my bed with my laptop in my lap and started finishing up my spring break homework. Yes, we have spring break homework, and it's only in our math class, my LEAST favorite class. Anyway, I was finishing up my math homework when I suddenly heard gunshots. Then someone screamed my name.

What. The.

I looked out the window to see what was happening, and I saw a bunch of guys in masks and the security guards pointing guns at each other. Then suddenly, my cousin Ehsaan darted into my room, followed by the rest of my family screaming. My uncle came around me and yelled something I couldn't hear. Ehsaan closed the lights off as my uncle stood by the door, my aunt, Nova, and Sirene were sitting on the floor with a frightened look on their faces. For some reason I was excited, and I don't even know why. It's like now I'm going to figure out what's happening. But everyone was quiet and my uncle was pacing back and forth in front of the door. I couldn't do anything except sit there, so I lay down on my bed and dozed off.

When I woke up my uncle was talking to someone outside the door, and my aunt was shaking me and telling me to wake up. I quickly got out of bed and stood up to see what was happening. My uncle told me to follow him, so I did and when we made it down the stairs I saw a bunch of men standing by the sofas and in the middle of the room, on our table, there was a leather box.

"Go ahead and open the box, Sarah," my uncle said.

I went and opened the box to find a bunch of stones and gems, and in the middle of the box, there was a bright red gem about the size of my thumb. Without thinking, I picked it up and took a closer look at it when I heard my uncle speak again.

"Congratulations Sarah, from now on you are the rightful owner of the Incredible Gem."

About the Author
Khadeejah Khan

Khadeejah Khan is a 12-year-old seventh grader and an aspiring Hafizha. She goes to MCC College Prep and lives with her parents and three pets. She has two birds and one senior cat. She has one sibling who is in tenth grade. She enjoys Badminton and her favorite subject is reading. Her favorite book series is *The Heroes of Olympus*.

Swans and Geese

By Khadeejah Khan

There was once a village on the outskirts of the city, where there lived a man with only a small farm to his name. The farm itself was unimpressive, with only a few skinny sheep and scrawny chickens and two cows. He had a horrid selection of crops which were wilted due to lack of proper care. He wished there were fish in the small, muddy pond that held only weeds. There was only one thing about his pond that was important: the swans. There were geese too, but in his eyes they were useless.

The swans were the only reason he still got business at his lonely farm. The village people thought that he was blessed to have the swans stay on his farm. The man didn't think so. If the swans wanted to bless him, then he would have abundant crops, and he would never work a day in his life. His father was the only one who believed in that spirit mumbo jumbo, and that was the only reason he hadn't started hunting the swans that lived in the pond. He knew none of the simple-minded villagers would forgive him if he hurt them anyway. He wished he could at least get his hands on some geese, but that was far too risky.

One dreary winter, after he had spent every last penny on seeds for new crops and got nothing but debt in return, the man realized he was running out of money. That was two weeks before the swans were to migrate, and all he had left were the ugly sheep and cows that produced barely any milk, but if he were to sell them for meat, he would get less than a coin for the thin, starving, animals. He sheared the wool once a year, at least making something to sell to the village weaver, who made warm winter coats with the wool. On one particularly cold morning, he noticed something. There were only geese in the pond! He had always assumed that the swans and geese migrated at the same time, but clearly, he was wrong. At that moment, he knew what to do. Set traps.

The man got to work netting and gathering, and when he was finally done, the sun had set and the sky glowed a hazy orange. He went inside, and for the first time, in a very long time, he had hope. He had hope that he could restore his family's farm to its former glory. It might not look like it now, but when his father was alive, there were abundant crops, lush green grass, and plump cattle. All of that combined had made the family richer than ever, living a life of comfort and happiness. But when an epidemic flew through the village killing his father and mother, his sibling ran away to the city, leaving him the task of taking care of the now barren land, he had lost all hope. But when the man went to sleep that night, though he had an empty stomach, his heart was full of hope, and that was more than enough.

HONK, HONK, HONK

The next morning, the man woke to a peculiar sound. Honking. He got up and rushed outside, both nervous and excited. When he finally got to the lake, his suspicions were confirmed, he had caught his first geese! To be exact 3 geese had hopelessly entangled themselves into the same net. The man felt a twinge of sympathy that quickly disappeared when he remembered how much they would sell for. Quickly, he took them out of the net and stuffed them into a wool sack, dragging them in the direction of his tool shed.

"Sorry, but a man gotta do what a man gotta do." The man said, shaking his head.

When he was done slaughtering the animals, he went into the village square and posted signs on the main market's doors and walls.

Less than an hour later, he heard a sharp knock on the front door, his first customer. He opened the door and saw Bernice, the market owner's wife.

"I need to buy all the geese you have!" She huffed, hurriedly reached into her satchel, and pulled out 30 gold coins. 10 for each goose. The man's eyes widened at the sight of the money, and he went to fetch the geese from the back. He gave her the bag and snatched up the coins like a greedy vulture. He spent the rest of the day wandering the market aisles for products that would help him fix his farm. When he went to sleep that night, he was content, this time with both his belly and his heart full. He spent the rest of the week catching and selling geese, until they too left for the south to join their brethren, the swans, who had already reached their destination.

But when summer rolled around and both the swans and geese came back, drought had hit and even his small income from crops was running out. He knew what he wanted to do, he hated himself for thinking about it, though he was desperate, surely he wasn't desperate enough to disobey his fathers dying wishes. But after three days of eating nothing but unripe corn he Even though he hated the idea, he was desperate and set traps out on the lake with only food for geese such as mixed corn, trying his best not to go near the swans. He also started dressing the geese for the market before he sold them to the customers, charging an extra 5 coins as a service fee.

He kept trapping and selling the geese with no problems until one day. That morning, he woke up to a different sound. A high-pitched *HONK, HONK, HONK* he heard. Curious, the man stepped out and went to the pond expecting a baby goose, but to his horror, he saw a swan. Who in the process of trying to get free of the netting had injured her wing. He stood there, contemplating the choices he had. One was to let the swan go, and risk getting in grave trouble with the villagers. Or to kill the swan and sell it to the customer, as the goose is scheduled for pickup that day. The man chose the latter of the options, telling himself that no one would notice. When he heard the knock on the door, his mind filled with guilt as he opened the door to reveal the village weaver, Edith.

"Are you going to give me my goose or just stand there and look stupid?" she snapped as she opened her purse and pulled out 15 coins. 10 for the "goose" and 5 for the dressing. The man forgot all about his guilt when he saw the shiny coins. He hurriedly handed her the so-called "goose" and took his money inside.

In the following weeks, word spread around town, about the delicious "geese " the man sold. He started setting out general traps, convincing himself it wasn't his fault if swans as well got trapped in the netting, as they were only for geese. As he kept doing this, the price shot up as more and more people wanted to try his delectable 'geese.' The man's guilt disappeared, and so did drought. His farm was getting better every single day, he no longer batted an eye when he caught a swan, and he filled his pockets with coins. His farm thrived with more cattle than ever before, the crops grew and the land flourished. All was well. Or was it?

The man started noticing the decline a few months after its peak. And that morning confirmed it, the farm was dying. Slowly and steadily the crops stopped growing, and the animals refused to eat. He took this as a challenge and started catching more swans to sell, to buy more supplies for the farm. But nothing worked. One night he had a disturbing dream, he saw his father, dressed in all black, as if he were at a funeral.

"Son, you must repent, apologize for your deeds, and maybe you will be forgiven." He said solemnly, shaking his head.

"But I didn't do anything, the swans got in my traps themselves!" The man retorted, refusing to repent.

"It is your decision, don't say I didn't warn you." His father turned and walked away into the distance, where he greeted swans on the way.

Suddenly the man had woken up in a cold sweat, he felt had groggy, and something else, but he couldn't quite name it. He walked to the pond, but when he got there, it was empty, he waded into the water trying to see if anything was there, getting stuck in the process. He looked around, and then down at his webbed feet. Wait... HIS WEBBED FEET?! The Man frantically yelled, but all that came out were high-pitched honks. He thought, someone will notice I'm gone, right? I won't be here forever, right? He heard footsteps and turned toward the noise, he squinted through the foliage to make out one thing. Himself. He screamed, no, honked in surprise when his human self grabbed him, stuffed him in a sack, and dragged him to the shed to be prepared for the market. He stopped flailing and honking and thought about what was happening. Is this the end? Is this how I die? He thought hopelessly, thinking about how he would be killed in the following minutes. When they reached the shed, and he closed his eyes, waiting for the misery to end. He heard a loud *THWACK* followed by a sharp pain. He expected death to follow, but it didn't. He continud to feel everything, right until the moment of consumption. Suddenly, he heard the howl of wind and the whispers of the bushes swaying with the breeze. He opened his eyes again and found himself at the pond, where saw his webbed foot stuck in a trap.

THE END

ABOUT THE AUTHOR
AMIN LALIWALA

Amin Laliwala is a 13-year-old boy who likes playing sports and playing video games. He is good at soccer and a little good at basketball. He likes playing outside in his free time. He also has a dream of becoming Hafiz.

This book is dedicated to my mom and dad.

—A.L

John Patt's Adventure

By Amin Laliwala

It was an average day in Ohio. John Patt and his friend Dave Gep were eating pizza at Liam's Pizzeria, the best pizzeria in Ohio.

"Mhmmm...it's so good," said Dave.

"The cheese is so...delicious!" said John. John Patts other friends Ron, Jake, Ben and Rick are training for their Basketball game.

"There's no point in going, we're going to win anyway", said Dave.

"This isn't any normal team," John said. "We are facing The Big Eagles."

"Well good thing we have a lot of time to practice today,"said Dave "And we already wasted an hour.. So we better hurry now," said John. School was off today because it was Saturday. John Patt, Dave Gep and their friends were not supposed to sleep because of the game, but John and Dave did. So now they are eating breakfast late while everyone is practicing.

After eating pizza, John and Dave walked to the court through extreme traffic. Even though it was 103 degrees out, they still practiced. "I wanna go home now!" said Dave "We aren't even in the court yet!" said John. When they got to the court they started practicing ."What took you guys so long!" said Ben "Uhmm we kind of woke up an hour late" said John nervously. "Well it's fine, just keep practicing," said the coach. After 50 minutes they stopped because it was game time. They all got on the bus and got ready for a very long drive to the Ohio Stadium, which was around 3 hours."You guys wanna watch a movie?" said John and Dave. Everybody said no because they were all sleepy.30 minutes later Everyone except John Patt and Dave Gepp were fast asleep. Meanwhile John and Dave were watching some random movie where giants take over the world "John if giants attacked us in real life what would you do?" said Dave. "Well that would never happen so i don't know?" said John. "Anyways i'm going to sleep until we reach the stadium."

When they got to the stadium they were excited but also nervous because there was a very big crowd. "I want to go home!" said Ben. John's team was called by some the best team in the state. They were facing The Strong Eagles, the second-best team in the state.

They are so good, they won 11 games in a row. And they're confident this is their 12th.

John's team has never played a team that is this good. There were still 20 minutes till the game and the whole stadium was already almost full. 20 minutes later the referee said "3...2...1....GO!.

The game started, and The Strong Eagles got the ball. John saw the player with the ball was about to pass, so he rushed to him, but it was too late. The player he passed to got ready to run to the hoop, but he made a bad dribble, so Dave got the ball and passed it to Rick, but the pass was too slow, so the fastest player on the Eagles caught it. He ran all the way to the hoop and scored a 3 pointer, which wasn't good. The Eagles fans were screaming so loud that it was causing an earthquake, the ground was going THUMP THUMP THUM P."That's not the crown thumping.." said the referee

He went outside to see what was going on, and he was shocked, it wasn't the fans causing the earthquake, it was a bunch of GIANTS heading towards the stadium! Buildings falling. Fire catching. 30 foot giants stomping towards the stadium. John can only think of 1 thing right now....RUN!

That's when the deafening alarm started ringing *BEEP... BEEP... BEEP. Everyone* was freaking out and screaming while they rushed to their cars." This is crazy!" said Ben. That's when John got dust in his eyes and by the time he got it out he could not find his friends, so he hid under the bleachers as he watched the giants take all the broken buildings and start forming a GIANT prison cell that was floating above the clouds. Behind the giant prison cell, he saw the giant's king.

He had a crown that controlled all the other small giants, he figured if he got the crown then he can let his friends and Ohio be free, and he can tell the giants to never come back ever again. Before that he had to make sure they didn't get him so he had to stay on guard but he accidentally fell asleep under the bleachers. When he woke up he didn't hear any thumping so he crawled outside, and he saw the glowing radiant prison cell with everyone in Ohio (except him) in it. And all the giants including the king were fast asleep under it. John read in a book that giants usually sleep a whole week before waking up again, so he knew this was his chance.

With a whole week, 168 hours of time on his hands, he decided to come up with a brilliant plan.

He decided to go on the king's head and push the crown off without making any noise. So overnight he created a giant mattress for the crown to land on so it

THE WORLD OF IMAGINATION 97

doesn't make noise or break. He had to make the mattress very big because the crown is 2 times his size.

The next morning, when he woke up, he decided it was time to execute the plan. He hopped on the king and crawled all the way to his head. He doesn't like the skin of the giants because unlike humans, their skin is really slimy and gooey like jelly. Once he reached the head he put the mattress in the perfect spot on the ground. He got ready and tried moving the crown, but even with all his effort, it wouldn't budge. Not even a little. He realized the king knew that this was going to happen, so he made it so only he can remove the crown!

John got demotivated, and he thought that he would never save Ohio, but then he realized that he still had 5 days left. John decided he still had a few more tries to save Ohio, so he went back to the house and fell on to the bed. He tried thinking of another plan overnight. When he woke up, he realized that the only way to get the crown is to fight the king.

He made a GIANT bell to wake up the giants, and then he made his own GIANT key to free everyone who is locked in the giant prison. When it was finally nighttime, he decided to try out the key and it worked! All the prisoners escaped the prison. After they escaped, they made their own custom weapons to contest the giants.

"We totally got this now!" Said John "Yeah lets do this!" said Rick.

When everyone was finally ready to fight, John rang the bell and the giants woke up. Everyone started fighting the giants with their tools and even after they gave it their all the giants acted like it was nothing. The military and the police with their tanks still could not stop them. They were just too powerful! They threw the tanks around like they were toys.

But even after that, everyone stood back up and started fighting! Everyone was giving their all but John realized that if they keep fighting like this same thing will happen over and over again. They will fight, lose. Have a bad mood. Get motivation to fight again, and lose again. He figured that they were impossible to fight, but not impossible to trick.

So this time while everyone else was giving it their all, fighting the giants, John and his friend Dave climbed on top of the giant and climbed all the way to the top. And when they finally reached the top, they found a big red spot. They figured it was the king's weak spot, so they got their stick and hit the red spot as hard as they could.

Yeah

They realized that the leader wasn't fighting as well as before, and then he got a flashback. He was watching a movie where 2 friends were fighting an evil dragon and his army. And when the dragon got weak, they were able to take his ring and control him and the army. John figured that this might work on the king so they tried it and the king started losing control over the army, John turned his army against him and defeated him.

He commanded the army to leave to another planet and never come back ever again. A few minutes after the giants disappeared John and the Eagles contintued the game and they won! John sat back and patted himself in the back. "Well this was a very long day i guess" said John "Yeah" replied Dave "Well at least it was a good ending". "Yeah...i guess"

A few years later John and his friends are all adults but they still get recognized for their work. John got a trophy and a statue of him holding the giants kings crown . John and friends all got on a very good basket-ball team together and continue to dominate. No one will ever forget John Patt who saved millions of lives.

THE END.

ABOUT THE AUTHOR
AFHAM MOHAMMED

Afham Mohammed lives in U.SA and he is currently in 7th Grade, in a school MCC, he is doing Hifz, and is done with most of the Hifz. He likes to play football, soccer, basketball, etc. He is also very hardworking in academics, and other stuff as well. He likes to write stories and essays. This is one of his stories.

World War II

By Afham Mohammed

T here was a 24-year-old brave man who used to live in New York. His dad was in the U.S. military, and was stationed in Europe to fight against Nazis so he also wanted to be in the army, so his dad told him to get training in Washington DC.

So he got training for 4 years in Washington DC, and he was told that he was going to be at Hawaii Army Base in 1936, after several years in the military he became a chief executing officer of Hawaii Army Base.

In 1939, it was told that Hitler was trying to conquer the whole continent of Europe, and Japan was trying to conquer more land in Asia, In 1940 David got orders from Washington D.C. that Japan would attack any of the army bases.

David was determined to protect his country and his base from any possible attack. He trained his soldiers rigorously and prepared them for any scenario. He also kept in touch with his dad, who was stationed in Europe, fighting against the Nazis.

One day, on December 7, 1941, David was having breakfast with his fellow officers when he heard a loud explosion. He ran outside and saw a horrifying sight: Japanese planes were bombing Pearl Harbor, the naval base near his army base. He quickly grabbed his rifle and ordered his men to take cover and fire back.

He witnessed the destruction and chaos around him, as ships were sinking, planes were crashing, and people were screaming. He tried to contact his superiors, but the communication lines were jammed.

He felt a surge of anger and fear, as he realized that this was the attack he had been warned about.

He fought bravely, but he knew that they were outnumbered and outmatched. He hoped that help would arrive soon and that his dad was safe in Europe. He wondered if this was the beginning of world war ll, and what the future would hold for him and his country.

As the attack continued, David saw a group of Japanese soldiers landing on the shore, armed with rifles and bayonets. They were heading towards his army base, intending to capture or kill anyone they encountered. David knew he had to stop them, or else they would overrun his base and slaughter his men.

He gathered a few of his loyal soldiers and led them to a nearby trench. He told them to stay low and wait for his signal. He then crawled out of the trench and ran towards the enemy, firing his rifle and throwing grenades. He hoped to distract them and draw their fire, while his men would ambush them from behind.

He reached the enemy line and engaged them in fierce hand-to-hand combat. He stabbed, shot, and punched as many as he could, but he was soon surrounded and outnumbered. He felt a sharp pain in his chest, as a bullet pierced his heart. He fell to the ground, blood gushing out of his wound, he called for help, but everyone was busy fighting.

As David lay dying on the ground, he saw a familiar face among the enemy soldiers. It was his childhood friend, Kenji, who had moved to Japan with his family when they were both 12. They had kept in touch for a while but lost contact after the war broke out.

David couldn't believe that Kenji was now his enemy and that he had come to kill him and his comrades. He felt a mix of sadness, anger, and betrayal. He wondered how Kenji could have changed so much, and how he could have joined the forces of evil.

He tried to speak, but only blood came out of his mouth. He wanted to ask Kenji why he had done this, and if he still remembered their friendship. He wanted to tell him that he was sorry, and that he wished things could have been different.

But he never got the chance. Kenji saw him lying on the ground and recognized him too. He felt a shock of horror and guilt, as he realized that he had shot his old friend. He wanted to run to him, and help him, and apologize. He wanted to tell him that he was forced to join the army, and that he hated the war. He wanted to tell him that he still considered him his friend and that he hoped he would forgive him.

Some of the loyal officers saw David on the ground, they took him to the nearest hospital out of the War, and the nurse took him inside the operation theater, three bullets were shot into his chest, but still, war was going on in the base.

Then the nurse tried her best to save David's life, but it was too late. He had lost too much blood and his heart had stopped beating. She said "He was a great man", pronounced him dead and covered his face with a white sheet. She felt a pang of sorrow for the young man who had given his life for his country.

Meanwhile, the battle at Pearl Harbor was still raging on. The Japanese planes had inflicted heavy damage on the American fleet and air force, but they had also suffered losses. The American soldiers and sailors had fought back with courage and determination, despite being caught off guard.

The Japanese commander, Admiral Yamamoto, told his soldiers, "soldiers destroy the america as much as you would like, today is the day of destruction";Then he planned to launch a third wave of attacks, targeting the oil tanks, repair facilities, and submarine base, so that fire can rage out. He believed that this would cripple the American naval power in the Pacific and force them to surrender.

However, he decided to cancel the third wave, fearing that the Americans had recovered from the initial shock and were ready to retaliate. He also worried that his own forces were running low on fuel and ammunition, and that they had lost the element of surprise.

He ordered his fleet to withdraw, hoping that he had done enough damage to achieve his objective. He did not know that he had made a fatal mistake, and that he had awakened a sleeping Giant beast.

The attack on Pearl Harbor had a profound impact on the course of the war and the history of the world. It had killed more than 2,400 Americans and wounded more than 1,100. It had destroyed or damaged 19 ships and 188 aircraft. It had also galvanized the American public and united them in their resolve to fight and win the war.

The next day, President Franklin D. Roosevelt addressed the nation and asked Congress to declare war on Japan. He called December 7, 1941, "a date which will live in infamy". He vowed that the American people would never forget or forgive the treacherous attack, and that they would ensure that justice would be done.

The Congress approved his request, and the United States officially entered World War II. They joined forces with Britain, France, Soviet Union, and other allies, forming the Allied Powers. They faced the Axis Powers, composed of Germany, Italy, and Japan.

The war would last for four more years, and would claim the lives of millions of people around the world. It would also see the development and use of the atomic bomb, the most destructive weapon ever created by mankind.

It would end with the surrender of Germany in May 1945, and the surrender of Japan in August 1945, after the atomic bombings of Hiroshima and Nagasaki.

safe in Europe. He wondered if this was the beginning of world war ll, and what the future would hold for him and his country.

As the attack continued, David saw a group of Japanese soldiers landing on the shore, armed with rifles and bayonets. They were heading towards his army base, intending to capture or kill anyone they encountered. David knew he had to stop them, or else they would overrun his base and slaughter his men.

He gathered a few of his loyal soldiers and led them to a nearby trench. He told them to stay low and wait for his signal. He then crawled out of the trench and ran towards the enemy, firing his rifle and throwing grenades. He hoped to distract them and draw their fire, while his men would ambush them from behind.

He reached the enemy line and engaged them in fierce hand-to-hand combat. He stabbed, shot, and punched as many as he could, but he was soon surrounded and outnumbered. He felt a sharp pain in his chest, as a bullet pierced his heart. He fell to the ground, blood gushing out of his wound, he called for help, but everyone was busy fighting.

As David lay dying on the ground, he saw a familiar face among the enemy soldiers. It was his childhood friend, Kenji, who had moved to Japan with his family when they were both 12. They had kept in touch for a while but lost contact after the war broke out.

David couldn't believe that Kenji was now his enemy and that he had come to kill him and his comrades. He felt a mix of sadness, anger, and betrayal. He wondered how Kenji could have changed so much, and how he could have joined the forces of evil.

He tried to speak, but only blood came out of his mouth. He wanted to ask Kenji why he had done this, and if he still remembered their friendship. He wanted to tell him that he was sorry, and that he wished things could have been different.

But he never got the chance. Kenji saw him lying on the ground and recognized him too. He felt a shock of horror and guilt, as he realized that he had shot his old friend. He wanted to run to him, and help him, and apologize. He wanted to tell him that he was forced to join the army, and that he hated the war. He wanted to tell him that he still considered him his friend and that he hoped he would forgive him.

Some of the loyal officers saw David on the ground, they took him to the nearest hospital out of the War, and the nurse took him inside the operation theater, three bullets were shot into his chest, but still, war was going on in the base.

Then the nurse tried her best to save David's life, but it was too late. He had lost too much blood and his heart had stopped beating. She pronounced him dead and covered his face with a white sheet. She felt a pang of sorrow for the young man who had given his life for his country.

Meanwhile, the battle at Pearl Harbor was still raging on. The Japanese planes had inflicted heavy damage on the American fleet and air force, but they had also suffered losses. The American soldiers and sailors had fought back with courage and determination, despite being caught off guard.

The Japanese commander, Admiral Yamamoto, had planned to launch a third wave of attacks, targeting the oil tanks, repair facilities, and submarine base. He believed that this would cripple the American naval power in the Pacific and force them to surrender.

However, he decided to cancel the third wave, fearing that the Americans had recovered from the initial shock and were ready to retaliate. He also worried that his own forces were running low on fuel and ammunition, and that they had lost the element of surprise.

He ordered his fleet to withdraw, hoping that he had done enough damage to achieve his objective. He did not know that he had made a fatal mistake, and that he had awakened a sleeping giant.

The attack on Pearl Harbor had a profound impact on the course of the war and the history of the world. It had killed more than 2,400 Americans and wounded more than 1,100. It had destroyed or damaged 19 ships and 188 aircraft. It had also galvanized the American public and united them in their resolve to fight and win the war.

The next day, President Franklin D. Roosevelt addressed the nation and asked Congress to declare war on Japan. He called December 7, 1941, "a date which will live in infamy". He vowed that the American people would never forget or forgive the treacherous attack, and that they would ensure that justice would be done.

The Congress approved his request, and the United States officially entered World War II. They joined forces with Britain, France, China, and other allies, forming the Allied Powers. They faced the Axis Powers, composed of Germany, Italy, and Japan.

The war would last for four more years, and would claim the lives of millions of people around the world. It would also see the development and use of the atomic bomb, the most destructive weapon ever created by mankind.

It would end with the surrender of Germany in May 1945, and the surrender of Japan in August 1945, after the atomic bombings of Hiroshima and Nagasaki.

They had left behind their families, their dreams, and their hopes.

They had also left behind a legacy of courage, honor, and tragedy, for their country, so that people can live in peace, with their full freedom in the Independent country.

The end.

BY, AFHAM MOHAMMED

About the Author

Abdul Kareem Syed

Abdul Kareem is a young author in 7th grade and, as of 2024, is memorizing the Quran to become a Hafiz. Let me tell you about this young author. Abdul Kareem's favorite sport is basketball. He has two siblings and lives in Chicago, Illinois. He enjoys writing stories like this one. His favorite genre to read is historical fiction. One of his favorite books is Scythe by Neal Shusterman.

For my best friend, who is always there to support me
—A.K.

THE FORGOTTEN ONE
BY ABDUL KAREEM SYED

I t was exactly 12 years ago when the house burned down and my parents mysteriously died, and somehow I managed to survive while being a baby. The reason why I said exactly 12 years ago was because today was my birthday, and there was nobody to celebrate my birthday except my aunt and uncle, who really didn't care about me. They can barely pay the house bills or afford any good food. All we eat is bread, and they give me the smallest portion. They don't want me to be with them because it increases the expense, and they really can't afford anything more than bread and bills. I just sleep on the floor, and they have their own room with a bed. Their son left them because they didn't treat him very well. I would do the same.

There's nothing to do at my aunt's house, so I like to go to the library and read books. I found this guy named Lucas at the library, and we became quick friends. He invited me to his house. He can't come to my house because we don't have anything. My favorite things to do at Lucas's house are to paint and cook. I just enjoy painting. I think it came from my mother because a few years ago, my Uncle John from New York came to visit me, but obviously my aunt didn't let him in, so he had to beg her, and she only gave him 2 minutes to talk to me and get out. He told me as much as he could about my parents, about how they looked, what they liked to do, and other stuff, but before I could ask him how they died, my aunt made him leave. I had begged my aunt to let him stay longer, but she refused, and I just like cooking because it's fun cooking with Lucas. Lucas has some new games on his PS5, like Fortnite, but I don't feel like playing video games.

I was going to school for the first time tomorrow, too. It's not the same school as Lucas's because the school he goes to is expensive. My aunt and uncle never sent me to school, but one day the law showed up and said that my uncle might get arrested if he doesn't send me to school because he's my guardian, and it's illegal not to send kids to school. So my uncle had to get a job, which he hadn't had in years because he got fired from every job he got because he looked poor and didn't have a heart for anyone l, but finally, after a long time, he got a job at a gas station far away from our house because we live in the middle of nowhere in the state of Ohio. Weird things happen here in Ohio; I just imagine a life back at the mansion my parents owned back in Chicago.

NEXT CHAPTER 2

Today was not just the day I was finally going to go to school, but also the day I was finally going to ask my aunt about my parents. I had enough; I wanted to know more about why it happened when it happened and if she knew anything. I got up from the floor and picked up the thin sheet I slept on every day, folded it, and put it away. I quietly went and brushed my teeth with a tiny dot of toothpaste because it was all I was allowed to use and an old toothbrush I had been using since I was a child. I waited for my aunt and uncle to wake up. It was about 6 a.m. when I woke up. After half an hour, I heard footsteps coming from my aunt's room, and she appeared from the corner. She didn't say anything; she just looked at me and went to the kitchen. I walked inside the kitchen, which was half the size of the living room, and saw my aunt looking inside the tiny fridge we had.

I cleared my throat, ready to talk, but before I could say anything, my aunt asked,

"What?" almost in an annoyed tone, but I continued to ask her,

"Uh, Aunt Mia, I had a question".

"Okay, what's your question?" she said, this time in a normal tone.

"I was just wondering what happened to my parents and how the house burned down. How do I not know anything?".

She said, "If you ever ask me that question again, you will be sorry, young man." I was furious and started to yell,

"I don't care!" She seemed a little surprised. "I'll ask you again. Aunt Mia: What happened to my parents, and why won't you tell me?!"

She was mad. She went to her room and came back with something I didn't expect.

She brought a belt and said,

"I warned you, you'd be sorry." I walked slowly backwards toward the living room, and she came after me. I ran around the tiny living room until I realized she wasn't going to stop. I knew I had to run for the main door. She yelled,

"Never ask me that again!" I rushed to the door and ran for my life. I rushed to Lucas's house to get some help. I tripped and fell the entire way even spraining my ankle. When I reached his house, his mom opened the door and was surprised.

"Oh my goodness! What happened to you?"

"I'll explain later, but I really need help with my sprained ankle and all these cuts." She immediately took me to the hospital, and they checked me up and put on some bandages and stuff.

Lucas's mom paid for the bills; they were rich; they had new cars, a fancy house, and everything. After I got back from the hospital, his mom asked me if I wanted to call the police on this. I told her no because Uncle Fred used to be in a gang and he could just send those people to kill me because he really didn't care about me,and I could handle the situation because it wasn't that big of a problem. I stayed at Lucas's house till five, then said that I would be going back to my aunt's house. Her mom said to stay, but I knew not to.

I walked home, and when I reached the door, I hesitated to open it because this specific thought kept coming to me about Aunt Mia, and if she would hit me again, well, it didn't matter now. I walked in and saw Uncle Fred and Aunt Mia on the dinner table. As soon as I came in, Aunt Mia got up from her chair and was coming toward me, but Uncle Fred stopped her and let me go to the living room. I lay there thinking about what I would do to find out about my parents. I got the idea to go there myself to see the burned-down house and find out what happened, to see if anything was left.

NEXT CHAPTER 3

I woke up the next morning at 4, brushed my teeth, and left the house. I had known the address since Uncle John told me I had it memorized: 6948 Bobbins St. I made my way there, asking people to get closer and closer until I was on the road to Bobbin St.; it was just a bit farther down this road. I walked down the road and saw a massive mansion; it was at least fifty times bigger than Aunt Mia's house.

Only the frame of the house stood; everything else was burned. I walked into it just to find lots of burned stuff on the floor. I looked around; there was nothing here; it really was completely burned down. I was at a really low point where I didn't know what to do. There was some guy walking down the street. I asked him, Sir, by chance, would you know what happened to this house?

"Yes, in fact, I do. I used to go to this house for some parties; I was a friend to the owner; he was really rich and had a massive fortune; he said he would be saving a lot for his child." I told him I was his son, and he was shocked.

"Oh my goodness! It really is! You look like him too! Oh, this is great. Here, I'll help you get your fortune from the bank." I walked with him until we came to the city downtown, and I saw a huge building that said J.P. Morgan Chase. I watched in amazement at the building; never had I ever seen such a big building in my life.

We walked inside to see a huge line, and we stood in line for a whole hour until we finally made it to the counter.

"Yes, hello, sir, how may I help you?" The guy said,

"Hi, yes, I think my friend here has a fortune. Could you check?.

" Yes, sir, uh, what's the child's name?" I said Oliver Patrick, my heart was racing. This could change everything; I wouldn't ever have to live with my aunt and uncle again!

"Oh yes indeed, Mr. Patrick, you do have a fortune,but I'm sorry you won't be able to inherit this fortune until you're the age of 18." I was pretty outraged; why couldn't I inherit it now? Well, it didn't matter now because no matter what I did, they wouldn't give me the money. The guy said,

"Oh man, it's fine. Just five more years to go until you become a millionaire! I walked with the guy back to the house, said bye to him, and made my way back to Aunt Mia's house. A tear rolled down my cheek as I cried there, walking back. It was the one way out, but it didn't work.

NEXT CHAPTER 4

I woke up the next morning motivated to find out more—another way to find out about my parents. I had the idea to look at the newspapers at that time. So I went to the library to ask the librarian (a person I could trust) where I could find old newspapers. I did my normal routine and made my way to the library. I'd been here multiple times; I memorized the way and knew shortcuts. I jumped over a fence, which was one of the shortcuts, and reached there in about five more minutes. When I entered the library, I went to the librarian's desk and asked her where I could find old newspapers.

"Oh, Oliver, there in the back beside the fictional book shelves. She smiled. I said thank you and went to the back.

I saw the fictional shelf, looked beside it, and saw a big stack of newspapers. I looked through them, looking for the year 2011. I looked through the years 2009, 2010, 2014, and 2023, but not 2011. I kept looking until I found it in 2011. I flipped through the pages until I found something that caught my attention. A huge fire was in a picture in the newspaper; it said, "There was a house that burned down on March 18, 2011; the owners were Pat John and Clara Sterling. I read two lines until I saw the bottom to see it was completely ripped. I looked through all the stacks of newspapers but found no newspaper that said 2011. I had looked through all the stacks of newspapers, but only that one newspaper that was ripped to the bottom. I prayed there was another. Nothing,absolutely nothing. I was so depressed at this point because nothing was going my way.

I thanked the librarian and left the library. When I reached home, I went straight to the living room, collapsed on the thin sheet I slept on every day, and went to sleep. The next morning, I woke up and did my usual morning routine, and I saw two letters in the mailbox throughout our tiny window beside the door. I went and walked to the mailbox and took out both letters. The first one was a bill, and the second one was from a familiar name I couldn't remember until I read the name again and thought, Uncle John!

CHAPTER 5

I opened up the letter and read it.

"Dear Oliver, I hope you are doing well. I wanted to let you know I know everything about your parents as well as what happened to your house. If you could come, I could tell you everything. Just convince your aunt Mia to bring you here. Don't lose hope,

Uncle John"

I couldn't believe my eyes. Uncle John knew everything! Atlast I would have someone to care about me. I needed to convince Aunt Mia to take me there. I wouldn't lose anything, and besides, I trust Uncle John way more than Aunt Mia. This was my chance to finally know everything and have a good life where there is actually somebody who cares about me. I sat on the ground, waiting for Aunt Mia to come out of her bedroom. When she came out, I asked her straight up, Aunt Mia, can you take me to Uncle John's house? She was surprised but said yes. She muttered,

"It'll be one thing off my shoulder."

I was going to Uncle John's house! The next day, at five, me and Aunt Mia left for the bus. When we got on the bus, we said nothing to each other until we reached the train station.

"Is this the one?" I whispered yes. This train took me straight to New York, so I said bye to Aunt Mia, and for the first time ever, she did something nice for me. She bought me a burger for the ride and just seemed not to care. There, I saw her walk away into the huge crowd of people. She didn't smile or say anything; she didn't seem like a bad person at that time. I fell asleep on the train and woke up just ten minutes before I reached. I just stared out the window, waiting to get there.

Uncle John was waiting for me because I had sent him a letter a day before letting him know I would be coming to New York. The train finally stopped, and everybody was rushing outside. I got lost in the crowd of people. I kept looking and looking for Uncle John. I couldn't see him anywhere, so I took a seat on a nearby bench and opened up the tiny box that had the burger in it. The soft bun, the fresh lettuce, and the juicy tomato all made the burger worth every bite. I ate it halfway until I noticed a face I thought was Uncle John. I rushed towards the guy just to find out it was a random dude. I was kind of feeling lost. These thoughts just kept coming back to me. What if Uncle John didn't get the letter, or what if he didn't care anymore?

But I was patient, and until I saw a familiar face, I slowly approached the guy cautiously because there was a chance he wasn't Uncle John. I immediately recognized the face as Uncle John. Finally, after such a long time, things were actually going my way. He gave me a hug, and we started walking to his apartment. He lived in a huge building that had a great view of Times Square. We walked inside the lobby of the building, walked to the elevator, went to the seventeenth floor, and went to his room. He opened the door, and we walked in. It was huge inside his room. I took a quick shower and saw Uncle John on his phone.

He got up and told me to put on my shoes. We walked to the elevator, went down to the lobby, and walked outside. He took me to a McDonald's and let me order whatever I wanted. I ordered fries, a coke, and a burger. He got an ice cream. After we ate, we walked to the apartment again and went to his room. I sat on the bed, and so did he. We both sat in silence for a minute or two until he said,

"You want to know what really happened?" Yes.

"Your father was a millionaire; he had fancy cars, a huge mansion, and everything you could imagine. He got this money because he owned a huge business that was very successful. More successful than all other competitors. So one day, to stop all this, one of his competitors hired an assassin to kill your father." I took a huge gasp and was astonished. He continued,Then one day, while your parents were asleep, one of the assassins set a fire on your house while your parents were in panic. An assassin was on a nearby hill with a sniper. He pulled the trigger two times, and both your parents were gone. I couldn't explain the feelings I was going through. I was heartbroken and at the same time hooked on to what Uncle John was saying. My brain and heart both wanted to hear more. Learn what had happened.

Uncle John continued,"luckily, the assassins didn't know that you existed, so they left as fast as possible. The nearby public came to the fire and took you outside. By the time the firefighters came, the house had been burned down. The people handed you to the authorities, and they sent you to your aunt Mia." I started weeping, but Uncle John said it was fine. I realized weeping wasn't going to do anything, so I stopped with the help of Uncle John. I asked him questions instead. Why did they send me to Aunt Mia and not you?" Well, you see, your aunt was a lot closer than I was, so they had to send you there. I asked him a few more questions until I came to the last, most important one.

"How did you find out about all this?"

"You see, when you were a child, I came to visit, but as you may remember, your aunt didn't let me stay, so I wanted to figure out the truth and went to the library, looked through the newspapers, and saw one newspaper that talked exactly about what I was looking for."

I stopped him right there. What did you do with the newspaper?

"Oh, nothing much, just ripped off a little more than half of the bottom of the newspaper." I was shocked. I told him about what happened to me in the library.

"Well, it really was a coincidence that you found the top half of the exact newspaper. I said, Wow.

"Remember, Oliver, never lose hope."

7 Years Later...

I sat on the sofa in my million-dollar mansion beside Uncle John, drinking an ice-cold Coca-Cola on this hot summer day. The sweetness and the coldness mixed together just made it twice as good. It had been two years since I had inherited my father's fortune. I had lived the last five years of my life with Uncle John, and by some miracle, I had made it to ColumbiaUniversity in New York. Uncle John had thought it would be best to send me to school, even if I started at the age of 13. I have many job opportunities, but I prefer to stay at home with Uncle John. It had been 7 years since I saw Aunt Mia and Uncle Fred. Uncle Fred had passed away in a gun shooting. He had joined another gang and died.

Aunt Mia still lived in the same house that I grew up in, all alone.

I sometimes wonder how Aunt Mia is still alive. I know because I wasn't invited to her funeral yet. I still visit Lucas every few weeks. With all this money in my possession, I am able to buy whatever my heart wills. I have a private jet and 32 luxury cars, which I keep adding more to. So going to Lucas is not a problem. Every night, I wonder where my parents are. I get a slight bit of hope that maybe they might have survived, or maybe Uncle John was wrong. I never brought up the topic with Uncle John until two days ago, when I found a letter in the mailbox that was about the same size as my hand. I opened it up and read it.

I know where they are. If you want to see them again, you must come to the same house where you grew up—the place that still haunts you. You must come at 7:00 in the afternoon. You may bring one person with you. I know that your Uncle John has told you about the newspaper story, but it is not true. They are alive, somewhere where I cannot tell you. Did you really think your parents would die so easily? If you did, you were wrong. I've known your parents since you were born. If you want to see them, then come.

-Mysterious Man.

On the front of the envelope was a arrow that looked like it was on fire. I was in complete shock. My whole life had been shaken. I told Uncle John about this, and he was up to go with me. I grabbed a backpack, put some essentials in it, and made my way to the place where I still get nightmares, Aunt Mia's house. I was going to find my parents, no matter what.

About the Author
Yousuf Ansari

Yousuf Ansari is a 12-year-old 6th grader at MCC Academy in the Hifz program, The school is in Morton Grove, Illinois. The reason he has made this story is because he wanted to see if he made a story, how it would turn out. Hobbies of Yousuf are bike riding, playing games, reading the Quran, and traveling. Yousuf has one older brother, who is in the Singaporean military, and one older sister, who lives with him and his parents. Yousuf's pets are 3 parakeets, and 1 beta fish. He has interests in computers, planes, electric cars, new tech, and coding. He also has a few achievements such as, winning 5 Quran competitions, writing this book, and fixing problems with tech. Yousuf has memorized 18 Juz of the Quran, and has been in Hifz for 3 years. The type of sports he likes is mainly Cricket and Soccer.

For my school and teacher, who helps me learn more and more.

—Y.A.

Portal Maze

By Yousuf Ansari

There was a time in 1973 in the USA where 3 boys who were named George, Joe, and Joseph, and they were friends playing soccer/football.

George was a very good player and the other 2 boys were not very good since they just started a month ago and George has been playing for about 3 years.

They were doing a 2v1 with George against Joe & Joseph, and they were having a really fun time until something unfortunate happened. A kidnapper told them that he had free candy in his car, and all of them thought it was true.

Then, the kidnapper was driving to his house and he locked them up in a room.

Only then the friends knew that they were being kidnapped, and they all had a lot of fear in their eyes, wondering about how they would get out and when they would.

All of their hearts were beating as if it was a plane flying at the max speed.

They tried to unlock the door, however they were not able to.

All of them were thinking of good ideas until they came up with another idea. They were thinking of breaking the door, so the 3 of them tried to kick and punch it as hard as they could and there was a bit of a crack on the door, but the door did not fully break.

But then they saw something: they saw that the kidnapper forgot his phone in the same room that he locked them up in. So they were thinking of calling the police on the phone so that they could get help, and that's exactly what they did.

They told the police about the entire situation and that's when the police arrived at the kidnapper's house.

The police confronted the kidnapper and the kidnapper said the reason for kidnapping them was because he wanted to help them practice real life scenarios if this were to happen. The police did not believe what he said, and that was for a good reason because what he said was not true at all. The kidnapper was arrested and put into jail for 10 years. After that, the friends discussed that it was time to go to their houses and go to sleep since it was a long day, and they were tired.

The next day, they all met up in the morning to play some soccer/football until something unusual happened.

There was a note on the field where they play that read, "Do not mix chocolate with an apple on the field."

As curious as the kids were, they decided to rip up the note and get chocolate from their houses and for 1 of them to bring an apple. When they all came back together to mix chocolate with an apple, something strange happened again.

There was another note that said, "You'll regret doing this!"

The kids felt a little anxious, but they still continued to mix the apple with the chocolate.

While they were doing it, they felt a bit nauseous, but they still continued.

When they were finished, a portal lit up, and it was horrifying for them, but they still went in.

Then, they saw a beautiful world with a bright teal sky, amazing rivers, and humongous trees.

They saw charming animals and white fluffy gorgeous clouds.

It was almost as if they were in a world in their dreams!

As they were exploring and trying to see as many wonders as possible, they witnessed a wild bear chasing a goat right in front of the green mountains that they were going to try climbing.

They were watching the incident happening while suddenly, the bear started running towards them! They tried to outrun the bear, but right as they looked behind them, they saw it was too late. The bear was already approaching them even though it was a long distance when it started chasing them. But just as they thought they would be injured or worse, a wolf started to come out running from behind a gigantic tree next to them. It actually saved both the bear and the kids from getting hurt by telling the bear that he should not try to injure the kids. After that, they all started giggling and decided to leave each other alone. The kids then thought about this world and realized it was a pretty nice place to stay, even animals could talk! But then they realized, "How will we get food?" "Where would we sleep?" and most importantly, "HOW DO WE GET BACK TO EARTH!?". They all started rushing towards finding a solution, but nothing was coming up. They looked, asked, watched, even tried getting an apple from an apple tree and getting cocoa beans to make apple and chocolate mixed again. But nothing was working, and that's because they were trapped there forever. There was no way of coming back. THEY WILL NEVER COME BACK.

About the Author

Abdul-Hannan Choudhary

Abdul-Hannan is a 12 year sixth grader hifz student who goes to MCC Academy. Abdul-Hannan likes to play fo otball.-A.C

For my baby brother, who I got some inspiration from.

—A.C.

Sudden Attack

By Abdul-Hannan Choudhary

My name is Zeus, and I was born with a gift. I can shoot electricity from my hand. Right now, I am in a warehouse because random people kidnapped me. And now I am sitting in a room filled with teens right now because I made a dumb mistake. I don't know how this even happened because my best friend Zane and I have superpowers. I can shoot electricity from my hands, and Zane can shoot flames from his hands. And plus, I could have just fried them, but I fell for their trick. And now I'm trying to think of a way to escape with a bunch of other kids.

This is how it all started. I was walking home from school with Zane when we saw some random man in an alley behind a store.

"Hey, who is that guy looking at us over there?"

I said "Please tell me how I would know? Let's just go home. I'm tired." Just when Zane finished that sentence the weird man said this.

"HEY, YOU KIDS COME OVER HERE NOW, I HAVE FREE MONEY!"

Ok now this is getting weird. First of all, I'm just trying to walk home with my friend and then there's some weird man in an alley telling us to come over to him. And I don't know why I even did that because they taught us in preschool to NOT go to strange people with big white vans, but I did so. But I was desperate to see what was going on, so I asked Zane.

"What is that?"

"Let's go check it out." Zane replied.

"I don't believe that a single bit. But I guess if anything goes wrong, we can destroy him with our powers."

Now little did I know that something bad was going to happen. As I walked up to the alley, I started to feel really weak, but I still didn't get a clue that something was up. When we got there, a piercing pain went through my body, and then we both passed out.

When we woke up, we were inside of a van lying in the back of it. I should have known. There was a big white van behind the man who was telling us to come to him. But where exactly are they taking us? The van had weird machines all over the place inside the van. There were big boxes everywhere. There was one that was open. I looked inside of the box and there was some weird blue juice inside, I took it out, opened the cap, and smelled it. It smelled so bad I cannot even explain it. I tried to shoot electricity at the man who was driving, but nothing came out. I was too weak. And I was some weird machine next to us.

"Zane," I whispered, so the driver could not hear me.

"Huh?"

"I think that thing over there is making us feel like this," I said.

"Yeah, I know, I can feel it man."

Around five minutes later, we stopped. It was a big warehouse." I have no clue why they brought us over here, man," Zane said. The driver got out of the car and opened the side door.

"GET OUT, COME ON HURRY UP OR ELSE YOU WILL REGRET IT!" He shouted and pushed both of us inside the warehouse.

When I got in, I looked around the warehouse, but nothing looked strange at all. Then the man took us into another room, and I could not believe what I saw. I looked at Zane and a look of horror was on his face. There were at least twenty other kids inside of the room. They all looked terrible, most of them had scars on their faces.

How did they treat these kids? I wondered.

As I was thinking the guard pushed us to the ground and left us there on the floor. Thoughts started racing through my mind, what if we can never escape? What's going to happen? Are we just going to stay here? Does anyone know about this? I kept on thinking and thinking until I fell asleep.

About three days later I could not take it anymore. One morning I looked around, everyone else was awake. I looked at everyone and said,

"Guys we can't let these people do this to us, we have to fight back, we have to escape!"

One of the kids looked at me and said." Yes, we've tried doing that a bunch of times and failed, we just ended up back where we were."

I looked at him and spoke.

"Do you know anything about this place"?

"Yeah."

"Well, tell me everything you know."

Ok, so one time when we trying to escape we passed a room, I think they were having some kind of meeting, they were talking about some plan where there's a bunch of other places like this, they have a bunch of kids and they're going to make all of us drink something, it's going to make us go crazy, we're not going to have control over ourselves, there is some crazy guy that wants to take over some big company. And then he's going to make us work for him while we don't even know it, because we are gonna be brainwashed."

"Oh, that's bad, but we're not letting that happen."

"What are you guys going to do?"

"Trust me, you'll be surprised.'

The boy looked back and spoke.

" Well, what are you going to do that is different from what we did?"

I reached out my fist and aimed at a vase on the other side of the room and shot a bolt of electricity out of my hand. The room flashed as it went across the room and shattered the vase. The kid looked at me with a face of confusion and horror like he had just seen a ghost.

"H-H-How'd you do t-t-that?"

" Do not worry, I am not some inhuman monster." I laughed.

Just then a guard stomped into the room, looked at the broken vase on the floor and barked "Who did that?!"

He said while pointing a weird gun looking thing at everyone. I looked at Zane and he nodded. We both knew this was our chance of escaping with these teens.

I shocked him so hard that his scream did not even leave his mouth. I kneeled and took the key from his pocket and motioned everyone to follow me and Zane. We all ran out of the room and saw two other guards running towards all of us.

Zane lit him up and he started screaming and just fell on the floor and stopped. The alarms started going off and guards started chasing us with the same weird gun-looking thing that the first guard had.

I turned around and fired everything I had. The hallway flashed with light and all the guards fell down and passed out.

"Everyone follows me!!" I screamed. Zane threw a fireball down the hallway and everything behind us lit fire. We ran down the next hallway and there was a whole new group of guards just standing there waiting there for us. I looked at them and spoke.

"What do you think you are doing, huh? Back off and I won't hurt you."

One of the guards stood there with a stupid grin on his face and said,

"What are you going to do if we don't move"?

I looked at him and said, "You don't want to know, trust me."

"Ok do what you are going to do, I don't care, it can't possibly be that bad."

"Don't tell me i didn't warn you" I raised my hand up and gave in everything I had. Electricity crackled through the hall and one of the lights on the ceiling broke off and landed on the guards who are now on the ground because I shocked them so hard. I didn't feel bad for them a single bit. We ran down a few more halls and found the exit. I used the key I got from the guard after shocking him.

I opened the door and ran out to make sure it was safe for the others. I told Zane to stay back to protect them. When I came outside there was one last guard standing over there. I would bet a thousand dollars, if he knew about my powers then he would've used this chance to run far away from here. But anyway, I had to deal with this last person.

He looked at me and said" You don't know how long I've been waiting to see you."

"You don't know how much I don't care."

"Silly boy, you do know you can't do anything right?"

"Your point?"

"You can't do anything; I can just take you right back to your cell with all the others."

"Try me, I dare you."

"Oh, you have some confidence, I like it"

He reached onto his shoulder and picked up his walkie talkie and said" Hey I need some backup to take this kid back to his room with the others."

No one answered him and he said again "hello?"

"Strange, looks like I have to take you back myself."

He took out the same gun thing as the other guards and shot it at the wall. It shot out a laser\bullet and it made a hole in the dumpster that was next to us in the alley.

"Huh, scary right?"

"No, you just shot yourself, the dumpster."

Before I knew it the guard shot the thing, it jerked my body backwards as the projectile found its way into my shoulder.

It hurt like crazy, I fell on the ground, and he came up to me and started dragging me on the ground. And then he picked me up and smashed me on the brick wall. My head was the part of my body that was hit first.

My head hurt so much; it was spinning. I couldn't see anything. Once I got my vision back, I was lying on the ground, I saw the guard looking down at me with a stupid grin on his goofy face. I lifted my hand up to his face and shocked him so hard that he flew up into the air like a foot and passed out on the spot. I got up and put my hand on him again and kept on shocking him. I was really mad, electricity started sparking around him and it sounded like bacon sizzling on a frying pan.

I got up and started walking back to where I had left the others. I had ripped off a piece of cloth from the guard's shirt and tied it on my shoulder to stop the bleeding. Once I got back, they were all gone. Ok, this is strange. I went inside the building and started looking for them. I had done all that to save them and escape this place and now they are all gone? I kept on looking but I found no clue where they were. Just then the door slammed shut. I went over to see what happened, but someone had locked the door.

"Who did that?!" I screamed.

"Me" A random voice answered.

And then the door slowly opened, and I saw a guard standing over there. But this one wasn't a normal guard. This one had a bulletproof vest, and he had a bunch of scary looking tools. One of them was a long knife with a taser at the end and a bunch of other things I had no clue about. I looked at him and pushed him over and ran out the door to the other side of the alley. He got really mad, he stood up and threw something at me. It was some kind of grenade, but it stuck to me like a magnet and a web of electricity covered me. But that didn't do anything to me, electricity only makes my power stronger.

So, with that power boost my eyes started glowing light blue and a big blast of electricity came out of me and the vest he was wearing was incinerated, it was turned into white powder. My blast was so powerful he flew off the ground and hit the wall behind him. He bounced off the wall and fell on the ground.

He looked at me and said, "Please have mercy."

"No"

"What?"

"WhAt "I said, mocking him and raising my hand in front of me.

"No please, mercy"

"I already said no," I said. He started screaming violently while I ended him. After that I started looking around for the others. After about a hour I found all of the others

"Where were you guys, you got me so worried."

Zane looked at my shoulder with horror where I had been shot and said.

"Zeus, what in the world happened to your shoulder?"

I said" It doesn't matter, we need to get out of here."

"Okay but where do we-."

Zane was cut off by a loud booming noise in the alley. "What was that?"

"Let's go check it out," I said.

"Okay but where do we leave them? "He said pointing at all the kids with which we had escaped.

" You guys stay right here, we'll be right back."

All the kids nodded. Me and Zane went to see what all the sound was. We ran down the alley and when we reached the end of the alley, we saw a bunch of the guards doing something with grenades. They were connecting them to a tripwire. One of the guards finished something he was doing and said, "They might have wiped out more than half of our guards, but they won't make it past this part. They can't see the trip wires either so when they come they trip and boom!"

"Zane"

"Yeah?"

"Should we jump them?"

"Yeah, but we should first play with them a little."

Zane raised his hand and shot a bunch of flames on the ground really close to them. All the guards got startled and started getting confused. I went right in front of them and said" Why are you doing all this"!? "None of your business" He barked back.

"Okay, you brought this on yourself."

He snickered and said" What are you going to do, huh?"

"I don't think you want to find out, trust me."

I raised my hand and so much electricity came out of my hand that his whole body just disappeared. The only thing that was left of him was powdery white stuff on the ground where he was standing.

Zane followed right behind me. One guard ran to me and tried to punch me, but I took his hand, turned it around and shocked him at the same time. He screamed in pain, so I shocked him with so much electricity that electric particles came out of his body, surrounding him. I saw Zane on the other side, he was going crazy. A guard came up to him and punched him and Zane fell to the ground. Zane held his hand on his face and got back up. He lit a guard on fire, I could not see anything because the flames were too bright, then punched him to the ground.

After we finished all the guards we went back to the other teens and called the police. They came a few minutes later, we showed them the juice stuff that they were supposed to make us drink, they did some tests on it, and it turned out that the juice was made of a bunch of illegal drugs that brainwashes people. They investigated the whole warehouse and found more illegal things. They called all the teens' parents and sent everyone to their homes. I was happy that all this was over.

"I hope this never happens again, Zane."

"I know right?" Zane said. "But it was fun to use our powers that much."

Finally all that is over so I don't have to worry about getting kidnapped again.

About The Author
Mustafa Farid

Mustafa Farid is a 6th grade student that attends MCC Academy. Mustafa's hobbies are playing basketball, video games and spending time with his cousins and baby sister. Mustafa also enjoys reading fiction books that involve mystery, suspense and thrill. The motivation for this story, "The Haunted Mansion," comes from previously read stories.

I dedicate this book to people who love reading spooky books.

—M.F.

THE HAUNTED MANSION
BY MUSTAFA FARID

It was the start of summer, when Mike and his friends who just got out of high school are going on a cross-country road trip. It was going to be the highlight of their summer. It's something they were looking forward to for months. No school, no homework, no deadlines, just three friends enjoying summer carefree.The plan is to drive from Chicago, Illinois to Santa Monica, California. It would take 40 hours which is 5 days. They got into Missouri and Kansas with no stops. In Texas, they went to a carnival for 2 hours. It took them another hour to get out of texas. They went to a gas station two times in New Mexico. When they got to Arizona their car had some trouble and broke down.

"What happened Josh?" asked Mike.

"I think the car broke down," said Josh. "I will go check it out."

"Ya it broke down," said Mike.

"Let me get a look at the engine," said Smith. It's messed up badly.

"Can you fix it?" asked Mike.

"No, I don't think I can." said Smith

"It's getting late," said Edward, " I think I saw a building we can stay at on our way here".

"Let's go check it out,"said Mike.

At a distance, they saw what looked like an abandoned house. When they got close to the house, they realized it was a mansion. They went inside and the place looked safe, so they stayed. In the middle of the night they heard a voice talking in the living room. When they went down they didn't see anyone or anything. It looked like there was no one there. Mike and his friends went back upstairs and fell asleep again. The next morning they went to check on the car. When they got to the car they tried to start it but it didn't work. They tried again and again but it wouldn't start. They checked the engine and there was a plug that was out of place.

"Do you think you can plug it back in?"asked Mike.

"No, I don't think I can," said Smith. "It's too far down."

Mike and his friend walked back to the mansion to find a rod to fix the car. They were searching for the rod.

They looked in the rooms but couldn't find it. When they got to the second bathroom they found a thin metal rod that could fit in the engine. They walked back to the car with the rod. They opened the hood of the car and stuck the rod in the engine but it was too short, they had to stay another night in the mansion.

"I'm bored", said Edward, "I'm gonna read something".

When Edward pulled out a book from the book shelf,the book shelf opened! They found a big secret room with a desk in the corner of the room, and in the middle of the room was a big bed that was made.

"The bed has no dust on it", said Mike, " That means the bed has been slept in recently..."

"Nah, that's really creepy bro," said Josh.

"Let's look around the room guys," said Smith, " Maybe we can find out if someone has actually been living here."

" Ok", said Edward.

The boys began looking around the room, looking under the bed, in the drawers,

and even inside the desks. They didn't find a single thing by the time they finally left the secret room. It was sunset so they went to the dinning room and ate some snacks. Then they went into their sleeping bags and fell asleep.it was three in the morning when they heard a sound coming from behind the bookshelf.. Where the secret room is. They got out of their sleeping bags and rushed to the secret room. When they got there they saw a white figure go through the wall.

"Did you guys see that?"asked Josh.

"Ya i did"said mike. " which room did that ghost go through?"

"I think that is the library room,"said edward.

Mike and his friends went to the library they split up and tried to find the ghost. Mike found a book on a shelf that had dairy on the cover and a lock that is keeping it closed.

"Look what I found here, Mike," said edward.

"What did you find?" said mike.

"I found a diary on which the cover says Tom Christopher,"said Edward.

"Hey guys, let's look for a hammer or a key so we can open the book,"said mike.

They looked around the library in books,under bookshelves,and in desks. They went all around the mansion. When they went into the basement they looked around and found a small key that looked like it would fit in the lock. They tried the key and it worked.Josh opened the diary and then Edward took it and started to read it.

"If you read this I am probably dead and a ghost now and I will kill you!"read edward

"That was pleasant."said edward

They didn't get much sleep that night. The next morning they saw Mike holding a knife and staring at all of them. Mike was right in front of a painting of a man in front of the kitchen table. When he steps towards them.

"Yo Mike, put the knife down!Josh yelled.

Then Josh throws a pillow at Mike so it would cover his face,then Smith goes on Mike and takes the knife and throws it.

"What happened?"asked Mike.

"Nothing, you just tried to kill us!"Josh exclaimed.

"Oh my bad." Mike said sheepishly.

"What about that knife?" asked smith.

"I was hungry so I found a knife and was about to cut something and then it went black and now I'm here,"said Mike.

"I think that knife might be connected to that ghost,"said Josh. "Let's go find something to break that knife."

Mike and his friends split up throughout the mansion when they came back Smith was holding the knife.They grabbed a rod and hit his hand.

"WHY DID YOU TAKE THE KNIFE!"Mike yelled.

"I was going to hit it against a wall thenI lost control of my mind,"said smith.

"Ok guys, no one touch the knife,"said Smith.

Mike and his friends go back on their search. This time they stuck together when they went back into the basement they found a stone brick and thought they would be able to use it to break the knife. They went back and got a wood log to stick to the knife. Mike took the brick and threw the stone on top of the knife.

"What! how did the stone break?," said Josh.

"I guess we have to go looking for something bigger and stronger than a brick,"said Mike.

They went to the kitchen and started to make a plan and to split up.

"Ok, me and Josh are together,"said mike. "Edward and Smith, you guys are together".

Mike and Josh went to the backyard and started to look for something bigger, sharper, and stronger that would break the knife.They looked behind bushes, above trees and under the patio.

"There's nothing here," said mike.

"This is so annoying,"said Josh

"Let's just go back inside the mansion,"said Mike.

Meanwhile, Edward and Smith went to the trophy room and started looking around. They opened the cases and were looking at the trophy. They were seeing which ones were most durable when they found a huge gold diamond trophy.

"Did you guys find anything,"asked Mike.

"Yup we found a pretty strong trophy,"said Edward. "How about you?"

Mike and his friend went back to the kitchen and came to the knife. They threw the knife and the trophy both dented a little. They threw it again and the trophy cracked a bit, the third try the trophy was broken into a million pieces.

"I'm done with this!"Josh said angrily. "I'm just going to throw it against the wall."

"DON'T TOUCH THE KNIFE MAN!"they all yelled.

Josh picks up the knife and is about to throw it when he stops and freezes for a few seconds. Josh turns around and looks at them, then he starts chasing them!Josh dives for Edward and cuts the bottom of his leg. Edward kicks Josh in the face and he drops the knife.

"Ouch my leg,"Edward says in pain.

"Oh are you ok I'm so sorry!"Josh exclaimed.

"Ya i think im fine but can someone get me a first aid kit,"Edward said.

"Hey smith go get it quick," Mike says urgently.

Mike wraps a cloth around the bottom of his leg, after they put Edward down to rest and go looking again.Th ey looked for a while in the master bedroom when Mike saw a white figure go up into the roof.

"Did you guys see that white figure go up in the ceiling?"asked Mike.

"Let's go in the attic and check it out,"suggested Smith.

They made their way up to the attic and saw a bunch of old things like stone carved knives and an antique bookshelf. Josh saw a black stone sword on top of a tall dresser.

"Hey guys do you see that sword lets stack up on top of each other so we can get it,"said Josh.

"Okay, get it on my shoulders,"said Mike.

They stacked up on each other and got the sword and made their way back to the kitchen. They woke up Edward and made their way back to the knife. They got a log and stuck it back on the knife then set the log on the table. Josh gave the sword to Mike then he swung the sword at the knife BAM the knife cracked, Mike swung again and BAM it cracked more , Mike swung a third time with all his might and BOM there's a blast that shot them all back the sword and the knife crashed.

"WE DID IT GUYS! Josh said. "Let's get out of here".

They made their way to the car, it started thankfully,and continued their drive to california. When they got there they stayed there for one week and they went to the beach. The last day they packed all their stuff and headed home.

The End

About the Author
Zayan Hassan

Zayan Hassan is smart and sometimes shy. He is memorizing the Holy Quran and his favorite subjects are Math and Social Studies. Zayan goes to MCC Academy and he is in 6th grade. Zayan likes to play cricket, but most of the time he plays soccer, and that is why he made this book. Zayan's favorite food is Mutton Biryani and he likes hanging around with his friends at ICCD. Zayan used almost all of his imagination in this book. Zayan has a mom, dad, and two younger sisters.

For Cristiano Ronaldo, who always inspires me every single day.
—Z.H.

THE RISE OF CR7

BY ZAYAN HASSAN

T HUD! Cristiano's soccer ball hit the window of the apartment building that neighbors his own. He hurried away before his cranky old neighbor, Mr. Johnson, yelled at him again for disturbing his peace. Cristiano went back home and started juggling the ball because he had no space for a backyard. After playing with the ball for a little bit, his mom called him for lunch and he saw his father reading a newspaper, while his mom was bringing the food on the table. When Cristiano was eating, he was curious about his dad being so attentive to his newspaper. After some time his dad realized that there was food on the table, so he put down his newspaper and started to eat. Ronaldo quickly ate his food and hurried to play soccer with his friends, but he was still interested in what was in the newspaper so he took a quick glance at the newspaper. A Soccer Match for ages 10-13. Ronaldo remembered the address 1624 west portugal street. Cristiano had fun with his friends in the training match by scoring a beautiful header and won the match 1-0.After the training match the coach said that there is a match for ages 10-13.Cristiano remembered that and he signed up. The coach also said that he will help them to practice for the game. One day when Ronaldo was playing with his friends. One new kid called Rooney came and he said that he is also playing. Cristiano didn't like him because he would always show off on everything and he was also a bad bully. One day in a training match Cristiano was doing very well. Rooney got jealous and slide tackled Cristiano's foot.

THUD!

6:30 am, 1999

Ronaldo woke up in a hospital and his head started hurting. He looked around and he saw his mom and dad giving the money for the bill.The doctor said that Cristiano's foot surgery was successful, but the problem is that it will be hard for him to play soccer. If he puts too much pressure on his foot, his foot may break and his parents were shocked because that was Cristiano's favorite sport. After hearing that Cristiano pretended he was sleeping because the second his mom heard that she turned her eyes to Cristiano. Cristiano thought about it and started being worried that he would never ever be able to play soccer for his entire life!

Cristiano woke up, brushes his teeth and gets ready to play for the soccer game. His parents also wake up for breakfast. His parents tried to make him confident and told him to try his best. Cristiano arrived at the soccer field. Cristiano had a fun game and they won 2-0. After the match

One man came and said whoever scores the most goals in a match will join a soccer club. Even though Cristiano wasn't fully recovered, he still wanted to play. Cristiano was so excited that when he was playing, he was dreaming of playing in a very big club and being extremely rich.

OUCH!

Ronaldo got fouled, so he got a penalty. His hands were sweaty, not knowing where to score, he became nervous. Ronaldo took a step and scored.

GOAL!

It was the last 1 minute of the game and Ronaldo's friend Muhammed, who was also very poor and lived next to Ronaldo's house, was about to score, but he passed to Ronaldo. Ronaldo stopped for a second, and kicked the ball. It touched the goalies hand and it felt like Cristiano couldn't make it but Rooney accidentally kicked the goalies hand and the ball went out of the goalies hand and into the net.

GOAL!

He scored. Cristiano and his team won 3-0. After the match, Cristiano asked his friend why he passed to him even though he could score. He said that Cristiano could play better in the future, so he passed to Ronaldo. Ronaldo said that he would never forget about his best friend Muhammad. After that Cristiano went to the ice cream shop and got a scoop of chocolate ice cream to celebrate. When Ronaldo arrived at his home, his ice cream was starting to melt when he was talking to his mother about the game. After telling his mother he quickly went to his father. Both him and Cristiano's parents were very happy and proud of him. Cristiano went to sleep and started dreaming about how many cars, houses and many trophies he is going to win.

About the Author
Aisha Hussain

Aisha Hussain is a 6th grader going to 7th, doing Hifz. She started writing this story at the beginning of the school year. Huda's characteristics are basically based of off mine. She also looks like me too. The baby jaguar picture is one of my favorite pieces of art ever made (in my opinion)! Part 2 will be coming soon. while you are waiting, I recommend reading the rest of these amazing stories written by my Hifz classmates, which you also might find interesting!!!

Dedicated to all the people out there who are fans of Wings of Fire!
—A.M.H.

DRAGON ACADEMY PART 1

BY AISHA HUSSAIN

Huda Khan was thrilled beyond measure when she received an invitation to attend a top-secret school that would teach her how to ride and communicate with dragons. She had always been passionate about these magnificent creatures and the thought of interacting with them was a dream come true.

Without wasting time, Huda packed her bags and headed to the school, where she was introduced to her four roommates - Crystal, Snowfall, Ariya, and Elyse. Crystal was full of energy and enthusiasm, while Snowfall was always sassy and had a bit of an attitude. Ariya was introverted but brilliant, and Elyse was outgoing, daring, and adventurous.

Over the next five days, the girls learned everything there was to know about dragons - how to ride them, take care of them, and even communicate with them. It was an incredible experience, and Huda felt like she had found her true calling.

But their joy was short-lived when they discovered that the school's head principal had been kidnapped by an evil sorcerer and his minions, who planned to use the school as their fortress. They also wanted to create an army of minions to help them take down their enemies.

Huda and her friends knew that they had to act fast to save the school and the principal. They devised an ingenious plan to rescue the principal and defeat the sorcerer once and for all.

The battle was intense, but Huda and her friends were determined to emerge victorious. They fought fiercely and bravely, and after a long and grueling fight, they finally defeated the sorcerer and his minions.

The school was saved, and the girls had proven themselves to be true heroes. From that day on, they continued to learn about dragons and how to interact with them. They remained best friends, knowing they had been through an incredible adventure together.

Actual Story:

My name's Huda Khan, and I'm 12 years old. I'm all about mythical creatures, especially dragons! I've got five siblings - two older and three younger - and we all live with my mom, dad, 3 grandparents, aunt, and uncle. We're a big family! I like playing chess, basketball, and reading books in my free time.

It's been tough since my dad's dad passed away two years ago in his sleep, at least he died peacefully but it's still sad. He was kind of the heart of our family, so we were initially struggling. But we're holding it together and managing just fine. We're not super rich, but we're not struggling either. We're somewhere in the middle-class-ish, you know?

Got it! So, let's move on from the intro and dive into the day. I was deep in my beauty sleep when that big ball of fire in the sky (a.k.a. the sun) decided to show up and shine super bright. Ugh, not the best way to wake up, am I right?

Anyway, I think it was time to wake up, but nope, it's just 2:37 am! And it's still dark outside, so what's that glowing? I turn toward my bedside and I have to shield my eyes from the brightness. It's an envelope!

My heart skipped a beat when I saw the name on it. Huda Khan, located in Champions Gate, Orlando, Florida 69678. I can't believe it's actually for me! My mind is racing with excitement, but also a bit of skepticism.

Gotta get it together and open it up to see what it's all about.

It says:

Huda Maryam Khan, we are pleased to inform you that you have been accepted to Dragon Academy, Where students learn to ride, interact, and care for dragons. A group of 5 will be placed in a penthouse based on their skills, traits, and personality, every quintet will acquire a mentor who watches over and keeps everything for the penthouse that you and your group will be living in for a semester...

I didn't even finish reading it, but who cares? I need some time to process this - I got accepted to a school that has freaking DRAGONS! And the best part? I'm getting assigned one too! I can't even believe it! Oh, hold up... maybe it's just my stupid little sister Noor playing one of her annoying pranks on me. Ugh, if only her handwriting wasn't so good, I wouldn't have fallen for it. *sigh* She got me there for a second. Just wait and see, she's gonna pay for it tomorrow morning, mark my words. "Little kids these days..." I mumble into my pillow, barely awake.

As I wake up in the morning, I'm thinking, "It's time for payback!" I head downstairs and find everyone in the living room, except for Mom. I assume she's in the kitchen, and thankfully, I'm right. "Hey, Noor know what this is?" I yell loud enough so Mom can hear, waving the paper."Ooh, what is it?" Sidrah (My 14-year-old sister) shouts back even louder. She comes running down the stairs snatching the paper out of my hand, ugh I forgot about her. "Hey!" I yell angrily, "Give it back!" "Hi!" She responds knowing I will get even angrier.

I forgot that I had yelled loudly enough for Mom to hear, and say, "I swear I am going to..." I start, "Huda!" My Mom says. Great, a lecture. Just what I need. "What were you saying?" Sidrah mutters under her breath but loud enough so I can hear, "Something like you were threatening me?" I shoot her a glare. It's all I can do not to slap her. "What have I told you about using that word?" my Mom says.

"Uhh, something about um...." I try. I honestly don't recall a word she has ever said about discipline. She sighs and says, "OK, everybody breakfast is ready." I grab the paper from Sidrah and stick my tongue out at her. She opens her mouth about to say something but turns on her heel and stalks off. "Phew," I think to myself, if she said something I would've been in big trouble.

So, I finished my breakfast and saw Noor heading upstairs to her room. I decided to check on Sidrah and found out that she was playing with my little brothers, Dawud and Ismael, in the yard. That was a relief because now I could take care of my important paper without worrying about her snatching it away from me. I dash up the stairs halfway through the hallway when it hits me. Noor can't be the one to write this letter.

I don't think she's smart enough to write so formally and professionally. Plus, all the envelopes are stored in the basement which is like 3 floors down from her bedroom. When I waved the paper, she didn't even seem to recognize it. If she did, I'm pretty sure she would've smirked. She's too lazy and scared to do all that work anyway. I'll just ask Mom, I don't have any other choice.

So, I sneakily go into my mom's room, and she's reading the Quran. Before she notices me, I quietly close the door and tiptoe back to my room. After a while, I return to her room and knock on the door. She tells me to come in, and I ask her if she knows what the invitation is from.

At first, she looks like she recognizes it, but then she quickly changes her expression to act like she doesn't know. It's too late though I've already noticed.

I think I figured out who did it - my mom. But why would she do that? I acted like I didn't notice her reaction and asked, "So, do you know who did it?" She replied, "No, why would I know? Now go back to your room and pray Zuhur." I drag myself to my room, plop on the bed, and let out a deep sigh. I highly doubt that my mom was behind it, but she knew something. I mean, come on, my mom pranking me? That's just ridiculous! I'm pretty sure she didn't do it.

Then who did, maybe it is real! No way it can't be, dragons are made-up creatures! Ugh, well I'll just finish reading the paper, but first I have to go pray Zuhur.

I walk to the bathroom thinking about the paper, make wudu, go to my room, pray, and then start reading the paper. Continuing from where I left off it says,

...Upon enrollment, each student is assigned one of four elemental affiliations: Fire, Water, Earth, or Air. Additionally, students are specified the unique opportunity to interact with the school's dragons on

campus. A special necklace is provided to each student which illuminates the formation of a bond between a student and their respective dragon. This necklace serves as an indicator of successful dragon bonding.

There exists a variety of dragon classifications, including MudWings, SandWings, IceWings, LeafWings, HiveWings, SeaWings, SkyWings, RainWings, NightWings, and SilkWings. It is advised that school supplies will not be necessary; instead, a suitcase containing personal belongings will suffice for a year-long trip worldwide. We kindly request your prompt response by July 27 as the academic year is scheduled to commence on August 26. This will allow us enough time to prepare your quintet and penthouses as per your requirements. We

appreciate your cooperation and look forward to your response.

HEAD PRINCIPAL:

Charlie Kentwell

Then my mom comes into the room and asks to see
the paper, I give it to her and wait patiently. It seems
hours before she is done, my eyelids start becoming
heavy and I am about to fall asleep when finally, she
tosses the letter back to me and says, "Why don't we
give this 'Dragon Academy' a shot?" She puts air quotes
around the name. I smile and agree. She offers to write a
letter saying I'll be attending the school this year. I nod
and say, "OK." Then she leaves to work on the response,
and I pass out. Ok, maybe that was an overreaction
but my brain thought that everything was too hard to
process so it just wanted to stop working for a while.

It's 3:00 P.M. when I wake up, how did I even fall
asleep? I try to recall how I did but I can't. Oh, I have a
guess it's the whole 'Dragon Academy' thing from my

dream. Ugh, if only it were real, imagine how cool that would be! Better pray Asr before Mom starts yelling at me for missing it. Thank God that I still have 10 minutes before Maghrib! I go to the bathroom to freshen up, and make wudu. Then I pray Asr and look for my Mom she isn't in her room, *gasp* but guess what is?

The invitation and the response note! My heart starts pounding hard against me.

Could this all be real? Was it, not just a dream? Am I hallucinating? I can't believe it, I move forward to touch the papers, thinking that I am just going to feel air but no! I can feel the warm and crisp invitation letter, written in gold letters. Its feeling is so soothing to my fingertips.

Tears suddenly cover my eyesight, I hug the letter, what a dream come true! My sister Sidrah walks into the room just as I finish crying, and says, "Ew, why are you hugging that weird letter, and omg, are you crying?" I roll my eyes and she says, "ASTAGFIRULLAH, oh, wait you're just searching for your brain in the back of your head until you realize you don't have one!"

She falls on the floor laughing her head off. Ugh, big sisters these days am I right? Dude, I wish I could just kick her in the stomach right now. Guess who would be laughing then, huh? Well anyway, I step over her, walk into my bedroom, and lock the door. I can't wait until August 26, 'cause that's when school is gonna finally start! My mom calls me down for dinner and smiles, I mouth "Thank you!" to her, "You're welcome!" She mouths back.

August 25th

Then the day of the journey begins, well... the day *before* the journey begins.

But anyway, it still is exciting! Tomorrow I am going to the best school in the world, Dragon Academy! Right now I am packing my bag and am about to be done, ok so the last thing on my packing list is... Quran Bag. Uh, I don't know if they will let me read the Quran, but what I have to put in the bag is my Quran, a prayer mat, a tasbeeh, and a device only to listen to the Quran + a pair of AirPods.

OK, that's done, now I can go and read the letter they said about how to get to the academy. Where did Mom say it would be? Oh, yeah her dresser, DUH! OK, here we go the letter says:

Greetings Huda Khan, I am your quintet's mentor, Alexis Crossley. Me and the rest of the staff of course are thrilled that you are

**joining Dragon Academy this year. However-
er, you will need a way to get to the Academy. It will be by jet you don't need to worry
about where because it will be at the front
of your driveway by August 25th, @ 6:00
sharp. Hope to see you soon.**

Your one and only mentor,

Alexis Crossley

Ooh, a jet I honestly have never flown in one before
this is gonna be awesome! Wait, a second! It says it's
gonna be here by 6:00! What time is it? OMG IT'S 3:00!
I have to tell Mom! I bet she has no clue what a single
word on this paper says! "MOM!" I yell. "Yes, Huda?"
My Mom responds. "The paper says the jet leaves at 6
today!" I say. "Uh-oh, did you pack all your bags?" She
says, "Yes, I did!" I respond. "Ok, put on a nice outfit,
come downstairs, and eat lunch!"

By the time I finish getting ready and eating my
lunch, it is 5:20. Oh good I'm 'on schedule' according to

my mom. I zip up all my bags, put on my sweater, adjust my quran bag and my basketball bag over my shoulder, and roll my suitcases out the front door. Surprisingly I see all my family standing outside waiting for me.

My 16-year-old brother Ali, Sidrah, Noor, Dawud, Ismael, and my mom. I give them all hugs and when I have to give Sidrah one we barely touch each other for even a second. Before I run to the pillar and try to get every essence of her off me and make a mental note never to touch that specific pillar ever again. I look over my shoulder and see Sidrah doing the same.

Then after I'm done saying goodbye, a jet materializes out of the air and it's time to go.

I open the door and oh! How beautiful it is inside! I rush to the window and wave one final goodbye smiling my ears off. I go to the pilot's station, but there is no pilot! How can this be? It turns out to be a deck where I can enjoy the outside air. I lean on the handrails and let the wind blow my hair behind me.

It feels so good! I have such good feelings about this academy. I go to the bedroom, examine it, and fall asleep on the bed. It's dark outside when I wake up, I go back to the deck, and... OMG! IT'S THE ACADEMY! I see jets just like mine going straight down, I catch a girl on a jet to my right waving to me and smiling. I wave back nervously, she has blonde hair with a few stands of brown, sea blue eyes and white skin. It also, I assume, has her name on the front of the jet, which says, "Crystal" in big bold letters. The jets even have our names on it, SICK! I look to my left and see a girl with red hair and brown eyes catch my eyes, and looks down at her nails and examines them as if she is bored, her jet says, "Snowfall".

The girl ahead of me has light wavy blue hair, gray eyes, purple glasses, and is holding a book, she eyes me nervously and quickly looks away, the front of the jet reads "Ariya". The girl behind me has brown hair in a ponytail, and has on athletic clothes, armbands, and those bands you put on your forehead (I forgot what it is called but I know it's not a headband). Why is she even wearing them? It's not as if we are heading to a travel game to play basketball, and totally not arriving at a secret dragon academy! Her name is "Elyse" She looks at me, waves her hand high in the air, and says, " 'Sup?" I smile at her and face back toward the academy, thinking that this is the best day I have ever had since my dad died.

I hope I fit in properly, and people don't hate me for being Muslim. I'm pretty sure there'll be other Muslims too. I start to worry, what if they do hate me? What if they send me home when they find out? What if my quintet doesn't like me? What if they bully me? What if my roommate pranks me, destroying my side of the room? Even worse, everybody finds a dragon and I'm the only one who doesn't? What if... ok, this has to stop. I should be focusing on the Academy and the Dragons!

What I can't wait for is to finally meet the dragons! It's soooo exciting! The jets are starting to land as we are about to hit the floor, a squeaky voice behind me says, "Greetings, human of earth, what is your name?" The voice makes me jump, I turn around to see a very tiny and weird creature holding my stuff. How in the world did he get here? I quickly but politely grab my quran bag from his hands just in case he puts it on the floor.

And respond by saying, "My-y name is-s H-huda K-khan." I stammer. "What a lovely name, mine is StrateBear!", "What a pleasure to meet you!" He responds putting out his hand for me to shake. I reluctantly hold out a finger ('cause his hand is so small!) shake it, and he says," I am your very personal escort here at Dragon Academy, the best school in the world!" He says. "Don't you agree?" He asks. I nod my head in agreement, he says "It only gets better every second, wait till you're inside!"

It is a long walk to the academy but very enjoyable, he is not the only weird creature here. There are different varieties of creatures. But tons of them look just like him but have a badge that says their name. When our walk to the academy comes to an end, we are standing right in front of the school. It has a fountain right in front of it that I am guessing is a SeaWing statue, water spurting out of the dragon's mouth. I look up expecting to see dragons flying up above our heads and I am not disappointed. There are so many of them, all very beautiful looking! Wow, that one with the blue and purple wings looks soooo cool! Oh, the one with green wings shaped like leaves is that even possible?!

Then the doors to the academy open, and 3 people riding dragons come out. The one in the middle says, "Greetings and welcome to Dragon Academy! My name is Charlie Kentwell. As you all know this academy is where you will be learning to interact, ride, and care for dragons. Today you will be assigned a dormitory, which you already know but just in case you forgot, is based on a certain element. Tomorrow you will be assigned a dragon. There are 4 dormitory elements: Fire, Earth, Water, and Air. Whichever element suits you best you will find the dormitory that is decorated based on that specific element. Have a nice day!"

Immediately, I go and sign up for the fire dormitory, and I see the 4 other girls that I saw earlier today doing the same. Snowfall, Ariya, Crystal, and Elyse. Then I am assuming our mentor: Alexis, comes to take all of us to our dormitory. On the way, she says, "Hello everybody, my name is Mentor Alexis, but please feel free to call me Alexis. I am the fire quintet's mentor because when I joined the academy just like you are now I chose the fire element. Oh, here we are now!"

She stops at this door that says, 'FIRE' and has majestic red, orange, and yellow patterns written above the door. Alexis opens the door, my god it is so beautiful inside! She says, "2 of you will be assigned a room each but Snowfall that one over there is a private one for you. Feel free to explore, your stuff has already been brought up to your rooms." I end up being roommates with Crystal, Elyse with Ariya, and of course, Snowfall gets a suite to herself.

Crystal suggests excitedly that we go check our new room and I nod as a yes. My and Crystal's room is on the second floor. We hurry up the stairs, skipping a few steps not wanting to wait a second longer to see our room. Crystal uses the key that was in the mailbox to unlock the door and opens it. WOW, one word WOW!

It matches my personality so perfectly, I turn to look at Crystal's half of the room and I'm amazed by what I see.

Apparently, she loves flowers, so she has what looks like a flower bed. A flower swing, flower pillows, and other flowery things. Anyways, back to my room. As I said earlier in the book, I love chess! I'm pretty sure they knew that, because there is a chess board on the dresser and a design on the wall where a hand is picking up a pawn (a chess piece that can only move one space), it looks sooo cool! I don't think I have ever told you guys this but I have an obsession for wild cats, especially Jaguars even better, the baby ones! So behind my bed is a picture of a baby Jaguar petting a butterfly that is sitting on a flower in a meadow. It is sooo cute! I guess they think books aren't my thing, cause there are only a few books.

I think I know who has a library, It's kinda obvious, Ariya the bookworm girl!

I think that I also mentioned that I love basketball at the beginning of the story, I am pretty sure they also know that. Because there is a basketball hoop pinned to the wall, plus my bed looks like a lit basketball court with a basketball going through the net that says: Eat, Sleep, Dunk, Repeat! Wow, just wow! It's like they know me more than I do myself.

I should start making new friends. I look at my chess set and glance at Crystal. What a good idea, now's my chance, I walk over to Crystal. But she comes to me first and says, "OMG, I love your side of the room, that jaguar is sooo cute! You have very good taste in things, wow you also like chess? Do you have a board, can we play if you do?" I responded, "Yeah, sure! I was just going to ask you that! I love your room too!"

After a whole game of chess (I won, in case you are wondering) she said that we should go visit the other dude's rooms, and I say, "Sure." We ended up going to Ariya and Elyse's room, and I guess I was right, on Ariya's half of the room there are 3 bookshelves and special gadgets that I don't know of. On Elyse's side, there are athletic equipment, training balls, and D-mans.

We decided not to go to Snowfall's room, cause she's literally standing right behind us in the doorway. Elyse quickly picks up one of those heavy-training basketballs and starts pounding it on the floor. She also says to us, "I don't think you guys want to stand here and watch me for 4 hours doing my daily training, you're probably gonna get bored." She winks at us, and just then Snowfall says, "You seriously do this every day for

4 hours?" Elyse responds, "Sure do, not only dribbling but I also do K-boxing,..."

She is interrupted by Snowfall saying, "URGH!!!" She storms out of the room angrily.

We all start laughing, we can't help it. I say (still laughing), "Good one Elyse!" She responds saying with a smirk, "Thanks!".

We all ended up agreeing to take my chessboard and go down to the living room to verse each other. We ask if Ariya wants to play but she says, "No thanks guys, I just found a book on the dragons and kingdom of Nethilor if you guys don't mind." "Sure you can read that instead, but later on if you still want to play you can," I say shrugging. I verse Elyse and end up winning (obviously), though it was a close call. I am about to ask her for a rematch when Ariya says, "Oh, that's just awful.".

All of us jump when she speaks, 'cause we were so caught up in the game we forgot that she was even there, Oops, my bad. "What's awful?" I ask. "Oh, nothing." She replies. "Oh, c'mon Ariya please tell us," Crystal says, nudging her knee. "OK, fine, it says: An evil sorcerer once ruled over Nethilor and used to make dragons and other species to his bidding, and if they didn't they would be publicly humiliated and whipped!" Ariya responds pushing up her glasses.

"Damn, whoever that evil sorcerer is, he means business." Elyse says, "Glad he isn't around anymore!" Crystal looks ready to cry. "Hey, why don't we check out the balcony?" I ask, trying to liven up the mood. Elyse notices Crystal, and says, "I bet you anything there is a pool!" "Ooh, now that sounds fun, c'mon Crystal!" I say. "Last one outside is a delusional squid-brain!" Elyse says. "You're on!" I say. Ariya hesitates but then surprisingly says, "Count me in!" "C'mon Crystal, we know you want to join in on the fun! Isn't that your thing, not the opposite?" I say. Crystal gives me a teary-eyed smile and nods.

We stay in the pool for like 4 hours when Ariya goes inside to check the time and comes running out saying, "Everybody get to bed, right now! It is 10:30, we have to get up at 8:00 on the dot tomorrow! Not even, it clearly says that we have to be on the *grounds* by 8!". Everybody rushes out of the pool thanking her, goes to their rooms and gets ready for bed.

Someone shakes me awake. I dumbly say, "Go away Noor!" But then I hear Crystal's voice and she says, "Who's Noor? Get up silly, it's me, Crystal!" I quickly wake up, rub my eyes, and say, "Thanks for waking me up, I probably would've been late!" "No problem silly, just get ready!" she says.

By the time all of us are done getting ready it's 7:30, "C'mon guys, I don't want to miss breakfast!" Elyse says. "Dude, chill out, we have 25 minutes!" Crystal says, "Okay, and?" Elyse says, "I heard that there are so many varieties of food it's going to take us 10 minutes to choose!" "Ok, we still have 15 minutes then if you are right!" Crystal says. I glance at my watch and say, "GUYS WE WASTED **2** PRECIOUS MINUTES!" "Let's go, NOW!" Ariya says.

We all run and dash down the stairs, this place is like a maze. We have made so many wrong turns that, every time we open a new door we hopefully smile but then it turns out to be a janitor's closet. Then the smiles slip away, I check my watch, again 5 minutes have been wasted! Just then we spot some kids across the hall going into a room with two large doors that are labeled above the doors as 'FEASTING HALL'! Yes, we have found it! Well actually did we?

We sprint down the hall, push the doors open with brute force, and enter. Trying not to trip over each other we grab onto the poles that hold hand sanitizers, panting hard Elyse smiles and says, "Well-*gasp* we fina-*gasp*-lly made *gasp* it!" with another huge in-

hale. "Yeah, *gasp* but we-*gasp* have onl- *gasp* -y
have 5 minu- *gasp* -tes to choose our *gasp* food!"
I say. "Ok, then we'd bette- *gasp* -r start cho- *gasp*
-osing now!" Ariya says.

We finish our food 1 minute before the announce-
ments start. Head principal Charlie says in the megaphone, "All 1st-year students need to be in the dragon
field by 2 minutes so you can be assigned your new
dragons, all 2nd-year students need to be in the training
courtyard so you can collect the same dragons that you
had last year and train with them. 3rd years need to be
in Mrs. Plumpberry's classroom by 8:15, 4th years need
to be in the graduation room for studying. Thank you,
and have a good rest of your day!"

"Few, I'm so glad that we spotted those kids or
we would've been starvin' the whole day!" Elyse says
standing up. "OK, we have about 2 minutes to get to the
dragon field so le-" I was cut off by Elyse's groaning
she says, "Ugh, we have to look for the field door, we
only have **2** minutes to do so!" "Uh, Elyse?" Ariya says,
"I don't think Huda was done talking yet?" "*Sigh*, Yep,
I wasn't," I say. "Well, you can continue," Crystal says.
"OK, anyways as I was saying, on our way to the Kitchen
I spotted a sign that said 'DRAGON FIELD' that was on
our right. It will prob take a minute to get there and a

minute to get across the field." I say pointing to the sign I was talking about. "OK, nice work spotting that Huda, or we would've actually been late this time, on our first day!" Elyse says with an apologetic smile.

I take the lead and we head down in the direction I pointed in. Push open the doors, having to block the Sun from our eyes to avoid going blind. OK, OK. I know what you're thinking but it's actually the sun this time, not an envelope to another secret school, okay?!?!?! All around us beautiful dragons are flying, running, and the babies playing.

"OMG, that one over there is soooo cute!" Crystal squeals. I look at the baby dragon she pointed to, it's a hybrid I think because it has I am guessing an IceWing's FrostBreath but black NightWing scales and a Sand-Wing's poisonous barbed tail. "I think that that baby is the most coolest and cutest hybrid that I have ever seen before!" says Ariya. I nod in agreement and say, "Yep sure is!" All of us jump when one of the teachers speaks because it's so loud, we turn around and see that she is holding a megaphone, "AHEM, AHEM CAN EVERYBODY HEAR ME? OK GOOD, I AM THE HEAD DRAGON TEACHER HERE AND I HELP STUDENTS PICK THEIR DRAGONS. MY NAME IS ISABELLA LEAH, BUT YOU CAN CALL ME BELLA. AS YOUR MENTOR

HAS MENTIONED IN THE ACCEPTANCE LETTER. YOU
GUYS WILL BE PROVIDED WITH A SPECIAL BOND-
ING NECKLACE THAT GLOWS WHEN INDICATING A
BOND BETWEEN A HUMAN AND A DRAGON.THE 2
TEACHERS BESIDE ME WILL BE AROUND TO ASSIST
YOU IF YOU NEED ANY HELP GIVE US A SHOUT! ANY
QUESTIONS?"

One girl from another quintet raised her hand and
Mrs. Isabella called on her. "My question is, if we don't
find our dragons today will you be sent home?" "WHAT
A SILLY QUESTION, FIRST OF ALL, WE SENT YOU AN
INVITATION "CAUSE WE KNEW YOU HAD THE PO-
TENTIAL TO BE A DRAGON RIDER, SO WHY WASTE A
TRIP? SECOND OF ALL, YOU SPECIFICALLY WILL FIND
A DRAGON TODAY AT 5:34 ON THE DOT! SO WHY
WORRY? ANY OTHER QUESTIONS? OK, LET'S START!"

We get assigned the teacher to Mrs. Isabella's right,
her name is I think Ms. Rosemary, she seems pretty hy-
per and nice. She hands us our necklaces and says, "Just
like Mrs. Isabella said, you guys are here because you
have the potential to be a Dragon Rider. Don't overthink
it, roam around, and eventually, you will find a dragon.
You guys got this when the gong sounds that will be
your cue to start Dragon Hunting. If you don't find it
today you will tomorrow, I promise. Good luck!"

The gong sounds through the woods, signaling the start of our adventure. Everyone rushes into the woods, but I stay close to my quintet. We're all nervous, but excited as well. We've been waiting for this moment for months, and it's finally here.

Suddenly, a deafening roar echoes through the forest, making us all jump. We look at each other's necklaces, searching for any sign of a dragon nearby. And then we see it, a very strong-looking LeafWing - Elyse's necklace is glowing! We can't believe it. It's finally happening.

Elyse is beside herself with excitement. "No way!" she exclaims. "This is so freaking exciting!" Ariya is next in line and she's already imagining what kind of dragon she'll get. "I hope I get a RainWing who loves to read," she says. "That would be awesome!"

But it's not Ariya's turn yet. Crystal is next, and when she realizes her necklace is glowing, she can barely contain her excitement. "I found my dragon!" she shouts, jumping up and down.

Ariya is quick to point out that there are no dragons around, but we don't let that dampen our spirits. We know that our dragons are out there somewhere, waiting for us to find them.

And then, out of nowhere, a colorful RainWing materializes behind Crystal. We all gasp in amazement as

Crystal turns around and sees her dragon for the first time. "Wow, Crystal, what a pretty dragon!" I exclaim.

After that excitement, we head in the opposite direction, listening for any signs of dragon roars that might help us speed up the finding process. We know that our journey is just beginning, and we can't wait to see what other adventures lie ahead.

Great to hear that our plan has worked out perfectly! It's now Ariya's turn, and as we wait in anticipation, the darkness of the night brings out the NightWings. A shy little NightWing emerges from the dark, her dark scales glistening with sparkles under her wings. She wears glasses and holds a book written in dragon language. As she approaches Ariya, she nudges her in a friendly gesture. Ariya pets the little dragon and notices her necklace glowing brightly. Isn't it amazing?

It has been 5 hours already, and I am the only one who hasn't found a dragon yet. I can still try tomorrow, but I am starting to lose hope even if there's still an hour left. Suddenly, we hear rustling leaves behind us, and we spot a ferocious SkyWing with scales that match someone's hair, which looks so familiar, but I just can't put my finger on it. We follow the SkyWing's direction and see Snowfall coming out from behind a tree with a hand on the dragon. The dragon's scales match Snow-fall's hair perfectly.

That's who it was! I should've known, duh. "Looks like Ms. Weirdo didn't find her dragon. Guess some-one's taking a sad plane trip home. Looks like the teach-ers were wrong about everybody having potential. The rest of you probably had 0.01%, but you..." Snowfall jabs me in the arm with her long nails. "had not a single drop. How embarrassing."

"No one asked for your opinion, Snow," Crystal inter-jects.

"Wait, you two know each other?" Elyse asks, point-ing to them.

"Yeah, she's my cousin. Her mom's one of the teach-ers here!" Crystal replies.

"No wonder she gets a suite and acts like she owns the academy," Elyse whispers to me.

"Snowfall, I have a question!" Ariya speaks up.

"I don't have an answer, but if you must...I don't have all day!" Snowfall replies rudely, but something seems off as if she added that last part to hide something.

"My question is, are they actually going to send Huda away if she doesn't find a dragon by the end of the day?" Ariya asks worriedly.

"None of your beeswax. If Huda or any of you really cared, you wouldn't be chatting with me. You would've been searching for one. But clearly, you guys don't. So, Huda, hope you have an exciting trip home," Snowfall says with a nasty smile, turning on her heel and stalking off with her new-found dragon.

"Oh, don't listen to her, Huda," Crystal says, trying to comfort me, but it doesn't work. "Why didn't you say anything? You don't actually believe her, right?" Elyse asks me. "Oh, me? I-i just..." I say, trailing off. "Look, we're really sorry we wasted 20 minutes of your time trying to get Snowfall to cough up information. But don't worry, we still have 40 left over," Elyse says. Crystal adds, "If you get kicked out of the school, I'll never forgive myself. So let's go find that dragon!"

"Thanks for the offer, guys, but I think I should get a head start back to school so that I can have enough time to pack my bags," I say, heading in the opposite direction of the dragons. "Oh, c'mon, don't talk like that!" Ariya says, pulling me back. "No, guys, really, I should get going," I say, making Ariya let go of my arm.

I quickly walk away before they can say anything else to try and stop me. I keep running until the academy comes into view and I can't see my roommates anymore. I can feel my face turning red, Snowfall was right it is embarrassing. Imagine what Mom is going to think when I end up at the doorstep and it has been only a day. I wish I'd never seen that stupid invitation. I knew it was too good to be true. I kick a tree so hard that the birds that were nesting in that tree quickly move to the next one, it makes me feel better to get all my anger out on something, even though it hurts a lot now.

I lay down next to the tree and sigh, and then I yell loudly in my brain (or at least I thought I did), "I hate this so much!" "I feel you, dude," A voice I've never heard before says with a strange accent. "Wh-who's there?" I say my voice shaking. I grab a stick that fell from the tree when I kicked it. "I warn you I'm armed!" I say trying to sound fearless, it's so dark I can't see a thing.

"Oh, you are going to need to do better than that to take me down," The voice says chuckling. "I command you to show yourself!" I say trying to sound demanding. "I don't take commands from anyone unless they are the human I share a bond with." replies the voice. "But if you insist I might as well." "Wait, what do you mean by, 'the human I share a bond with' I don't understand what you mean," I ask the voice. "Do you not know what's going on today? Today's the day that the humans will be bonding with us dragons. Didn't Chief tell you that?" asks the voice. "Woah, hold on. What do you mean by us dragons? And who in the world is 'Chief'?" I ask confused.

"Are you not a dragon?" asks the voice. "Wha- of course, I am not a dragon! Does it look like I am?!" I say. "You are literally speaking Dragon right now! How could you not be a dragon?!" the voice asks. "I'm speaking Dragon?! Are you ok? 'Cause it doesn't look like it!" I say. "Are you saying I'm speaking Human 'cause the human I share a bond with..." I cut the voice off by saying, "Why do you keep saying that?!?!?! You make no sense!" The voice replies saying, "Can you let me finish!" I nod and the voice continues, "You are speaking Dragon, I have never learned Human before. The human I share a bond with is supposed to teach me it, and I'm supposed to teach them Dragon. Are you with me so far?" the voice says.

"Are you saying that I'm a dragon? 'Cause I'm not. Who are you?" I ask the voice.

The remaining leaves on the tree rustle and a figure jumps out of the tree and lands right next to me. The figure has icy-blue wings dotted with jet-black scales. Her sharp, curved claws and the spines along her back were also icy bluish-white. "You're not but I am." the mysterious voice says. I just stand there with my mouth open, shocked is the word. The dragon closes my mouth and says, "The name's Whiteout, nice to finally meet y-you... What's your name?" the dragon, I mean Whiteout asks. "M-my n-name i-is Huda," I say still shocked.

"Oh, nice to finally meet you, Huda!" Whiteout says excitedly. Out of nowhere, a bright light shines in front of us. If you guessed that my necklace is glowing, then you are absolutely right! "OMG! This is so cool! It's happening Whiteout, it's actually happening!" I say ecstatic. "No way! You're my human buddy and you already know how to speak Dragon! Wait till Everfrost hears about this! That means I can learn Human right away! We're even the same age, right? (I nod) We're one step ahead of everybody, Huda!!!" Whiteout says joyfully.

"Ok, now that we have actually found each other, wait... the teacher never said what to do when we find our dragons, did your Chief tell you dragons?" I ask pointing at Whiteout. She shakes her head.

"Well, I'm pretty sure we're supposed to meet back at the place we started when the gong sounds, so..." I say. "Wait, where is your quintet?" Whiteout asks.

"Well..., it is a long story," I say. "We have time," Whiteout says, nudging me with her wing. "Go on, I'm listening," she says.

"Ok, so, it all started when we found Ariya's dragon. Ariya is a girl from my quintet... and then I heard you, that's it," I tell Whiteout starting from when Ariya's necklace started glowing, till when we started our conversation.

"Wow, ok, that's rough. I feel bad for not finding you earlier," she says.

"At least we found each other, I can't wait to see Snowfall's face when she sees you!" I say, "You know what's even cooler? You're a hybrid, you're not just any average hybrid either! You're the two coolest dragons mixed together! An IceWing and a NightWing! Wait, shouldn't we start heading back now?" I say.

"OK, maybe we should calculate it. 20 minutes were spent fighting with Snowfall, 7 with me, 5 when I revealed myself, and 14 right now plus telling me the story. So that leaves us... with 13! One extra 'cause I was calculating." Whiteout says.

"Do you know how far the walk is from here?" I ask her.

"Not really..., but I can check?" Whiteout says as she flies to the top of the tree. "It's a really long walk from here, we better get going if we want to make it!" she says flying back down. We head toward the academy and are out of breath when we arrive.

Everybody is already there by the time we arrive. Ms. Isabella is checking names on her clipboard and frowning at the last name (probably mine) that isn't checked. Ariya is looking everywhere (probably searching for me). Elyse is on her phone texting (probably me, but I left my phone in my bag). Crystal looks worried and asks Elyse something (probably asking if I responded, which I didn't, in case you were wondering). Ms. Rosemary is recounting everybody, and when she stops at the last person, she frowns and starts counting again (probably because I'm missing). Snowfall is smirking and checking her watch (probably waiting for me to get in trouble and be sent home).

"Should we come into view now?" I ask Whiteout.

"Yes!" she says with an excited smile.

"OK, on the count of 3. 1...2...-" I was cut off by a loud blood-curdling scream to my left, which sounded like Crystal. Me and Whiteout rush towards Crystal to help her, but she is fine. "HELP!" a desperate voice says, we turn around in time to see a very ugly and disabled RainWing materialize out of nowhere and take our Head Dragon Teacher, Mrs. Isabella...

To Be Continued...

About the Author

Abdul Raqib Majid

The author, Abdul Majid, is an action and fantasy writer that takes time on most of his stories. He is a very wise and educated author that has a very nice teacher, Ms. Safa Subhani. He really loves playing a mobile, PC, and Xbox available game called Roblox. His top favorite games are Blox Fruits, Plane Crash Physics, and Hair Salon Simulator because he loves giving people old grandpa hairstyles. He also has a dad (obviously), a 10-year-old sister, and a nice and loving and caring mother. He lives in the northwest side of Chicago, Illinois.

FIVE BRAVE HEROES
BY ABDUL RAQIB MAJID

O nce upon a time there was a happy village in a country called Drawland. But one day there was a really big hole in the ground, and the police went to look at it. Suddenly, a big zombie rose out of the ground.

Storm Headerman, a 12 year- old boy, was frightened by the vicious beast. "What is that?!" Storm said.

His friend J.J went over to look at the horrible beast. "Don't do that! That has a higher risk of getting killed!" Storm shouted.

"I don't care." J.J argued.

"Fine then, go get eaten stupid. I'm not being responsible."

"Well then, let's see about that!"

J.J raced to look at what's happening. There were piles of dead officers everywhere, and it smelled very filthy. "P.U! It smells like the public restrooms at the pool!

"Having fun there goofy?" Storm teased his comrade.

"Shut up!"J.J shouted.

Just then, the zombie rose out of the ground.

"Uh-oh, somebody got a frowny face!" J.J teased.

The zombie roared in fury, and attempted to grab him, but slipped and fell on the mud.

"Ha-ha!" J.J yelled at the silly green specimen.

The zombie screamed at J.J, and leaped at him, but landed on someone's car. "This zombie is even dumber than I thought!" J.J exclaimed.

Suddenly, the zombie started glowing green, then it turned into a zombie brute. The newly transformed zombie ran at J.J, but J.J managed to dodge the zombie but fell on the ground in exhaustion. "Darn, I need to start moving again or this zombie will tear me apart!" J.J said. The zombie ran at him, but fell and soon, he later died from getting stabbed in the back. "You can count on us now. We're not gonna hurt you." an odd and unfamiliar voice called out from the behind view of J.J. "Who is this? And what do you want?" J.J called out. Out came a very fat man and, good lord again he had a package of hot & spicy noodles! Are you serious?! You need to hit the gym man, I'm saying this for the last time, hit the gym! "Why are you such a fat man?" J.J teased the funny looking person. The fat man tried to threaten the innocent troublemaker but another voice called out for him to put down his weapon, and out emerged a weird ghost. "Ahhhh!" J.J yelped in fear. The ghost told him to calm down. "Chill out, man. I'm not gonna hurt you." "What are your guys' names?" "My name is Goofy," said the ghost. "My name is Fatty," said the fat man. "Oh, so why do you have hot & spicy noodles? Is that your weapon?" "No, that's just something to eat. I really love noodles!" said Fatty. "Bruh, so that explains why you're so fat." J.J said. He started to go back down the hill, but he was scratched behind by an explosive zombie. "Owww!!" J.J moaned in pain. Storm went up to see what was going on. The zombie was gonna scratch him, or bump into him and cause an explosion, but Storm took out his galaxy staff and knocked the zombie out cold. There was a ticking sound on the rocket. The zombie exploded and left out green goop from his body. "What's that green stuff, Storm?" J.J asked him. "It's radioactive waste that was causing the zombies to grow so quickly." Storm explained. "Well then, let's go eat some zombie flesh!" Storm and the gang proceeded down the hill, but they were stopped by a dying soldier. "You can't go back down, it's too dangerous!" The soldier yelled at the slayer group. "But we're just going back down the hill because we are zombie slayers!" J.J explained. The soldier shot 2 times at J.J, later killing him. Storm didn't dare say a thing when the soldier glared at him and barked "You youngsters aren't old enough to be slayers! They are the chosen ones, and they get to do what they want!"

They continued their way down the hill and looked for more zombies, and Fatty yelled out "Watch out!" Storm took his staff and hit the zombie but it had no effect. "Is this an invisible shield generator zombie?!" The zombie had zero damage, but Storm immediately knew his answer and used his ultimate galaxy laser gun and shot his high power laser beam. The zombie collapsed on the ground and careened into the river. Storm spotted an old truck that was still working and grabbed the keys and took away speeding into the horizon. Along with Goofy and Fatty of course. When they were halfway to their base, they heard a noise that sounded like metal grinding against even rustier metal. When Goofy looked at the back of the truck, there was a corrupted zombie at the trailer. Goofy got terrified and yelled, "INCOMING!!!" Storm looked at the back of the car, pulled the emergency brake, and all of them hopped out of the truck and Storm went into Galaxy Storm mode. He pulled out his Savage Tornado attack, and then came a really strong wind, it almost blew Goofy away.

The zombie roared like a pixelated goofy ahh AI robot and teleported away and left behind a special glitch generator. Storm picked it up and went back to the truck. The truck sputtered when Storm put the key into the engine. "Darn it, what's going on?" Storm muttered inside his breath. Storm tried fiddling with the car system, desperate to get the truck to work again. Storm put the key back into the truck and a car system warning popped onto the screen that read, "OIL IS RUNNING OUT. PLEASE FILL THE ENGINE UP NOW OR ELSE THIS TRUCK WILL HAVE TO BE DEMOLISHED. THANK YOU FOR PAYING ATTENTION." Where are we gonna find oil now?" Storm thought in his head. "What happened to the truck?" Fatty called out. "Out of oil. You boys need to stick together and scavenge for an oil jug and a funnel." "YESSIR!" the boys yelled out. They ran as they went along their upcoming journey to find oil. Goofy started digging in the ground to find oil. Like, that's gonna work. "WHAT ON EARTH ARE YOU DOING, GOOFY!?" Fatty barked at Goofy. "Bro, I'm just trying to find oil. Maybe it's somewhere buried in the ground. No one knows for sure." Goofy tried to scare Fatty by sprinting towards him. "Quandale Dingle here!" Goofy yelled out. His name was a good choice for him. Fatty started dashing like a Roblox Blox Fruits player and went to snitch on Goofy or something. Fatty went to Storm and blurted out of nowhere, "GOOFY WON'T WORK WITH ME!!!" Such a baby! I've seen people better manners than him. Anyways, so when Fatty blurted the complaint out to Storm, Storm immediately ordered Fatty to call Goofy. Goofy then came to Storm and told him that if Fatty even snitched on him, he would then immediately tell Fatty that he is a blabbermouth and would spread rumors about what he did back in elementary school. If you don't know what he did, I will explain later in the story. Goofy started acting like Andrew Tate or something. "Hey Storm!" Goofy barked, I mean Andrew Tate 2.0 barked. Storm said "Yeah, what's up?" "What color is your Bugatti?" Goofy asked. "AAAAAAAAAAAAAAAAAAAAAAAAA!!!!!" Storm yelped like a hyena. Behind them was a whole crowd of zombies ready to fight for their own lives. Storm went out and screamed and started sprinting at the zombies. Goofy found a Glock on the ground and used it to fight the zombies. But he was interrupted by a big black cloud in the sky. Out emerged the zombie alpha. A zombie alpha is basically a zombie boss but bigger and can speak and can warp in time.

About the Author

Aiza Murtaza

Aiza Murtaza is a 6th grader at MCC Academy. I wrote this story because I wanted to motivate people that they should not give up and accomplish their goals. My favorite sports are basketball and badminton. My favorite hobbies are sleeping and doing art.

For my very kind classmate A.S. who inspired me to write this story.

—*A.M.*

THE SPECIAL STONE

BY AIZA MURTAZA

Once there were two best friends named Texas and Paris. Texas was brave, bold, and active, while Paris was kind and caring. Despite their differences, they were always on a mission to do something new, help everybody, and solve problems. But the problem they were facing now wouldn't be easy to solve. They were running out of water, and the reason was that the stone had disappeared. To solve the issue, they had to find the stone. As soon as they heard about it, they decided to meet at the park to discuss it.

"I wish we could do something about it," Texas said.

"I don't think there's any way we can solve this problem," Paris sighed.

"Hmm, actually I just remembered that I did some research yesterday and found an article about the stone and where it would be," said Texas.

"But are you sure that you read the right article?" asked Paris.

"Yeah, I'm sure!" Texas said.

"But are you extremely sure?" Paris said again.

" YEAH, I DID!" Texas said annoyed.

"Ok, ok calm down when should we start?" Paris said.

"Let's start tomorrow. We'll start our journey early in the morning," Texas exclaimed.

They slept early that day, woke up at sunrise, and headed out to get the special stone. While they were going out, they noticed that the clouds were turning gray, and the sky was turning dark, and then in a boom it started to rain. With a loud clap of thunder, the thunderstorm began. The lightning was loud and horrifying! There was terrible weather and the lightning made it worse, so they quickly ran and rushed to a nearby gas station. They stayed there until the weather was good and clear. Afterward, they continued their journey, but this time they had to find the cave. They walked and walked until they saw the cave. Upon arrival, they went inside. The cave was not like any other cave. It was spooky and frightening, but it wasn't like any other cave; it was different and had ancient-like symbols on the walls, which was unusual because they had never seen them before. While they were walking, they noticed many cracks in the floor, the more they walked the more the cracks got bigger and then it came to a point when lava started bursting out of the floor. The lava was bursting with its bright colors and ashes were everywhere. They were scared and frightened, but they knew they couldn't turn back. So, they went on.

"How are we going to get past this!" screamed Paris.

"Hmm, I don't know," said Texas, panicking.

They both tried to look around to find something to escape the lava.

"Wait, I see some blocks. We can use them to get past the lava!" exclaimed Texas.

"But it's such a big risk!" screamed Paris.

"It is, but there is no other option, and we came all the way here. We have to take the risk," said Texas.

Paris wasn't too happy with the decision, but they had to do it anyway. It wasn't easy, but they managed to escape. After they had passed the lava part, they now had to go through lasers, and while they were there, they saw the bright purple stone shining bright. So as soon as they saw they knew they hurried to the next obstacle.

"LASERS!" screamed Paris.

"This isn't too bad, all we have-" said Texas, as Paris rudely interrupted.

"This isn't too bad? How do you expect me to pass that? It's impossible!" exclaimed Paris.

"If you had let me finish my sentence, then you would know what to do," said Texas aggressively.

"Well, as I was saying, if you follow me and follow the same steps as me, then we can grab the stone and get out of here," said Texas.

"Ok, I guess so," sighed Paris.

So they went through the lasers. There were many of them, so they had to be careful while going because they didn't know what would happen if they touched the lasers. It was a little easy for Texas, but it wasn't as easy for Paris. They sneaked past the lasers, but it came up to a point when there was one laser underneath Texas, so she jumped over it and told Paris to do the same, but Paris didn't hear her, so she accidentally hit the laser! As soon as she touched it, everything started to collapse! All the rocks were falling and crashing, and everything was getting destroyed! The lasers were gone, so they quickly took the stone and ran as fast as they could. Everything was crashing and falling, so they were afraid they would get hurt. So They ran and ran as fast and quickly as they could to get out of this mess. It took them a really hard and long time to get out of there but they still managed to leave, and when they were finally out of the mess, and were finally free, they felt so relieved.

"WE DID IT!" Both of them screamed, trying to breathe and get some air.

"Now all we have to do is go back to the city, put the stone there, and get water back," said Texas.

"AGAIN!" screamed Paris.

"Yeah obviously, if we can get through that thunderstorm and all the troubles we had in the past, then we can do it again." says Texas.

"Ok, fine!" exclaims Paris.

And so they went back to the city. After taking a few breaks, they finally arrived back in the city. Their announcement was met with skepticism at first, but when they placed the stone where it belonged, it began to shine, and in just a few seconds suddenly water began to pour out of the fountains, and the rivers started flowing again. Everyone was overjoyed!

Knowing that they had once again saved the city and accomplished their goal they were happier than anyone could be!

"We did it once again!" Paris exclaimed excitedly.

"Yes, we did," replied Texas.

About the Author
Humza Rahman

Humza Rahman the great is the author that wrote this awesome masterpiece. He is a great person. He loves the Holy Quran. He is also interested in Harry Potter.

For Aariz Rangoonwala, for always being a good friend and always having my back and always putting a smile on my face.

—H.R.

The Moment of Epiphany

By Humza Rahman

Bob and Tim who are good friends and partners in crime come from a very similar background. They are currently in Chicago Underground Tunnels, provided by an evil company that they work for. They are in urban New York. The year is 1990.

"Let's rob a house," said Bob.

"There is a house in the neighborhood I have been observing. It has a lot of valuable goods there. Full of booty," said Tim.

"Where is it?" asked Bob in excitement.

"It's near the police station," Tim said.

"Wow, that's where it is.......," said Bob in surprise.

"Good night!" said both of them to each other, as it was late at night after a long day of crime they had committed.

It was not easy to fall asleep with the excitement of what they had planned for the following day.

"Tomorrow, let's rob that house; I think it is a great idea," said Bob.

"Oh, he is deep asleep," said Bob.

The next day.

"This is the police, open your doors, we are armed" exclaimed a loud voice.

"Ya, and we have rifles," said Bob and Tim.

"This is the third time this week the police have found us," said Bob.

"At least we still have a billion dollars left," said Tim.

"HANDS UP, WE ARE COMING for you. Prepare to spend the rest of your tiny little life behind bars,"said the FBI.

"GET IN THE VAN," exclaimed both of them.They escaped by tricking the police by running away from the other door in their house.

This is how they got to this point.

Story of Tim

Tim was a nice boy, who was good at studies. He got straight As and had a perfect GPA in his elementary and middle school. His life took a turn when he started high school. To Tim, high school was a jump from nurturing and nice teachers to a very cruel place. It was not the math or any subject he was finding hard, it was the bullying, hard disciplinarian and harsh teachers.

He turned to a life of crime.

Story of Bob

Just like Tim, Bob's childhood was very fun, and he was a courteous, happy kid. Bob was a talented young man, loved by his teachers. High school was certainly not as he expected it to be. He was bullied for having small eyes and being petite. He dropped out of school, and one day he rammed his house with a car. As he used to live in New York, he was wanted by the New York Police Department. He stayed away from New York after that incident.

How Tim and Bob met each other.

So now the way they met was that they both joined the E.P.S.H. (Evil People's Safe Home) in New York before they moved to Canada. That's why they got shipped through Canada by erupting the border. Then they went through Wisconsin, so that people would investigate only in Wisconsin, and they could be safe in Chicago. Now, their company (E.P.S.H.) was so rich and wealthy that they earned forty percent of the company share. That means the whole company, including international branches, pays them around three billion dollars a year, so they evenly split the amount among themselves.

Soon, they planned out a grand heist. Later that day they looted an ice cream shop, seven clothing stores, a paint store, five Walmarts, two Targets, and finally an Amazon Go. The total time of the robbery was approximately 4 hours long.

Then they saw it.

It was the police!

They knew if they didn't run, they'd be done. So they ran for their lives, by their master plan to trick the police. Then they got in the van, and went to a dealership. They bought a blue and fast Bugatti and ran away to their underground tunnel.

The very next day, they got inside the van and went to rob the same house that they had talked about a couple of days before.

"Let's specifically take the red gem worth about 69,784 dollars," said Bob

"That's the smart thing to do, I guess," said Tim

Deep inside Tim and Bob felt something wrong about it, and wanted to stop, but the fun of robbing made it hard to quit.

"We can do this forever," said Bob.

"Fine, we will talk about it later; we're here already," said Tim as they reached the house.

They got out of the van, and they started to get the gadgets and tools out of the van. That's when they noticed their lock picking device was misplaced!

They used the big gadgets, and they went inside. As soon as they entered, they destroyed all the cameras. Then they went to the mini-vault, nothing unusual for them. When they opened the vault, they were in for a surprise, a police man was waiting there for them with guns. The police gave a warning and then started shooting, but Tim and Bob were wearing armor to protect themselves, so they were safe. Then they led the police out of the building by moving their truck to the other side.

Then they quickly got the gem they have been eyeing on into their truck. Then they got the gem in their truck safely. Then they saw an elderly man, and they pushed him off the roof, but he lived for a little more.

They saw him scream and say "You are doing wrong man, you shouldn't be killing me. Look at my pain!" So they rushed him to the hospital. Then they had an epiphany about what they were doing. It was wrong.

That's why they went to the police station, showed them their ID, and the police sent them to jail. Once he was in jail, he met his cellmate, Tim. So they got sentenced to 20 years in jail. Then they got released, and the reason he got only 20 years was because they promised to tell them where the E.P.S.H. was and all their secret tunnels were. By then, they were 40 years old, and the year is 2010. They both were able to meet with their whole families again, and they reunited with their families.

They had still made money in jail and had 1 million dollars, so he bought a jet and a yacht and donated it to a charity.

Then Bob finally ate some very yummy Momos after 20 years with his family.

He went to a construction company to build a building for his business so that he could have a good life. Then he went to visit his dads side of the family, and he saw his cousins and his aunts and uncles, and he went out for dinner as a family. He did the same with his moms side too. Then he promised his parents he would never rob again. Although he still lives with his family, he still made sure to see his friend Tim, but his parents thought that Tim led him into being a robber, but Bob insisted that it wasn't Tim. He said it was himself who made wrong choices in the past and opted to do things that were easy and not right. So his family believed him and loved Tim and welcomed him to their house. They became family friends.

After that they lived a very good, righteous life.

About the Author
Hafidh Abubakr Shethwala

Abubakr Shethwala is in 6th grade and is 11 years old. Abubakr attends the school MCC Academy, and he is also in Hifz. Some of Abubakr's hobbies include playing sports, bicycle riding, reading books, and reading the Quran. Some of Abubakr's favorite sports include playing basketball, soccer, and football. Abubakr's main achievement is memorizing the entire Quran and earning the title of Hafiz. Abubakr is the oldest of three siblings and he is interested in the *Harry Potter* series.

For all the teachers I ever had, for helping me use my creativity.

—A.S.

The Mega Robotic Aliens

By Hafidh Abubakr Shethwala

I woke up this morning and everything seemed totally normal. The beeping of my alarm is starting to hurt my ears because it's WAY too loud, the sound of pans clanging together downstairs in the kitchen, and the voice of my mom calling me down to eat breakfast. I turned off my alarm, brushed my teeth, and went downstairs to the kitchen.

My mom gave me my cereal, and I sat down to eat. I quickly ate my cereal, wore my jacket and shoes, and started walking to school.

When I got to school, I went to my homeroom really quickly because I was getting late. The rest of school went fast because it was the same boring stuff that happens every day.

When I got home it was 4:00, and I was exhausted, so I took a nap. I woke up at about 6:30, so I was pretty—no, REALLY hungry— so I went downstairs to eat dinner. To my surprise, everyone was on the couch watching the news.

"What are you watching?" I asked, while I sat down on the couch beside them.

"A spaceship just landed on a nearby farm," answered Dad.

"A *spaceship*?" I asked in disbelief. Sure enough, there was a giant spaceship on the ground, with a bunch of people surrounding it.

"I know, right? Aliens, or whatever creatures are in there, are probably not even supposed to be real!" He exclaimed.

"Shhh," said Mom. "They're saying something else."

Dad and I both turned around and watched the TV. The news reporter had returned to the screen and started talking again.

"As you can see," said the news reporter, "a giant spaceship, filled with who knows what, landed in the middle of Froberg Farm here in Texas."

She was about to say something else, when the door to the giant spaceship fell to the ground. Everyone moved back a few inches, startled by the loud *thump* that followed it.

The next thing I saw were a few figures walking down the door like they were some movie stars or something.

Nobody said a word as we all stared at the figures that were slowly coming down to the people staring at them in fear. Nobody moves an inch. No one screams, no one runs away. It's like we're all paralyzed with fear by just looking at those figures that are almost at the bottom of the giant door.

When the figures finally got to the bottom of the door, the camera zoomed in on them, and I could finally see what those figures actually were. I gasped upon looking at it. I looked at Mom and Dad, and could tell they were shocked as well. They look like aliens—no, robotic aliens—and they. They wear some very big armor that looks bigger than the aliens themselves. The armor looks like it's made from some shiny gray or black minerals or something like that.

One alien was being surrounded by a lot of others, and he was being carried on some kind of red pillow. I'm pretty sure he's the leader, because he sure looks like one. There was one more alien to the left of him, holding a giant speaker and a microphone.

When the alien holding the speaker and the microphone got to the bottom with the leader, he gave the leader the microphone and put the speaker down beside him. The leader held the microphone and spoke into it.

"Dear citizens of this astounding planet, my name is Zorgon, and me and my army are here to take over the Earth," He said. Everyone gasped, on the TV, and my family.

"Do not try to stop us, for we know all of your weaknesses, we are stronger and smarter than you, and we have technology that was made in another world," he said.

Immediately following his statement, he applied pressure to his armor, causing it to transform into a massive technological suit.

After the transformation was done, he pressed a button that opened up the middle of the suit to reveal some kind of cannon. After that, he pressed another button that seemed to charge up the cannon with some orange particles. Finally, he pulled a lever and a giant, fast, and strong laser beam went soaring through the sky, and it hit a nearby tree. The tree exploded, sending leaves and bark everywhere.

This time, everyone yelled, screamed and shrieked. Everyone tried to run away, but they hit some sort of force field.

"Oh yeah," Zorgon spoke again, no longer in his tech suit. "I almost forgot to tell all of you that no one will be escaping."

Everyone looked back at Zorgon, horrified.

"This force field is stronger than 1,000 people combined, so no matter how hard you try, you will not be able to break through," he informed everyone. This seemed to frighten everyone even more.

"All of you have a choice," continued Zorgon, "either give in and become my minions, or say no and be imprisoned in my jail cells for the rest of your lives. If you accept my offer, come to the front and kneel down to me. If you don't accept my offer, then prepare to be imprisoned for eternity."

Half of the people went to the front and kneeled down to him. The others stayed back. "You have all made your choice," Zorgon said.

Afterward, a group of aliens appeared from inside the spaceship with some kind of ruby-colored handcuffs. They went to the people who were running around, trying to get as far away from the aliens as possible. The aliens chased them everywhere, eventually catching them because apparently they don't get tired.

They took them all inside, but not before they noticed that there still was one man hiding behind a tree. One alien left the others to go get the last person. The man started to run away, throwing things at the alien behind him.

Every time the alien got hit he hardly flinched, until the man, who was starting to slow down, threw a water bottle. The bottle opened midair, spraying the alien with water.

This time the alien stopped, crackling and sparking. After a few seconds, the alien exploded, sending pieces of metal around him.

The man stood in shock, surprised that it actually worked. More aliens ran to catch him, and the man couldn't find any more water bottles. The aliens took him in with the others, and that's when I noticed that the person holding the camera was hiding behind a car.

Right when the man was taken in the spaceship, the cameraman took a run for it.

I don't know what happened after that, because when he started to run, he dropped the camera, and the screen went black.

Mom turned off the TV, and I could tell she was worried.

"It's going to be okay, Max," she said.

"Yeah," said Dad, "As long as you're with us you'll be safe."

That night, after dinner, I laid on my bed, but I couldn't sleep. I guess I was just feeling terrified. Not only that, but I kept thinking about all the people who were being held prisoner and the ones forced to work as slaves for Zorgon.

I got up from my bed, knowing that I must be brave. I went to my closet, took out the water gun I received on my last birthday, and put it inside my favorite green backpack. After that, I opened my bedroom window, and jumped outside.

I knew I couldn't destroy Zorgon all by myself with all those other robotic aliens surrounding him, so I started thinking of a place where I knew I would be able to acquire an army of my own. Finally, I thought of one. It was the perfect place, it was only a few blocks away from here, and I think it's really close to Froberg Farm.

So I looked back at my house, wondering if I'll ever see it again. After taking a little time just looking at my house, I started walking to the field where me and a whole group of other kids gather at the break of dawn every weekend. From there, we will all gear up with equipment and everything else we might need in our quest.

Afterward, we will all stealthily sneak into the spaceship, destroy Zorgon and his army, and save the world.

The final battle is soon to begin..

TO BE CONTINUED......

ABOUT THE AUTHOR
AISHA NOOR AFZAL

Aisha Afzal is in 5th grade and is 10 years old. She goes to a Muslim school named MCC Academy, and her hobbies are making slime and writing stories. One interesting fact about Aisha is that she has a twin sister. Her favorite foods are sushi, biryani, ramen and seafood. Her favorite colors are teal and lime green. Aisha is also currently in Hifz and would like to finish soon!

Dedicated to anyone who comes across this story.

—A.A.

A MORISCO FAMILY

BY AISHA NOOR AFZAL

The beaming Granada sun pierced through Maryam's window forcing her to open her eyes. The fragrance of the fresh bread her mom was baking pushed her to get out of bed and wash up. She joined her parents, grandfather, and sister in the courtyard near the hibiscus tree. Maryam devoured the bread with olive oil from her grandfather's orchard. She sipped her delicious Andalusian tea. When Maryam and Fatima's mom wasn't looking they both snuck more sugar cubes into their tea. They both LOVED sugar!

After they ate, Maryam's grandpa finished the last few lines of the poem he was writing in the language Aljamiado. The Moriscos, *little moor*, was what the Spanish called secret Muslims who had made a language called Aljamiado to talk to each other because the Spanish king and queen forced everyone to become Catholic. No one was allowed to speak Arabic, or practice Islam or Judaism. They could speak to each other in Aljamiado without the soldiers understanding them. Maryam and her grandfather always loved to write poems together. It was their favorite thing to do with each other. Maryam could not imagine the world without her grandfather. Maryam and her energetic younger sister, Fatima went outside and decided to make a mini toy boat with wood and string.

When they finished making the boat together, Maryam and Fatima put it in the mini pond in their garden and watched it float around the water near the water lilies. After they got bored of watching the mini boat they came inside to sit with their grandfather. Her Grandfather said excitedly, "The poem that I have been writing about the Prophet []for two months is finally complete.

"Alhumdulilah!" Maryam and Fatima cried.

The whole family gathered and started singing the poem together. "Mashallah! This is a beautiful poem" Maryam's mom said after they finished singing.

A Few Months Later...

" Maryam and fatima come help me pick some more hibiscus flowers so I can make some

More tea for your grandpa". Her mom said. "Ok" Maryam and Fatima shouted.

As they were picking the flowers king Philip screamed "everyone come to the town square."

Maryam was really curious what he was going to say, so Maryam and her family stood in the town square with all the other people.

"Not a single Muslim will be allowed to practice Islam in fact all Muslims will be searched

and expelled".The king shouted. The town was terrified,especially Maryam and her family.

Maryam's heart melted out of sadness. After the king announced the sad news the soldiers

went door to door making sure no one was practicing Islam, so if someone was showering,

praying,reading Quran,or even if they looked clean on jumuah the soldiers would kill them.

They also made all the masjids into churches which hurt Maryam's family the MOST because they used to walk to the Masjid everyday for all the prayers. Maryam had to have a secret name so that the soldiers would not know that she was Muslim her home name was Maryam and her outside name was Mary. Maryam's family fled to Morocco because they were not safe in Granada when the king expelled all of the Muslims in Spain.

He also took all of the little kids that were four years old and younger and gave them to the church to be raised by Catholic nuns. When the soldiers came for Fatima, she clung onto her moms dress and screamed until they took her away. Maryam's mom and dad ran after the soldiers but they threw them to the ground and marched away. The pain in Maryam's heart was unexplainable. She loved Fatima so much, Fatima would always hang out with Maryam and they would always walk around the streets of Granada together. But now the only memory Maryam had left of Fatima was the mini toy boat they made together.

Maryam and her mom held hands the whole walk to Morocco because they were so sad that they took Fatima and cried the entire journey. All they could remember was when they took Fatima from her mother's hand as she screamed out of fear.

After they took Fatima, Maryam's grandfather hid the poem in the wall of their old home and they kept living in Morocco for the rest of their lives.

A hundred years later... builders began to demolish Maryam's family home to build something else and found the old poem that Maryam's grandfather wrote.

The Aljamiado poem:

"Oh beloved, Oh Muhammad

blessings be upon Muhammad and on the family of
Muhammad

Oh Lord, send your blessings upon him and increase
our love for him raise us among his people under the
banner of Muhammad

Oh beloved, oh Muhammad blessings be upon
Muhammad and on the family of Muhammad

Your word will come forth, your prayer will be heard,
embrace the greetings of peace   that I offer these are
the deeds of Muhammad

Oh beloved, oh Muhammad

blessings be upon Muhammad, and on the family of
Muhammad

God bless the chosen one, our beloved Muhammad,
upon him be peace

although I am but a weak servant, my lord has power
over all things

God bless the chosen one, our beloved Muhammad,
upon him be peace."

*Based on a true story and inspired by the manuscript
found and performed as the Morisco Memory.*

About the Author

Asma Afzal

Asma Afzal is in fifth grade and goes to MCC Academy. She loves cooking, crocheting, knitting, and crafting. She also has a talent for making random, crazy things. Her favorite food is ramen and tteokbokki. She has a twin sister and comes from a family of five. She loves playing with cats, and has a passion for reading. Her favorite colors are navy blue and green. She is in hifz and hopes to finish soon.

To all the people who love to read.
—A.A.

THE MISSION

BY ASMA AFZAL

I am so bored. Mom and Dad are working. Leilah is sleeping. I can't go outside because it is snowing. I hate winter break. I could call Noor. I forced myself to get out of bed, unplug my iPad, and call Noor.

" Hey Isra! Summer called me, we have a new mission," said Noor over the iPad.

" Hey Noor! Ok come over now!''

"Sure! Let me tell my mom and I will be there in a minute.''

I hung up. It is nice having your best friend next door. After a few minutes the doorbell rang. I ran down the stairs and opened the door for Noor. She came in, took off her jacket and shoes and followed me upstairs. We sat upstairs on my old, worn, white bed. Sunlight was streaming in through the window. I heard a loud, disruptive cry come from the door.

"I guess Leilah is awake." I said

Noor and I made Leilah breakfast and fed her. We got some chips and juice, gave Leilah some toys to play with and went back to my room.

"Let's go." Noor said.

I shoved my bed over with a grunt and looked at the tile, it looked old and intricate. The edges were frayed and browned. There was a beautiful design of a realistic yet whimsical flower. I brushed my finger on one of the petals and the wall slid back revealing an old stone passage.

"Let's go!" Noor and I said in unison.

We left a note on my bed saying where we went.

" Ready Isra?" said Noor

" Yeah!"

Exactly when our weight shifted onto the stone, the torches lit up. We dashed into the dimly lit passage and ran past the fountain and into a curvy hall.

We ran until we reached a large room with three doors. We went through the middle one and reached a door. Noor and I scanned our eyes and the door opened. We walked into the lobby. The walls were adorned with gadgets in clear showcases. The walls were white with green accents. We walked up a few stairs and halls until we reached a grand door that read "*Summer Armstrong CEO assistant*"Noor knocked on the door.

"Come in" said a high pitched voice.

We opened the door and walked in.

"Hello, how are you guys?" Said Summer.

"Good. You?"

"Good, thanks. Let's jump straight to why I called you here. We need you and two other girls to go on a mission to steal a potion at a school that is controlling their students minds. You have two hours to get ready. Here they are." She said pointing to two girls that just walked through the door, one had ocean blue eyes and the other had long, silky, pitch black hair.

"Hey! My name is Sara." said the one with the black hair.

"And my name is Lily!" Said the one with blue eyes, energetically.

"Hello! My name is Isra." I said.

"And mine is Noor." Noor chimed.

"Good. Now that you guys have met, go and prepare." said Summer.

We walked out the door and into the launch room. The shelf's were stuffed with backpacks, food, maps, and best of all— gadgets!

There were all sorts of gadgets. From watches to foldable cars. We chose backpacks and filled them with gadgets, food, maps, and waited until it was time to go.

We walked over to the launch tubes. We each stepped inside our own tubes; as I stepped into my tube I closed my eyes because I was claustrophobic. I kept them closed all six seconds. After it was over, I opened my eyes. We stepped out of the tubes.

"Where are we?" Sara asked.

"Let me check," I said, tapping my watch. A 4D image popped out of my watch.

"It says *Gemini Middle School,*" I said.

"Let's go! School starts in five minutes" said Lily, looking at her own watch.

We walked towards the entrance. I felt nervous. What if...."PINGG" the bell rang. We dashed down the hall looking at our schedules. I spotted room 211 and shot through the door. Right as I sat down, a loud "PING"erupted from the speaker. The first half of the day went by quickly. Most of the teachers were very strict, however I liked the art teacher. She was fun and nice. I got in line for hot lunch. The food looked DISGUSTING. I wished I had brought lunch. I looked around, the walls were a faded and stained yellow. The room was huge. I sat down at the table where Noor, Lilly and Sara were sitting.

" Hey guys! How was it?" I asked

"It was okay" said Sara

"Yeah" said Lily

"Do any of you guys know where we are going after school?" Asked Noor

"Someone named Mrs. Wang will pick us up" said lily

"Ok. Let's go. The bell is going to ring."

The day went by swiftly. At the end of the day, M rs.Wang picked us up and took us to her house. The car ride was awkward. Mrs.Wang took us to her house and showed us our room for the night. There were 2 bunk beds. I fell asleep as quick as Leilah takes to eat a cookie. The next day we arrived right on time. We skipped assembly and cautiously walked up the stairs and down the hallway. We dropped our backpacks on the floor, while Sara tapped her watch and a green ray of light scanned the hallway. Sara walked up and down the hallway until she heard a "BEEP! BEEP!"

"SHHHH!" exclaimed Noor

We stepped towards the spot that made the watch beep.

I tapped on the wall. There was a hollow sound. I saw an oddly giant frame with an anti-bullying poster inside.

"Hurry!" Lily cried. "The bell will ring in 4 minutes!"

I feebly lifted the frame and looked under. I saw a small corridor that was very short. I motioned to Noor,

Lily, and Sara to come forward. We crawled into the corridor and stood up (I hit my head in the process). We tread along the passage until we reached a door that had a "CAUTION! FACULTY ONLY!" Noor slowly opened the door. Me, Lily, and Sara followed her. Behind the door was a small room the size of a closet with another door that had a lock on it. Lily pulled a chip out of her bag while I tried to find an outlet. She inserted the chip and tapped on her watch. Suddenly the door fling back, exposing a dark room with a large table in the center that was engulfed in vials, bottles, and other items that were filled with abnormal liquids.

"Which one is it?" asked Noor as we inspected the objects.

We scanned all the items and put the ones that caused our watches to beep, into a plastic bag that I pulled out of my pocket. Just as we were about to leave the room, a brittle and cold, "Look who we have here!" came from behind us. I flung around. In front of me was Ms.Smith, the principal.

"AHHHHHH" we cried as we ran for our lives.

Ms. Smith chuckled and ran towards us. She caught up to us and held us by our arms. I yanked my arm away with all my strength and kicked Ms.Smith in the stomach. Me, Lily, Noor, and Sara ran back the way we came until we reached the frame. I pushed it forwards and we crawled out of the passage. We ran down the stairs and out the building. I gasped for breath. After we all caught our breath, we stepped into the tubes that appeared in front of us. I closed my eyes until we reached headquarters. I stepped out of the tube and gave the plastic bag to Summer who was standing in front of me.

"Good job guys! You can go home now." She said,

I looked at Noor "Let's go home!"

The End

About the Author
Yusuf Ahmed

Yusuf Ahmed is a 5th grader in a school called MCC in a special program named "Hifdh." He is the youngest sibling out of three siblings. He initially wrote this story because he was forced to, but he started liking it after. Ahmed's hobbies include reading and riding his bike. His favorite drink and food is mango lassi and halwa puri.

For the people who like reading and riding their bikes too.

—Y.A.

THE DARK POTION
BY YUSUF AHMED

Tom Myter and his family were driving to his family friend's house in his new car his family bought about four months ago. It was sunny outside. A bit too sunny that Tom was almost sweating from the heat of the sun. As they were driving to their family friends' house, Tom, who was sitting in the back seat of the car, overheard his parents whispering to each other.

"Remember last time about what Vakaam tried to give to Tom? What if he does something similar this time?" Tom's mom whispered to Tom's dad.

Tom realized what they were talking about immediately. The last time they went to his family friend, Vakaam's house, Vakaam offered Tom this gleaming, bubbly green drink to Tom which Vakaam said was just soda. Still, Tom stared at him suspiciously, then finally, Tom stepped out of the room without drinking the "soda" and then showed the drink to his parents.

Half an hour later, Tom and his family reached Vakaam's house, which just looked like an average house. They approached the door and Tom rang the doorbell. They waited ten seconds then finally heard footsteps coming towards them. The door opened and they greeted their family friend, Vakaam. Vakaam was a young man who was normal-sized and had a clean-shaven face.

They entered Vakaam's house which was small and modern. There were a few paintings and pictures on the walls which some were, according to Vakaam, a forest preserve Vakaam went to in mid-fall.

There was a good smell of food which made Tom immediately hungry. Vakaam requested Tom's family to sit down, and they talked for what seemed like an hour (because of how hungry Tom was) but was actually 20 minutes. Then finally, Vakaam led them to the kitchen to eat. While they were eating, Vakaam put a drink on the table next to Tom which Vakaam got from somewhere in a different room that Tom had never gone to, because Vakaam restricted him from going in there. The drink that Vakaam put on the table was a Canada Dry can, so Tom grabbed the can, opened it, and without realizing what was in the can, he drank the drink and then felt a tingle in his body. The drink also didn't feel or taste like Canada Dry. The texture of the drink was thick and it tasted like medicine. He looked back in the can to examine what the drink was, and he saw a gleaming, bubbly green drink, the same drink Vakam offered to Tom the last time they came to Vakaam's house!

Tom left the kitchen and rushed to the bathroom to spit out what was left in his mouth while he heard his parents calling to him, "Tom, where are you going!?" "What happened, Tom!?"

Tom didn't reply. He reached the bathroom and spat out what was left in his mouth. But it was too late, he already drank it. He also felt a weird feeling in his eyes, so he looked in the mirror that was in the bathroom, but he just saw his normal, pale green eyes.

When he went back to the dining room, his parents asked Tom, "Where did you go? What happened?"

"Look at what's inside that can," Tom replied, sitting back down on his chair. Tom's parents looked at the liquid inside the can and gasped.

"What did you give to Tom!?" Tom's dad exclaimed at Vakaam.

"It's just soda," Vakaam lied.

"Then what is this!?" Tom's dad showed Vakaam the can.

Vakaam looked inside the can and sighed. "It's a potion," Vakaam responded. Tom's dad was completely stunned by the statement he had just heard. He made a face that Tom had seen before: a face he makes when his mind fills with questions and hatred.

"What kind of potion!?" Tom's dad finally said, extremely eager to find the answers to all the questions he had in his head. Vakaam stayed silent, he looked so worried about what was going to happen to him. "WHAT KIND OF POTION IS IT!?" Tom's dad shouted at the top of his lungs so suddenly it made everyone in the room flinch.

"A potion that can make anyone a magician... and it cannot be reversed," Vakaam said in a low voice, so worried he started chattering his teeth. Tom's family became bewildered by what Vakaam just said. Their temper greatly increased. Tom's family highly disliked all magicians. They call magic "a cheat in life", and always say, "Be happy the way you are...without magic". They see all sorts of people using magic by tormenting one another.

"YOU WERE A MAGICIAN THIS WHOLE TIME AND YOU NEVER TOLD US!?" Tom's dad roared. Vakaam gave a deep sigh.

"Yes," Vakaam said, quivering. "I can teach Tom magic if you want," he insisted.

"NO," Tom's dad barked. "WE CANNOT HAND OUR SON TO YOU MONSTER!"

Tom could see that his mom was in deep thought about whether they should send Tom to learn from Vakaam.

"C'mon, let's get out of here, Susan," Tom's dad said, walking towards the door.

"David," Tom's mom said.

"Yes?" Tom's dad asked.

"I think...I think it's a good idea for- for Tom to learn magic from Vakaam."

"Susan, we can't let that mon-"

"David, it's the only choice we have! No one will allow a magician into any school." Tom's dad stood there speechlessly in deep thought.

"Fine, but not today," Tom's dad responded.

Vakaam stood there in astonishment. He would never have thought that they would accept his offer. Tom's family left Vakaam's house without saying goodbye. They entered the car and drove home. Tom still felt a weird feeling in his eyes, so when Tom entered the house he rushed to the bathroom once again to observe his eyes.

He inspected his face and saw that there was something off about his eyes. It looked as if his eyes were turning brighter. He went up to his mom and told her about them. She shook her head and said, "I don't know what Vakaam did to you."

Later that night Tom went to his bed to sleep. He laid down and put his blanket on. He closed his eyes, but couldn't sleep because of the weird feeling that he had in his eyes. He got out of his bed and opened the light and approached the mirror that was in his room. He checked the mirror and noticed that his eyes were striking, emerald green! He went to his parents' room but figured out that they were already sleeping, so Tom just went to sleep too.

When Tom woke up he went to the living room and Tom's parents spotted Tom's eyes, stunned.

"What happened to your eyes?" Tom's dad asked. "Was it that monster?"

"Yeah, probably," Tom replied.

They drove to Vakaam's house and rang the doorbell then saw Vakaam greeting them, but Tom's family didn't answer. Vakaam looked delighted about him teaching Tom magic. Tom's parents told Tom to go inside, so he went inside Vakaam's house and closed the door.

"Are you here to learn magic from me?" Vakaam asked.

"I think," Tom answered.

"Okay, then let's start. So first, you will need a wand, wait here, I'll get it," Vakaam said, going to the room he forbade everyone from going in. A few seconds later he came back holding two wands for Tom and himself.

"Here is your wand," Vakaam said, handing Tom one of the wands he brought from the forbidden room. "Okay, so first you will need to have the proper grip of the wand," Vakaam said. He went to Tom and showed him how he was supposed to hold the wand. He went to a tissue box and took out a tissue from it. "Now, do you see that tissue? You will have to pick that up without any physical contact with it by saying '*Trodius*' and by focusing a lot on it. Like this. *Trodius*!" Vakaam demonstrated.

"Okay. *Trodius*!" Tom yelled. The napkin barely moved. Tom couldn't tell if the napkin moved because of the wind or if it moved because of the spell.

"I obviously wouldn't expect a beginner to learn a spell on the first try," Vakaam mentioned. "Try again. Try focusing more."

"Alright. *Trodius!*" Tom shouted. It moved a little bit, he had to admit. "Oh my god! It actually moved!" he cheered.

"Very well. I also absolutely wouldn't have expected you to learn your first spell on the second try," Vakaam stated. "Keep practicing it."

For the next 5 hours, Tom learned and practiced new spells. Then after his class was done, his parents picked Tom up from Vakaam's house and asked Tom how it was. Tom said it was good. His parents became disappointed because they never liked magicians and Tom is becoming one.

For the next couple of months, Tom did the same routine: learning spells and practicing them, learning spells and practicing them, learning spells and practicing them. Also, by now, everyone knew Tom as "The magician that hates magicians", but Tom actually liked being a magician.

One day, when Tom went to Vakaam's house and figured out he wasn't there, Tom went into the restricted room and searched what was in there. He found wands, potions, and other magical items. He kept walking until he reached the end of the room and found a piece of paper on the ground at one of the corners of the room. Tom picked it up and examined the paper, which was labeled "The Plan to get Tom killed and to frame the good magicians". Tom was shocked by this discovery. He thought Vakaam was innocent. He read the entire paper and then saw from a window in the room that Vakaam arrived at his house. Tom quickly put the paper into his pocket, ran to the living room, and pretended he was practicing spells, waiting for Vakaam innocently. Vakaam entered the house, greeted Tom, and then started Tom's class.

A few days later Vakaam went outside with Tom to start his evil plan that was going to be executed. It would be by gathering a powerful magician and walking with them and Tom far away in the forest where no one would see them as an excuse that it would just be a walk. After he did that, he would kill Tom and the good magician. When they are both dead, he would lie to everyone by telling them that the good magician betrayed everyone and killed Tom so Vakaam had to kill the powerful magician so he wouldn't kill anyone else who was innocent in the world. Tom had prepared for Vakaam's evil plan so that right before Vakaam would try to kill Tom, he would stun Vakaam before he attacked Tom. After he did that he would then tell everyone about Vakaam's vicious plans.

Vakaam drove to the good magician, Thomas's house, which was even smaller than Vakaam's house. Vakaam called Thomas to come outside. Thomas, who was a man that was a little old and a little short and who was wearing a green outfit and a blue hat that had a pointy top, greeted both of them and they walked into the woods together.

"How is your magical education going?" Thomas questioned Tom as they entered the woods. The woods had tall trees and a bunch of broken branches on the ground. The trees were so long and big that there was barely any sunlight.

"It's been going pretty good," Tom replied.

After about 5 minutes, Tom saw Vakaam slowly take out his wand from his pocket behind his back, but before Vakaam attacked anyone, Tom said "*Trodius*" and brought Vakaam's wand to Tom. Vakaam flinched and his eyes widened.

"What's happening?" Thomas asked, widening his eyes also. He looked first at Tom, then Vakaam, then back to Tom.

"He is trying to kill both of us," Tom responded.

"Where is your proof," Thomas asked disapprovingly.

"Here," Tom said, taking out Vakaam's paper from his pocket and handing it to Thomas.

He read the entire paper carefully, and after he finished reading the paper, he dropped his jaw and looked at Vakaam. Vakaam started running away as fast as he could, dodging trees and branches, but it wasn't too long before Thomas yelled *"Stunadius"* which stunned Vakaam, making him fall to the ground as if he just died.

Tom and Thomas brought Vakaam's stunned body and called the police using magic. They watched as the magical police car came through trees, bumping along the way. The cops came out of the car and put Vakaam in it. Tom and Thomas also rode with the cops to the prison. They reached the prison and entered it, revealing an old and rusty room. It was cold and it was dark inside of it.

Right before the cops were about to put the magical, green handcuffs (that were summoned by the cops) on Vakaam, he leaped backward, sprinted hastily behind the police officer, took their wand that was located in the cop's back pocket, and quickly said *"Shirorio"*, which is a spell that makes everyone near him blind for the few seconds, including Tom and Thomas. Tom took out his wand before Vakaam could go anywhere and then said *"Stunadius"*, pointing at where he saw Vakaam before he became blind, but accidentally hit a police officer. He knew that because when the police officer got hit, he made a noise that Tom could tell was not Vakaam's voice, and also because he could hear footsteps running. When Tom and the others could see again, they looked outside to see where Vakaam went, but they couldn't find him, so they assumed that he teleported away and they just left him, hoping he wouldn't do anything vicious again.

Tom, thanks to his intelligence, now knew why Vakaam had made him a magician, taught him how to use magic, and made him a powerful magician: it was because a lot of good magicians knew about Tom and if Tom died by a good, powerful, and famous magician, people will think that the good magician betrayed Tom and everyone would think Vakaam was actually a good magician.

Tom told everyone about Vakaam's evil plan starting with his parents. Tom learned magic from Thomas after Vakaam's disappearance. After one year, Tom could beat Thomas in a fight, and in another year he was amongst one of the most powerful magicians in the world, but after about another year, he became the one-and-only most powerful magician in the world.

ABOUT THE AUTHOR
MUHAMMAD ABUBAKR ATIF

Muhammad Atif is more commonly known as Abubakr. He's 11 but I'm not sure you would think so. He goes to MCC academy taller than most kids his age but short to himself. He moved to Chicago when he was 7 but lived in New Jersey before. Why he wrote the story: he didn't live in the best neighborhood but it was perfect to him. There was a little gang violence where he lived, and his house even got robbed three times. He started playing basketball when he came here. He has two siblings, a sister and a little brother. Finally, he likes gaming but is also is trying to make a business.

I dedicate this story to those who want everything and more.

—M.A.A.

THE NEIGHBORHOOD'S SHADOW

BY MUHAMMAD ABUBAKR ATIF

I woke up and slammed my alarm clock. I was trying to wake up at 11:00, or at least 9:00, and it was 6:00 right now. I had forgotten to turn off my alarm clock, so now I had to stay awake because I couldn't go back to sleep after waking up.

"Turn that infuriating thing off!" My mom yelled from her room, her voice muffled but clearly irritated. I woke her up with my alarm.

"Sorry, Mom!" I called back, rubbing my eyes. I stumbled out of bed and into our small, cramped bathroom. The linoleum floor was cold under my feet, and the mirror above the sink was speckled with age. I splashed some water on my face, trying to wake myself up fully.

As I was getting ready for my weekend job, my mom poked her head into the bathroom. "Can you take off today and you can spend it with me? I made your favorite breakfast—blueberry pancakes with chocolate chips."

I sighed, feeling a pang of guilt. "I'd love to, Mom, but we need the money. I can't take off."

She gave me a sad smile. "I know, honey. Just thought I'd ask."

As I walked to work, which was about a thirty-minute walk because we didn't make enough money to afford a car, I thought about how tough things were. The streets were lined with old houses, some with boarded-up windows and overgrown lawns. I had a bike, but I rarely used it.

About ten minutes before I got to work, I ran into the same group of kids who always made fun of me at school and tried to bully me into joining their gang. They were dangerous, or at least the people they worked for were.

"Hey, loser!" the gang leader sneered.

They threw all of my work materials onto the ground and snatched my watch off my wrist, tossing it down the street. "Go fetch," one of them said with a smirk.

My watch wasn't expensive, but it was a gift from my dad before he passed away, so it was very important to me. As they were leaving, they shoved me to the ground and laughed as they walked away. I usually shrugged it off, but lately, it had been getting on my nerves.

When I finally got to work, I was met at the front by my best friend, Damian. Like me, he was poor and worked hard to support his family. I worked at a grocery store as a cashier, and Damian was the janitor.

"Hey man, rough morning?" Damian asked, noticing the dirt on my clothes.

"Yeah, those guys again," I muttered, trying to brush myself off. "Thanks for covering for me yesterday, by the way."

"No problem," he said, giving me a sympathetic look. "We gotta stick together."

I worked for ten hours and got paid fifty dollars a day. It wasn't much, but it helped. After work, Damian and I usually hung out. We were too poor to afford boba or coffee, so we went to the library to talk and get something from the vending machine there.

The library was a quiet refuge from our hectic lives. The musty smell of old books filled the air, and the dim lighting made it feel cozy. We sat in our usual corner, munching on cheap snacks.

"Why do you put up with those guys?" Damian asked, concerned in his eyes.

"I don't know, man. I guess I'm just trying to avoid more trouble," I replied, staring at the table. "I don't want them to go after my mom."

We talked until the library closed, then I walked home. It was around 10:00 p.m. when I got there, and my mom was usually asleep by then, so I quietly headed to bed.

On weekdays, my routine was different. I woke up at 6:00, and my mom left for work around 5:30, but she always left me half a bagel or some milk. School started at 8:00 a.m., but since I walked everywhere, I left around 7:00 a.m. and got to school in about fifty minutes. The streets were often empty that early, with only the occasional car passing by. The cracked sidewalks and graffiti-covered walls were a constant reminder of where I came from.

I usually didn't see Damian until about 8:20 a.m., but the teacher never marked him tardy. "Why are you always late?" I asked him one morning.

"Don't worry about it," he replied with a shrug, a mysterious look in his eyes.

As I walked into school, the gang was right there. I tried going the opposite way, but it didn't work. They pushed me around, calling me names and trying to convince me to join them. I didn't budge, but the daily harassment only got worse, and finally it began to wear me down. I stayed home for a week, in hopes that they'd forget about me.

When I returned to school, they were waiting. They dragged me into the hallways and beat me up so badly I ended up with a fractured arm. They laughed at me, threw my lunch in the garbage, and bashed me with name-calling. The more they did it, the more I tried to ignore them. I started making excuses not to go to school, but my mom eventually caught on and made me go.

"I can't keep running," I thought to myself, the dread gnawing at my insides. One day, the gang cornered me after school. They all had baseball bats.

"Our parents got a call from the principal," the leader, Jamal said. "We know you snitched on us."

"No, I didn't," I stammered, trying to make sense of what was happening. "I swear I didn't say anything."

Jamal's eyes narrowed. "We don't believe you. You have two options: One, we beat you up right now and every single day from now on, no matter where you are—at home, at school, or anywhere. Or two, you join our gang and you don't get beaten up, except when you make a mistake. Which option will you choose?"

I went through some hard thinking and decided what I was going to choose. I chose option two.

After the weekend, I saw them for the first time without being beat up or hurt. I was so amazed and thought this might be the way to go. But they didn't talk to me much at school. After school was a whole different story.

They told me my first task was to quit my weekend and weekday job. "How will my mom and I live off five hundred dollars a month?" I asked.

"You chose this option, not us. But we'll make sure you make enough money. Trust us," the leader said with a smirk.

"Remember, don't talk to us in school. We're not friends; you're our employee now. Get that in your head. We gave you an easy way out, but if you mess up, you'll be beaten up badly. Got it?"

I nodded, feeling a chill run down my spine. "Got it."

"Good. Now, we need you to go to the other side of town and pick up a package for us," the leader said.

As I was going I contemplated how much danger I was in, like the consequences for messing up I will, you know, get beaten up. So I thought I am gonna make a plan and go to the city with my mom and Damian will hold them off for me. I walked to the other side of town, feeling a sense of unease as I went to pick up the package. As I walked, I thought about my plan to escape with my mom and Damian. I knew it was risky, but I had to try.

I arrived at the designated location and picked up the package. As I turned to leave, I was confronted by the gang's leader. "What's taking so long?" he asked, his voice cold.

"I'm just getting the package," I replied, trying to keep my cool.

The leader's eyes narrowed. "Make sure you get it back to us quickly. And don't think about trying to escape."

I nodded, feeling a surge of fear. But I knew I had to keep my cool if I was going to make it out alive.

As I walked back to the city, I couldn't shake the feeling that I was being watched. But I didn't let it deter me from my plan.

When I arrived back in the city, I met up with my mom and Damian. We quickly made our way to a safe location, where we waited for the gang to track us down.

As we waited, I could feel my heart racing with anticipation. But when the gang finally arrived, they were not alone. They were accompanied by a group of community leaders, who had been tracking their activities for some time.

The leader of the gang sneered at us, but the community leaders stepped forward, their faces firm. "We've been watching you," one of them said. "We know what you've been doing to these kids. And we're not going to let you get away with it."

The gang's leader smirked at them, but the community leaders were not intimidated. They threatened to take action against the gang if they didn't leave and turn themselves in.

The gang was shocked and outraged. They had never been threatened like this before. They looked at each other uncertainly, and for a moment, I thought they might actually listen.

But then, one of them stepped forward, his eyes blazing with anger. "You're just trying to get us in trouble," he said. "But we're not going down without a fight."

The community leaders stood firm, and the gang began to argue among themselves. It was clear that they were divided, and that their leader was losing control.

As we watched, the gang's leader stormed off, followed by most of the others. The rest of them looked at each other with uncertainty, then slowly backed away.

The community leaders turned to us, their faces relieved. "It's over," one of them said. "You're safe now."

My mom hugged me tightly, tears streaming down her face. Damian grinned at me, his eyes shining with relief.

We all hugged each other tightly, feeling a sense of joy and freedom that we had never felt before. We had finally escaped the gang's clutches, and we were going to start a new life together.

From that day on, we all worked together to build a better life for ourselves. We got jobs and started our own businesses, and we became involved in our community. We helped others who were struggling, and we worked together to make our neighborhood a better place.

And as for the gang's leader, he eventually turned himself in and was given a chance to reform. He became a positive influence on his community, and he even helped others who were like himself, angry and violent.

In the end, we all learned that there was a better way to live than through violence and fear. We learned that by working together and supporting each other, we could overcome any obstacle and achieve our dreams.

And as for me, I realized that I didn't have to be afraid anymore. I could stand up for myself and fight back against those who tried to hurt me. I was strong enough to overcome anything that came my way.

And so, our story came full circle. We had started out in a place of fear and uncertainty, but we had ended up in a place of hope and freedom.

About the Author
Areeb Hussaini

Areeb Hussaini is a young boy who has a series of imagination and likes to draw. He also finds video games fun and entertaining. Areeb Hussaini lives with four other family members, his mom, dad, and two brothers. Areeb is the middle child. His favorite show is *Ninjago* and favorite game is *Roblox*. When his teacher explained to him that they would be writing a book, it was a chance to finally release his imagination into the wild so other people can also view his work. His mom encouraged him along the way as he was writing this book so that he would never give up on his dream work.

Dedicated to Mom.

—A.H.

THE HOODS

BY AREEB HUSSAINI

In the magical city of Fortimone, a group of brave individuals called the Hoods stood together to protect their cherished home. Leading this courageous band were DarkZeytras and DarkMortagon, wielding their unique weapons with skill and determination.

DarkZeytras held two sharp swords, swift and sharp, while DarkMortagon swung a massive spiked ball, a mighty weapon indeed. Together, they swore to defend Fortimone against any threat that dared to emerge.

Among the Hoods were other members, each with their own special talents. There was Blaze, who could command fire with great intensity, and Aqua, who had mastery over water. Earthquake possessed incredible strength, able to shake the ground itself, while Gale could manipulate the wind to great use,Then there was Lightray who had the elemental power of light, And many other hoods in the army.

Their unity formed a strong bond, and they were prepared to face whatever challenges came their way. However, lurking in the shadows was a dark presence that threatened to disrupt their peace.

In a distant realm, a Hood named Metalgear harbored sinister intentions. Betrayed by his own kin, Metalgear divided into forbidden arts, summoning creatures known as reapers from another dimension. Their goal: to create chaos and destruction in Fortimone.

When the reapers descended upon Fortimone, panic spread like wildfire. The Hoods rushed to defend their home, but the battle was fierce and dangerous. DarkZeytras and DarkMortagon led the fight on both sides, their fight was fierce, but Metalgear's cunning tactics brought heavy casualties on the Hoods.

Among the chaos, Blaze's flames clashed with the icy moves of Frostbite, a reaper of chilling power. Aqua fought fearlessly against Torrent, a reaper whose sandy attacks were relentlessly thrown on the battlefield. Earthquake's strength collided with Spawn, a reaper who could control the forces of nature. While Gale's winds battled against Cyclone's zapping attacks.

In the heat of battle, Metalgear set his sights on DarkMortagon, his weapon poised to strike. With a mighty blast, DarkMortagon fell, his brave spirit extinguished, leaving the Hoods reeling in shock and sorrow.

DarkZeytras, consumed by grief and rage, tapped into his inner darkness, his power swelling to match the magnitude of his loss. Metalgear, sensing the shift in power, smirked with wicked satisfaction, confident in his superiority.

"You think you can defeat me, Metalgear?" DarkZeytras's voice , his eyes blazing with fury.

Metalgear chuckled darkly. "Your sorrow blinds you, Zeytras. You are no match for me."

Their battle erupted with a ferocity that shook the very city of Fortimone. DarkZeytras's blades danced with deadly precision, each strike fueled by the memory of his fallen comrade. Metalgear countered with calculated strikes, his moves of dark magic caused destruction.

As their clash continued on, the other Hoods fought valiantly against the reapers, their elemental powers clashing against the otherworldly forces. Blaze's flames roared against Frostbite's icy assaults, while Aqua's water clashed against Torrent's relentless tide. Earthquake's tremors shattered Boulder's defenses, and Gale's winds buffeted Cyclone's swirling attacks.

In the midst of battle, DarkZeytras and Metalgear exchanged words amidst their clashes, their voices cutting through the chaos.

"You cannot defeat me, Metalgear!" DarkZeytras shouted, his determination unwavering.

Metalgear laughed mockingly. "Your bravado means nothing, Zeytras. You will fall before me like all the others."

But DarkZeytras remained resolute. With a roar of defiance, he unleashed a torrent of dark energy, overwhelming Metalgear's defenses and sending him crashing to the ground.

Metalgear, battered and broken, looked up at DarkZeytras with a mixture of fear and defiance. "Finish it, then. End me."

DarkZeytras hesitated, his heart heavy with sorrow. But then, with a grim resolve, he raised his blades, his eyes filled with regret.

"Forgive me, Metalgear," he whispered, as he delivered the final blow.

As Metalgear fell, the reapers retreated, their leader defeated and their purpose thwarted. The citizens of Fortimone cheered as the Hoods emerged victorious, but their hearts remained heavy with the loss of their fallen comrades.

DarkZeytras stood amidst the aftermath of battle, his breaths heavy and his heart weighed down by the loss of DarkMortagon. The once bustling streets of Fortimone now lay in ruin, but the Hoods had prevailed against the dark forces that threatened their home.

Aqua approached DarkZeytras, her expression somber yet filled with admiration. "You did it, Zeytras. You saved us all."

DarkZeytras nodded, his gaze distant. "But at what cost? We've lost one of our own."

Blaze stepped forward, his fiery aura flickering with sorrow. "DarkMortagon was a true hero. He'll be remembered for his bravery."

Gale joined the group, her voice soft yet determined. "We'll honor his memory by continuing to protect Fortimone. Together, as Hoods."

Earthquake, his expression stoic, spoke up. "Metalgear may be defeated, but we must remain vigilant. Who knows what other threats may lurk in the shadows."

Lightray, her radiant energy pulsing with hope, added, "As long as we stand united, Fortimone will endure any challenge."

DarkZeytras nodded, a sense of determination rising within him.

The Hoods stood amidst the ruins of Fortimone, their hearts heavy with the loss of DarkMortagon. As they mourned their fallen comrade, a new threat loomed on the horizon.

A shadowy figure emerged from the darkness, his presence striking fear into the hearts of the Hoods. Shadowbane, a sinister villain shrouded in mystery, stepped forward with a wicked grin.

"Well, well, well," Shadowbane sneered, his voice dripping with malice. "What do we have here? A group of pathetic heroes, mourning the loss of their precious friend."

DarkZeytras narrowed his eyes, his grip tightening on his swords. "Who are you, and what do you want?"

Shadowbane chuckled darkly, his form flickering like a shadow in the moonlight. "I am Shadowbane, the bringer of darkness. And I've come to claim Fortimone as my own."

Blaze stepped forward, his flames flickering with defiance. "You'll have to get through us first, Shadowbane!"

The villain's laughter echoed through the night, sending shivers down the spines of the Hoods. "Oh, how amusing. But I assure you, defeating you will be child's play."

With a wave of his hand, Shadowbane summoned a horde of shadowy minions, their eyes gleaming with horror. The Hoods braced themselves for battle, their determination never ending.

The clash was fierce and intense, with Shadowbane's minions overwhelming the Hoods with their small numbers. But the heroes fought with courage and skill, pushing back against the tide of darkness.

DarkZeytras leaped into the fray, his swords slashing through the shadows with precision. "We won't let you destroy Fortimone, Shadowbane! We'll protect our home at all costs!"

Shadowbane's laughter echoed through the chaos, his eyes gazing with cruel amusement. "Foolish heroes! You cannot stop the inevitable. Fortimone will fall, and I will reign supreme!"

But the Hoods refused to back down, rallying together with unwavering determination. With each strike, they pushed Shadowbane and his minions back, inch by inch.

As the battle raged on, the citizens of Fortimone emerged from their homes, inspired by the bravery of the Hoods. Together, they stood united against the darkness, their hope shining like a beacon in the night.

And as dawn broke over the city, Shadowbane's forces began to crumble, their dark power waning in the light of day. With a final roar of anger, the villain vanished into the shadows, his threat thwarted for now.

The Hoods stood victorious once more, their spirits lifted by their triumph over evil. As they surveyed the city, now safe from harm, they knew that no matter what challenges lay ahead, they would face them together, as one.

As the Hoods celebrated their hard-won victory over Shadowbane, little did they know that the shadowy villain was far from defeated. Deep within the darkest corners of Fortimone, Shadowbane plotted his return, his thirst for revenge burning brighter than ever.

Meanwhile, in a forgotten corner of the city, Metalgear lay dormant, covered in rust and forgotten by all. But fate had other plans for the fallen Hood, as Shadowbane stumbled upon him during his search for allies.

Shadowbane's eyes gleamed with wicked delight as he approached Metalgear's prone form. "Well, well, what do we have here? A former ally, cast aside and left to rot."

Metalgear stirred from his slumber, his eyes flickering with recognition. "Shadowbane... What do you want?"

The villain grinned, extending a hand to help Metalgear to his feet. "I seek vengeance against the Hoods, and I believe you can help me achieve it."

Metalgear hesitated, memories of his past loyalties conflicting with the bitterness in his heart. "And why should I help you?"

"Because together, we can defeat our common enemy," Shadowbane replied, his tone laced with persuasion. "With your knowledge and my power, we can crush the Hoods once and for all."

Metalgear considered Shadowbane's offer, his mind clouded with doubt and uncertainty. But in the end, he knew that he could not deny the opportunity for redemption.

"Very well," Metalgear said, his voice tinged with resignation. "I will help you defeat the Hoods."

Together, Shadowbane and Metalgear devised a cunning plan to ensnare the Hoods and crush them beneath their combined might. With Metalgear's knowledge of the Hoods' weaknesses and Shadowbane's dark magic, they would be unstoppable.

Meanwhile, the Hoods reveled in their victory, unaware of the looming threat that awaited them. But their celebration was short-lived, as all the reapers who had fought against them approached with a plea for mercy.

"We... we don't want to fight anymore," Torrent, Frostbite, Spawn, and Cyclone stammered, their voices trembling with fear and uncertainty. "Please, we beg of you, spare us and allow us to join your team."

The Hoods exchanged glances, their hearts filled with compassion for their former enemies. After a moment of deliberation, they welcomed the reapers into their ranks, extending a hand of friendship to the once-villainous creatures.

And as the reapers joined the Hoods, a new chapter began for the courageous band of heroes. Little did they know that their greatest challenge lay just ahead, as Shadowbane and Metalgear prepared to unleash their wrath upon Fortimone once again.

As Shadowbane and Metalgear plotted their next move, they sought out two more allies to boost their ranks. In the darkest corners of the realm, they found Nightshade, a evil sorceress with mastery over shadows, and Brimstone, a fearsome warrior wielding flames of pure destruction.

With their alliance solidified, Shadowbane and his allies prepared to unleash their fury upon Fortimone once more. But little did they know that the Hoods and the reapers had forged an unlikely bond, united in their determination to protect their home.

Under the guidance of DarkZeytras, the Hoods and the reapers trained together, honing their skills and preparing for the inevitable showdown. Despite their differences, they found strength in their unity, their shared goal binding them together as allies.

As the day of reckoning dawned, Shadowbane, Metalgear, Nightshade, and Brimstone launched their assault on Fortimone, their forces descending upon the city with relentless fury.

But the Hoods and the reapers were ready. With DarkZeytras leading the charge, they rallied to defend their home once more, their determination unwavering in the face of overwhelming odds.

The battle that ensued was fierce and chaotic, with fire and shadow clashing against light and elemental power. DarkZeytras and Metalgear faced off once more, their swords and rusty mechanisms clashing in a duel of epic proportions.

Meanwhile, Nightshade's shadows enveloped Aqua and Blaze, testing their resolve as they fought to break free from their grasp. Brimstone unleashed torrents of flame upon Earthquake and Gale, their strength and agility pushed to their limits as they countered his fiery onslaught.

But amidst the chaos and destruction, tragedy struck as Cyclone sacrificed himself to save Blaze from a devastating attack by Brimstone. With a final, heroic gesture, Cyclone summoned all his remaining strength to create a barrier of wind, shielding Blaze from harm at the cost of his own life.

As Blaze watched in horror, Cyclone's sacrifice filled him with a newfound determination to honor his fallen comrade. With a roar of defiance, he unleashed a torrent of flames upon Brimstone, driving the villain back with sheer force of will.

And as the sun set over Fortimone, casting its golden light upon the battlefield, the Hoods and the reapers emerged victorious once more, their home saved from the clutches of evil.

With Shadowbane and his allies defeated, the city rejoiced in the triumph of its defenders, their courage and determination shining bright in the face of adversity. And as they celebrated their hard-won victory, they knew that no matter what challenges lay ahead, they would face them together, as one.As the dust settled and the echoes of battle faded, the Hoods stood amidst the rubble, their hearts heavy with both sorrow and happiness. Blaze mourned the loss of Cyclone, his brave sacrifice etched in their memories forever.

But amidst the sorrow, there was also joy. Fortimone had been saved once again, thanks to the bravery and unity of its defenders. With tears of both grief and relief, the Hoods turned to their fellow citizens, who emerged from their homes to witness the aftermath of the battle.

The streets of Fortimone filled with loud cheers as the entire city celebrated the victory. Citizens embraced one another, tears of joy streaming down their faces as they realized that their home had been saved from destruction once more.

The Hoods stood at the center of it all, their weary faces illuminated by the glow of victory. DarkZeytras raised his swords high, his voice ringing out above the tumult of the crowd.

"Today, we have triumphed against the forces of darkness!" he declared, his words echoing through the streets. "But let us not forget the sacrifices made by those who fought beside us. Cyclone may be gone, but his bravery will never be forgotten. Let us honor his memory by rebuilding our city stronger than ever before!"

The citizens of Fortimone cheered in agreement, their voices rising as one in a chorus of unity and hope. Together, they began the task of rebuilding their beloved city, their spirits lifted by the knowledge that they had faced the impossible and emerged victorious.

And as the sun dipped below the horizon, casting its warm glow over the city, the Hoods stood shoulder to shoulder with their fellow citizens, ready to face whatever challenges the future might bring. For in Fortimone, they knew that as long as they stood together, they could overcome anything that came their way.

About the Author
Yusuf Jilani

Yusuf Jilani is a fifth grader at MCC Academy. He wrote this story because he has a passion for writing thrillers. He is an avid reader and a writer. He wants to write many books one day and become a bestselling author. His work includes *The Coding Complication* and many comic books. He is currently a contestant of the Betty Award Spring writing contest. Yusuf Jilani enjoys playing football and drawing.

For every reader, who enjoys reading a book over and over again.

—Y.J.

The Crime at Night

By Yusuf Jilani

O nce upon a time, in the dead of night, there was a man standing on a dark street that appeared to be deserted. No lights shone from any of the large houses, making them look very spooky. The cunning man stood camouflaged with black clothing in the darkness outside the largest house, which he very well knew was filled with gold and money. And he intended to steal it.

There was something very unusual about this robber. During the day, he was amazing and clever. But at night, he was unstoppable. He had special abilities that seemed like magic. One of his abilities was to summon weapons when he willed. Another was that he could grab objects and teleport them anywhere he wanted.

He was standing in front of the house's back door because entering from the front door was too risky. *I could have taken out the two security guards, but then they would have probably set off an alarm,* he thought. But just as he opened the back door with a key made of stone that he made using his special abilities, he came across two heavily-armed guards.

"Hey fellas," he said. "So, can I please have your gun," he pointed to the guard on the right. And with amazing speed, he took the guard on the right's gun, broke it into two with incredible strength, and knocked both of the guards out. "Thank you," he said.

"Well, that was easy," he continued. He stole a great amount of riches and escaped. But he didn't realize that someone was on his tail...

6 HOURS AGO...

Mike Brown was called, unexpectedly, to the Smith family's house. He assumed what he had to do there. Probably stop a bad guy.

Mike worked for the Crime Stopping, Criminal Investigating, Spy Agency, as known as CSCISA. He was a rookie spy, and he knew this was his chance to prove himself and make his mother prouder. Growing up, Mike had learned a lot from his mother, a retired school teacher. He could never forget her precious words, "Strive to be the best in whatever you do and always make the right decision no matter the cost." That's why he had wanted to be just like Mark Stan, the best spy in the history of CSCISA. He had heard about so many thrilling missions Mark had completed so effortlessly. Mark had been Mike's motivation in joining CSCISA. But who knew, Mark would go rogue. The whole agency knew Mark's name.

Mike asked the driver of the car he was in when they would get there, and he said five minutes. In a little bit, Director Bob Thomas would give him a dangerous assignment. Soon they arrived. It was 5:13 p.m. He walked up to the front door of the big house.

When he entered, there were guards everywhere in the fancy house. An assistant led him to the living room. Director Thomas was there along with a man and woman.

"Agent Mike," the Director said, "your mission is very important. You have to follow a robber when he steals stuff from this house."

Mike was surprised. "That's it?" he asked. "I thought you said this mission is important."

"It is," the Director said. "The mission file will give you a lot more information than I can." He handed Mike a red file.

The file said that the robber had special powers at night and was incredibly dangerous. It did not say his name, but it did say that his lair was close by.

"We put guards everywhere," said the man, who was probably Mr. Smith. "But, he will likely be able to get past them. Once he gets away, you have to follow him to his lair and catch him."

"Please ensure to get back all the valuables he steals," said Mrs. Smith.

"Don't worry," said Mike reassuringly. "I'll stop him."

Mike got a lot of high-tech equipment. For six hours, he was trapped in the extremely fancy master bedroom. "*This is taking too long,*" he thought.

But then, he heard a noise. It sounded like something breaking. Mike crept downstairs. Then he saw a man. He was wearing black clothes. He had knocked out two guards. The robber said, "Well, that was easy." He went to the pile of gold in front of him. When he touched the gold, it vanished. Mike gasped. Then, the man ran away. Mike took his gear and went after him.

The man hopped onto a motorcycle and sped away. Mike put himself and his gear into his new, high-tech car and went after him. He put his car into stealth mode and his car became silent and hard to see.

Soon, the man got to his lair. He drove his motorcycle into it. Mike parked his car and activated his high-tech suit. His car blended in with its surroundings. His gear shrunk and he put it in his suit.

Mike followed the man into his lair. It was a dark, big space. When he entered it, lasers pointed at him. He kept dodging them until they were confused. Mike took this chance to use his suit to hack the lasers and shut them down. "*That was cool,*" he thought. The motorcycle was lying in front of a door.

When Mike opened the door, he saw a huge pile of riches, some lab equipment, and a huge machine in a big, damp room. In front of the machine, the man was holding a floppy disk. The man inserted the disk into the machine. Something appeared on a large screen. Then the man said, "Hello, Mike."

Mike was shocked. "How do you know my name?" he asked.

The man replied, "I know the identities of everyone at your agency." The screen was showing the names of everyone in the CSCISA. The man laughed. "You don't know me, Mike? After all the history I have with CSCISA?"

"What are you talking about?" asked Mike. "Director Bob doesn't even know your name!"

"The whole agency knows my name," the man said.

"No, we don't," said Mike.

"Yes, you do. My name is Mark Stan," said the man.

"No!" said Mike.

"Yes," said Mark, grinning. "My powers aren't magic, they are the agency's tech. They are hard to detect at night. That's why I only use them at night."

"How did you get here?" asked Mike. "Your new director framed me. He wanted my job. Bob was always jealous of me. He framed me for working with shady crime organizations. The old director, Sam Lance, fired me. Bob got rid of him too somehow, but the agency imprisoned him. Then he aimed for the top. He got the director's job. He knew I would come back to get my revenge. That's why he put so much security, and now he put you on my tail too." Mark explained.

"That's right," said a voice. Director Bob was right behind them. "I put him behind you, Mark, because I could track Mike. Thank you, Mike. You have made everything much easier."

"Hello, Bob," Mark growled.

"Bob, why?" Mike asked.

"*Director* Bob, Mike," Bob said.

"You got that job wrongfully," said Mike, growling like Mark.

"It doesn't matter," Bob said. "Now I can eliminate both of you."

"No way!" said Mike.

"Oh, yes way," said Bob. The door opened and a bunch of spies ran in.

"He's right," said Mark.

"Exactly," said Bob. "Mark says I'm right. Do you agree, Mike?"

"Actually, Bob, I was talking about Mike," said Mark. "*He* is right."

"See, Bob," said Mike. "*I* am right."

"No. You aren't," said Bob. "I am. Get them!"

The spies surrounded Mike and Mark. Mike knew what he had to do. Make the right decision, no matter the cost.

"You wanna do this?" asked Mike.

"Yes, I do," said Mark. "Let's go!"

"YYYYYYAAAAAAAAAAAAAAAAA!!!!!!!!!" they both yelled.

Mike used his suit to paralyze the spies around him. Mark took out a tranquilizer dart gun and shot all the remaining spies.

Bob was frightened. "You got my spies, but you won't get me!" He ran to the door.

"Oh, no ya don't, Bob!" said Mark. He threw a ball at Bob.

Crash!

"Well, let's take this guy to the agency prison hall, right?" asked Mark. Bob was tied to the machine.

"Yeah," said Mike. "He needs to think about what he did."

They returned to the agency building. It was a tall, glass building in NYC. They opened the door. Mark turned his suit invisible, along with a tied, knocked out Bob. He went around the metal detector. They entered the elevator and pressed "Prison Hall."

The doors opened. There were two signs. The first one said "⧉ Prisoner Delivery & Cell Monitoring". The other one said "Cells & Ultra Prison ⧉". "Come on," said Mark, and all three of them went to the left. A door said, "PRISONER DELIVERY."

"This is the one," said Mike. He opened the door.

Five men were there. "Hello," one of them said. "Where is your prisoner?"

"He is right here," said Mike. Mark deactivated the invisibility mode of his suit.

"Mark Stan!" the men said, raising their guns.

"No, he's not the prisoner," said Mike. Mark pressed a button on his watch. Bob appeared.

"He is," said Mark.

"Director Bob!?" asked the men.

"No," said Mark. "Just Bob."

"Bob got Director Sam and Agent Mark fired, so he could become director," Mike explained.

"I also want to return this to you," said Mark, handing one of the men the floppy disk. "I also kindly request that you release Director Sam and put Bob in the same cell that he was in."

"Hello, everyone!" said Director Sam, later that evening. "I was imprisoned falsely because of our former Director Bob. However, now justice has finally come and *I* have to apply justice too. It's my job as the director. So first, I'd like to give back Mark Stan the job of Ultra S.W.A.T.!" Everybody clapped as Mark went up to the stage.

"Also," continued Director Sam, "we have to recognize the person who solved this case. I am promoting Mike Brown to become partners with Mark Stan in Ultra S.W.A.T.!" Everyone clapped for Mike as much as Mark. Mike's mother stood right in front of the crowd, cheering the loudest.

"So," said Mike. "Welcome back."

"Thanks," said Mark. "I couldn't have done it without you."

ABOUT THE AUTHOR
KINZA MARFANI

Kinza Marfani is in fifth grade and goes to MCC Academy. She is the oldest sibling out of three and comes from a family of five. She enjoys cooking, crocheting, making things, and enjoys horror stories and movies. She also enjoys spending time with her family and loves cats. She is in hifz and hopes to complete the Quran at least in two years. She has a passion for drawing and writing.

This story is dedicated to the people who are like me and love to create.

—*K.M.*

After Dark

By Kinza Marfani

I know this isn't how usual stories start, but this is my first time writing one. I'm writing it because my doctors recommended it to help me recover from memory loss. Some parts I just can't remember but I hope you, the reader, enjoy it anyway. I am currently writing in my hospital bed in the journal that my mom brought me from the 'Gift Shop' downstairs. This is the story of how I fell into a 5-year-long coma:

My name is Hana, I am 11 years old, and my family just moved to Seattle, Washington. My dad's job requires moving to different places every few years. I am an only child and since we have to move every few years it's hard making friends. As I lay on my bed, my phone's ringtone startled me. I picked it up and Inaya and I chatted for almost half an hour. But as I ran downstairs for lunch, my parents were discussing my school plans for tomorrow.

Frustrated, I whined, "Amma, do I have to go to school tomorrow? We just moved here yesterday."

But my parents were firm. "Yes, Hana. You haven't had a full year of education in five years. You have to go to school. We can't afford you missing another year," my mom said. I grudgingly agreed and continued eating my lunch while my dad chuckled at my antics. Later that evening, I ran upstairs to check my supply list and realized I needed a protractor and a calculator.

"Amma, I need a protractor and a calculator," I whispered-screamed to my mom.

But my mom had already taken care of it and talked to my teacher about it. I smiled awkwardly and ate my dinner quickly before going to sleep, excited for my big day tomorrow.

I woke up early, took a shower, wore my uniform and hijab, grabbed my bag, and left for school so I wouldn't be late on my first day. When I walked into the classroom, I was met with stares, whispers, and giggles from my classmates. But I held my head high and sat down.

Ms. Linda took attendance and explained the school's policies. In art class, I sat next to a girl named Suzie.

She said "Hi," but I didn't respond. I waved to her, and continued with my class. After class, I stayed in the bathroom stall for half an hour because I didn't want to take the bus home and be made fun of again. While walking home, some kid snatched my hijab off my head. I yelled at him to stop but he ran away laughing. I cried and ran home.

When I got home, I ignored Amma's question about my day and went straight to my room. She followed me but I pretended to do laundry and said I was fine. I didn't eat dinner and went straight to bed.

The next day, the same kid who pulled off my hijab started telling everyone about it. Suzie told him to shut up and sat with me at lunch. She invited me over to her house and I accepted. When we got there, Suzie's mom told me to make myself feel at home before leaving the room. I started to explore around a bit and there was just garbage and things in her closet and drawers. I looked inside her closet to check if she had nice clothes. Or, at least that's what I *thought* I would do until I saw this weird misplaced tile at the end of her closet. I picked it up thinking about putting it back, but this time in order until I saw a small little passageway with a whole lot of stairs, and at the end of it it looked like a door leading to somewhere, I was eager to go through there even if I had to squeeze my big body into that hole, in fact, it even felt as if it was calling to me. I started walking closer and closer to the hole until I heard footsteps that sounded like someone coming up.

"Suzie!" I quickly whisper-screamed to myself and closed the closet door.

SCREECH! Went her door as she entered the room.

"What are you doing in the closet?" She says

"Oh umm, nothing!" I quickly say.

Whew, that was a close one. Suzie's mom makes sandwiches for us, and then it's time to go home. At night it's very hard to sleep, and tonight it was even harder! I kept thinking about that tile. I wanted to go inside so badly yet I couldn't. The next morning I got to school very anxious, knowing I couldn't return to her house, but having some hope she invited me back.

I'm at lunch (a week later)with Suzie and a group of people I barely know. Suddenly, Suzie leans over and invites me over to her place again. I can hardly contain my excitement as I call my mom and get the green light to go. Fast forward to arriving at Suzie's house, and her mom is making me sandwiches again. I excuse myself to find the bathroom, but instead, I make a beeline for

Suzie's room. As I step inside, my jaw drops - her room is spotless. I can't help myself as I make my way over to her closet, only to hear Suzie calling my name. I panic, and before I know it, I've passed out.

It's around midnight when I wake up and I'm still stuck in Suzie's closet. I try to make my way out, but as fate would have it, I fall and hurt myself. I manage to wrap a piece of my dress around my foot and continue walking, but I have no idea where I am. I take out my phone to call my mom, only to have her call me first. I answer softly, and my mom frantically asks where I am. I have no idea, and I scream, dropping the phone. When I pick it back up, I decline the call and continue walking, only to come face-to-face with a creepy, earthquake-ridden scene. I hesitate, but my limbs seem to have a mind of their own, eagerly propelling me towards the looming staircase. As I descend the stairs, a sharp pain twists my stomach, causing me to collapse onto the ground, groaning in agony. Sweat beads on my forehead as I gasp for air, my body trembling with exertion. Suddenly, everything goes black, and I am plunged into darkness. Panic claws at my throat as I call out into the void, my heart pounding with fear.

After what feels like an eternity, the lights flicker back on, illuminating a small door that is barely visible in the dimly lit room. Without a second thought, I fling the door open, revealing a space that is eerily similar to Suzie's room. My heart sinks as I realize that my friend is nowhere to be found. Panic sets in as I frantically search the room, my mind racing with a million questions.

As I stumble through the door, I am suddenly overcome by a feeling of suffocation. The walls seem to be closing in on me, and I struggle to catch my breath. My vision blurs as I gasp for air, my mind consumed by a sense of dread. I feel as if I am losing my grip on reality, forgetting even the most basic things, like my own name and how to breathe.

In that moment of desperation, a figure appeared out of nowhere, clad in a tattered black cloak that fluttered in the breeze. My heart raced as I realized that I was not alone, and I braced myself for whatever was to come.

As I timidly whispered "Um, hello" into the darkness, my heart raced with fear and confusion. Suddenly, I saw him approaching me, but something was off. He seemed to be floating, and I couldn't make out his face. But what sent shivers down my spine was the huge, disturbing smile that spread across his face.

Without warning, I found myself backed against the wall, struggling to speak as my throat thumped wildly.

His shadow loomed over me, and I knew I had to run. But each step I took seemed to bring him closer, and my screams for help went unanswered.

As he closed in on me, I wished I hadn't dropped my phone when Mama called me. I wished I had never been curious enough to venture into this place. But before I could think any further, I tripped on my stupid untied shoelaces and tumbled headfirst into a pit I hadn't noticed before.

The fall left me in a coma for five long years, and I couldn't help but wonder if I'd ever wake up again.

ABOUT THE AUTHOR

UZAIR BIN OMRAN

Uzair Bin Omran is a 10 year old that loves to read books especially *Diary Of A Wimpy Kid* and the *Who Would Win?* series. He has one older sister and one younger brother. Uzair Bin Omran wrote this story about two friends lost in time so that he can donate the money to Gaza.

This story is dedicated to people who love to read.
—U.O.

TIME TRAVEL
BY UZAIR BIN OMRAN

Once upon a time in a lush green forest, there lived a two friends whose names were Hamza and Haroon. They had a cozy two story house with a basement that was locked since they bought the house. One day as Hamza was cleaning the house, he found a key in one of the draws. Then he called Haroon down and showed him the key.

"Do you think it leads to the basement?" Asked Haroon.

"I dunno," replied Hamza.

"Let's try at least," he added. Then the both of them went to the basement door. Hamza put in the key and the door opened then the both of them looked at each other and they went down the stairs.

In the middle of the basement there was a book, "What is this book," Asked Haroon. "Why are you asking me that?" Replied Hamza. Then Haroon found a staff and started messing around. "Stop messing around," Said Hamza. Then the book opened and it said,

"Who dares disturb me, you will be punished!" Then the book opened a portal and Hamza and Haroon ran upstairs but it was too late they got sucked in the portal then the portal closed.

Meanwhile Hamza and Haroon were zooming through the strange portal they saw a bright light up ahead they both braced themselves and fell out of the portal. When they got up they saw giant mountains, volcanoes and dinosaurs. Then they saw a group,of cave people walking towards them and the caveman started to talk to each other.

Then one of them picked his mace and smashed it on the ground but Hamza and Haroon dogged it then Haroon used his staff to knock out the caveman. Then cave men started to attack Haroon and Hamza. Hamza picked up a spear and started to fight the cave people.

Meanwhile, there was a group of hikers hiking in the forest. Then they saw Hamza and Haroon's house. They saw that the door was open so they walked. They went into the basement but nobody was there. Then they saw the book it started to talk to, then they ran out of the house Then they called the authorities and told them what they saw.

A while later the authorities showed up and they told the hikers to go home. Meanwhile Hamza and Haroon made the cave people retreat. Out of nowhere a volcano exploded and that caused a chain reaction. Hamza and Haroon started to flee from the volcanos.

As they were running away a stampede of dinosaurs came in their way. They had to stop even though lava was flowing from behind and the ground was shaking.

After the stampede got out of their way they started to run again. Meanwhile back in the present the authorities were searching the basement when the book started to talk again.

" Who goes there?" Asked the book. The police got so scared they ran upstairs and got in their cars and drove off. Meanwhile in the past Hamza and Haroon thought they got away from danger for a bit then suddenly a T-rex was charging at them.

It roared at them and again they started running away from the T-rex. By now Hamza and Haroon were both really tired and the T-rex was getting closer and closer. Then suddenly a spinosaurus jumped on the T-rex and that gave Hamza and Haroon more time to get away from the T-rex. Then they went into a cave and stayed there for a little while to rest.

After a while they got out of the cave and tried to find a way to get back to the present. Then all of a sudden the book that brought them here was in front of them. It said,

"I am the one that brought you here so if you want to go back to the present you have to complete these trials."

"What trials?" asked Haroon.

"THE TRIALS OF TIME!!!!!" yelled the book.

"What are the trials?" asked Hamza.

"You will see," said the book.

Then the book teleported them to a colosseum in front of them there were two gladiators ready to fight them. Then the book said, " if you can beat them then you can go home." "Deal," Said Haroon. And the both of them got ready to fight. As they got ready one of them charged at the both of them but they dodged the attack.

Then they both tried to attack their enemies but they dodged both of their attacks. They tried to strike again but their enemies dodged again and again and again. Then the gladiators started to attack Hamza and Haroon, but they dodged then Hamza struck one of them and they died then Haroon struck the other one. In the end Hamza and Haroon were victorious.

Then the book said, " You may have got past them but now you both have to get past me." Then Hamza and Haroon took one big gulp and went into battle. They tried to use their swords but the book was so swift it dodged all of their attacks.

The book used its powers on Hamza and Haroon and it tried to knock them out. But Hazma and Haroon dodged all the book's attacks. The book got angry and shot a portal at Hamza and Haroon. But they still dodged the book's attacks.

Then Hamza struck the book and it turned into a portal and they stepped in the portal and they found themselves in the basement of their home. They went upstairs and found a giant mess. Then Haroon said, " Time to get to cleaning I guess." Hamza laughed and the both of them got to cleaning.

THE END!

ABOUT THE AUTHOR
ZAFAR SAIYED

Zafar Saiyed is 11 years old and has a great memory. He is in fifth grade, good at sports, and does the memorization of the Quran. His religion is Islam. His dream is to go to Mekkah and Medina. He also has three siblings. He also wants to become a hafiz.

Dedicated to my parents.

—Z.S.

THE FAKE GHOST

BY ZAFAR SAIYED

O nce upon a time, there was a man named John Arbal and his pets, Orrie and Field. John had a brother named Devin. John's cat really liked ice cream and was lazy. Orrie was a dog and he chased his tail, played fetch, or drank out of the toilet. John makes dinner, goes to get groceries, and tries to convince Field to be active. John also had a brother, Devin, who works on a farm. Both were invited to collect their cousin's fortune when he passed away. Their cousin's name was Elcom.

When John and his brother arrived at their cousin's house, it looked haunted with lightning in the background. It had big windows that really needed cleaning. "The guy who lives here probably owns a ghost," said Field with an uncaring voice. The house was a whole castle with flickering lights. They went in, and they were greeted by a butler. "Greetings, you were expected," said the butler. They went in. The butler showed them the last recording of their cousin Elcom.

The Last Recording of Elcom

He said in the recording, "Greetings cousins, I have known you for such a long time. I've set a challenge for you which is to sleep here. If you can survive the night, you get to keep my fortune," said their cousin. The night was on. I gave my brother company by giving him Orrie. The butler assigned our rooms. My brother and I couldn't sleep that night because we were thinking about who was going to win the fortune. My brother barricaded the doors; he was creeped out for some reason. Field was looking for food. When he opened the fridge, a zombie walked out and said, "No way out," looking at the barricaded doors. My brother ran straight through the wall screaming like a little child. I also ran with Orrie following my brother Devin.

"AHHHHHHHHHHHHHHHHH!" my brother screamed. Field said, "Eh, this challenge is harder than I thought," in a lazy voice. While the chase scene was going on, Field ran into a statue that followed every movement he made. He had an idea to use the statue. On the other side of the story, John and Orrie came across three doors. They picked the middle door and saw a line of Frankenstein monsters. Same with the other doors. Another chase scene was involved. Wonder how they're going to survive a whole night like this? It was 12:43 at night. Back on the other side, Field's idea was to simply scare the zombie with the knight. Field first borrowed Orrie's help. He took a white cloth and stepped on Orrie's shoulders and put the cloth on top. "Steady boy," said Field standing on his shoulders. The zombie came, and he actually was scared, backing down. As Field started to walk up, a chandelier caught the cloth and he was revealed. The zombie realized it was Field and Orrie quickly, and again another chase scene broke out. "Wow, these chase scenes are tiring me out," said Field with a tired voice.

Back to John, Devin, and the Frankenstein monsters. The Frankenstein monsters kept chasing John and Devin until they came across another door. They were both hoping this door did not have any more monsters. "Are you ready, brother?" said John with a scared voice. "I am," said Devin with a terrified voice. They opened the door and thankfully, it was just a bunch of bats. They tricked the Frankenstein monsters into going in and John trapped them inside. They were not going to be inside for a long time because many Frankenstein monsters were pounding on the door, which was weak and about to break. So John and Devin had to think of a brilliant idea. It was only 1:33 am at night.

The Mysterious Room

Meanwhile, Field and Orrie had to get rid of the zombies, so Field and Orrie opened random doors. From one of those doors were dozens of bats. Not baseball bats, but creepy furry bats. They both stepped aside and made the bats go on to the zombie. "Great," said Field relieved. Field felt accomplished, so he started to find the kitchen to find something to eat. He found a door that slid downward, and he found a stairway that led upward. He found a whole electric system with different wires and a lot of circuits and lights. He went back up to warn John and Devin.

Back to John and Devin. Both brothers barricaded the doors. Then they ran for their lives. Both ran into the zombie, or so they thought. John started screaming and hitting the mysterious thing. Then the mysterious thing was Field. John immediately felt guilty. "Really, John?" Field said with a disappointed face. Orrie smelled the path to the secret electric room. On the way there, they ran into the bats. Remember, not baseball bats, but creepy furry bats. "As a wise one once said, don't make it hard for one, but make it easy for one," said Devin with a tired attitude. "I was going for a celebration meal," said

Field. Then another chase scene. Field had a brilliant idea to dress up as a bat and trick the other bats into going into the chimney. Then Orrie was back to sniffing the way to the electric room.

When they reached the mysterious electric room, John was amazed. "What could this be for?" said Devin. "I don't know!" said John. They exited the room with curiosity and question marks on their heads. They heard a sound in the distance. They looked up and saw the zombie.

The Surprising Truth

They ran for their lives; the door was broken where they locked the Frankenstein monsters. They hid behind the door. Surprisingly, they fell for the trick again. They barricaded the doors even more so they wouldn't come out whatsoever now. Now they just had to find a way to trap the zombie for good. There weren't any bats in stock anymore. It was 3:54 at night. "I don't know if there's any pet store open at this hour at night," said Field with a disappointed face. "I don't really think this mansion is haunted. I think someone wants to scare us out so they can keep our cousin Elcom's fortune for themselves," said John with confidence. So they all sat down and brainstormed ideas of how they could stop this. Then a loud thumping sound came from down the hall. It was the Frankenstein monsters and the zombie at once. Then Field suddenly had an idea. The zombie followed Field and Orrie while the Frankenstein monsters chased the two brothers. "Nowhere to run, nowhere to hide!" said the zombie. Then the knight that followed every movement that Field did walked and punched the zombie so hard that he went flying into the Frankenstein monsters and crashed into the wall. The Frankenstein monsters broke into pieces, which were electric monsters. "So that's what that room was for!" said Devin. "And this is the guy behind all this," said Field. The zombie was actually wearing TWO MASKS. One mask was the zombie one, and the other mask was the butler. The guy was "COUSIN ELCOM!!!" everyone said, surprised. "Who won your fortune? Yeah, don't leave us hanging." "Neither of you. Huh, the cowardly faces you all had." Then Field kicked him to the ceiling angrily. They got their sleep and went home. Then they lived normally and happily ever after.

THE END

ABOUT THE AUTHOR
INAYA SALEEM

Inaya Saleem is a girl who loves arts and crafts and loves making slime. She is the middle child and has a family of five. She is 10 years old and goes to a private Muslim school, MCC Academy. She is in 5th grade and one of her most favorite things to do in her free time is make puzzles and sketch. She has two pet birds named Fall and Flora. Her favorite foods are noodles, dumplings, sushi, haleem, and seafood, and her favorite colors are purple, violet, baby blue, and light pink.

This story is dedicated to all the people who have, or had, hardships in their lives.

—I.S.

A New Life: Fatima's Story

By Inaya Saleem

"Ugh," I groan.

"What is it Fatima?" my mom says. "Why aren't you touching your food?"

"I don't want to eat rice *again,* we've been eating this for like 3 months!" I whisper quietly so that the soldiers don't hear us.

"Fatima," my Abba explains, "you should be thankful we at least have food!"

"Your Abba is right Fatima. In fact, right now many people don't even have food!" Amma tells me.

"Okay, Amma," I say and continue eating my food.

"Yuck!" I think.

"Wahhhh," Noor cries.

"Shh quiet down hold the soldiers might her you" I tell Noor as I quickly cover her mouth.

"Othay, but I jot hurt," Noor says.

"Here," I say as I put a piece of cloth and wrap it around on her scar.

"There we go,is that better now?" I ask her

"Jup" says noor with a smile

"Ok,Fatima,Noor,go to sleep"orders amma

"Yes Amma" me and noor say

We then both lay on the floor and pick up a piece of cloth

I start to put it on myself when Noor says"I'm so cold!" So I put it on noor.

The next morning I wake up to the sound of crashing and banging

"Assalamualaikum,what's that sound?" I ask my parents

"Where am I?"i think to myself

"Oh I'm in the closet." I say while getting myself out of our so called *closet* which is actually a bunch of pieces of wood stuck to each other

I then get out the closet and look around the room,but surprisingly i don't see my parents

"Mama, Baba, where are you!?" I say while looking around the room again

"Wait a second,where's Noor!?" I say frantically while looking behind myself.

I then finally see a trail of blood going all the way to the corner of the room

"OH NO" I say while following the track of blood.

Then I see my parents dead bodies and the piece of cloth I gave to noor last night covered in blood

"NO" I scream while seeing the treacherous site

I quickly cover my mouth when I hear some soldiers screaming "check to see if there any others left,remember If you hear them,spot them,and kill them"

Then from under my parents dead burned bodies I hear a little faint voice crying

"NOOR!?" I quickly whisper in surprise and shock knowing that if scream the soldiers will come and kill me

I quickly start to search under my parents bodies and then see Noors tiny bloody mushed up face

"NOOR" I say in a bit of relief.

"Come on let's get out of here"i explain to noor

I then imagine amma and Abba covering noor while the soldiers came to kill us and my parents quickly hiding me in the closet so the soldiers don't catch me and kill me

"Why didn't I wake up earlier!"

"If only I did, maybe mama and baba wouldn't be dead!"

"Why did they protect me and die themselves!"

All these thoughts jumble into my head as I crawl while carrying noor in my hand

"Wahhhh" Noor Continues to cry while I think

I then all of a sudden realize how loud noor is screeching so I quickly put my hand on her mouth to quiet her down.

Then I hear a bomb crash

"BOOMB"

"BANG

"CRASH"

I Wheeze as smoke covers my way

I start breathing heavily

My legs start to bleed,and my arms start to burn

I then collapsed to the ground...

8 years later...

8 years.

It has been eight years since that "incident" hap-pened. I still remember everything as if it were yester-day.

A lot has changed since then.

I now live in Chicago now, and got moved here for college

My sister,Noor, goes to a normal school and nothing gets bombed.

I also have a friend named Sarah,

And turns out she's also a refugee from iraq.

And...yup that's pretty much it

I've also heard about a place named Starbucks but you can't have it cause it supports Israel.

I heard that it is really good, or, it *was* really good

Oh yeah, and there's also a place named McDonald's that's good too

But, that also supports Israel, so sadly I never got to have it

How? I don't know. But it just does.

Sometimes I really wish I came to America earlier and tried all of the stuff.

In fact, now that I think of it, it would be really nice to have lived here all of my life

But I guess I should be really grateful that I even got to be here

And apartments here are so big compared to my old house, I've got my room and so does my little sister!

Believe it or not, there is so much food here! I LOVE and I mean LOVE my new house here!

Also for school you can choose what you want to do!

I chose business so that i can make money and give it to gaza and Palestine and fix the homes there

I remember that one day in 12th grade when I they called me .

I was in our small class of like, nine people and we were all studying for a scholarship at literally anywhere!

We didn't even care if it was a good quality or a bad quality college because honestly,we wouldn't care.

I remember how in the middle of our class they called my name and how confused I was and how happy my teacher was.

I remember that they then told about the news and about how I was leaving in 3 days, I was so happy

After that had a party and that was the first time I ate rice, and it was so good compared to like, the one can of some mushed up thing that 5 people shared together.

After the party I then told noor the news and she was so happy her face was beaming with light and her smile was so big.

We both then paced the few little things we had in a piece of cloth and went to sleep.

The next day,we woke up at around 3:00 am and started to walk away from Tel al-Sultan, the name of our refugee camp.

After that, we took our leave and left.

Bye by Gaza, bye bye...

About the Author
Muhammad Mateen

Muhammad Mateen wrote this story because it was a school project. His hobby is to play video games all night on weekends. He has two younger brothers and one older brother. He has an African gray parrot.

THE HEADLESS HORSEMAN

BY MUHAMMAD MATEEN

Once there was a kid named Henry. Henry was a professional horse rider who won every horse adventure. Henry's best friend Liam was also a good horse rider who did adventures with Henry.

Henry And Liam were in a corn maze when they heard a neigh from the other side. This was not a normal horses neigh because this one was louder than any horses.

Henry and Liam Thought it was just a sick horse in pain so they just ignored it. After they both left the corn maze they saw a tent with a trail of blood. Henry and Liam went to see why there was blood by the tent.

When Henry and Liam Went inside the tent they saw an animal hanging by the neck while blood was dripping down its toes.

Henry and Liam got scared so they ran away. While Henry and Liam Were walking home they were shocked and disgusted by seeing the animal hanging with blood dripping. When Henry and Liam got home they decided to tell Henry's mom. When Henry Told his mom his mom started laughing and told them it was a slaughter house.

Henry and Liam Went outside and felt bored so they went on a horse ride, Henry rode his horse Hoof Hearted. Liam rode his black spotted horse spots. When Henry and Liam were riding they heard the same neigh from the maze.

This time they got scared because they were in a dark forest. Liam told Henry we should go back but Henry insisted that they should go. Liam finally agreed on going with Henry to find where the noise came from. After 5 minutes they heard a neigh again. This time Liam didn't feel scared so they continued riding.

Henry and Liam felt tired so they decided to go back home. While they were going home they saw an all black horse with a rider under the dark tree. Henry got shocked and asked the rider who was there but the rider didn't reply. After a second the horse did the scary loud neigh.

Henry and Liam realized it was that horse that was making all those noises. After the rider started chasing Henry with his horse. Liam was scared so he was going back home as fast as he could with his horse. Henry saw him running so he followed him. The horse man followed Henry and Liam but then stopped because they were by the village. After Henry and Liam went back to the village, they went to see mom but when they were going Henry and Liam randomly fainted unexpectedly.

After They woke up they saw they were getting cured by the nurses.

Henry asked the nurse what had happened and the nurse said they both fainted.

Henry then asked Liam if he was okay but Liam didn't respond.

Henry thought he was just sleeping but Liam was just shivering and didn't talk.

After Henry and Liam recovered they tried to remember what happened but apparently The horseman was a reaper which had removed their memory of what happened.

Henry and Liam went on a horse ride again when they saw the reaper. But they didn't know that it was the reaper. Henry asked the reaper aka the horse rider who are u but he didn't respond. When the reaper came closer Henry and Liam Realized it was the horse rider that was chasing them earlier today.

Henry rode his horse as fast as he could but the horse lost balance and fell and broke his leg. Liam went back to Henry but Henry said to go on without him. Liam didn't want

To leave Henry there but he went without him. Liam went back to the village as fast as he could and went to get help. He got some people to come with him but by the time he went where he last saw Henry he was gone and his horse was dead just laying there. Liam knew it was over so he went home and told everyone in the village Henry Is dead. Everyone gathered around Liam and His mom to cheer them up but Liam would never be happy.

THE END

ABOUT THE AUTHOR
MOHAMMED YAHYA PATHAN

My inspiration was reading books. There was this one day when I was thinking how it will be if I make a story. I can make like anything. I can make my type, too.

Boxing 24/7

By Mohammed Yahya Pathan

Mike was 17 years old and he was a senior in high school. He had this bully, Jake, a very mean kid who would throw lunch at people, steal money, and do that. So that night Mike was eating dinner he wondered, what to do, he told his dad what to do. The next day, his dad puts him in a boxing club so he can fight and get revenge. It was the first day of boxing, and he did not know what to do but day by day he got better and better one day he went to school to fight, but eventually, he lost and got beaten up badly he got sad, but that did not stop he kept on going to the class and after 6 months of training he was officially ready. So he comes to the school and tells everyone how he is about to get revenge on him. Everyone thought he was joking because the last time he got beaten up his nose was bleeding, his lips were cracked, and his shirt was full of scratches and mud but this time it was revenge time, said Mike. Jake just laughed at him, well see about that buddy, said Jake. Fight fight fight screamed the crowd, Mike punched him like crazy, and he almost won when suddenly Jake punched him and knocked him out. The crowd went crazy when they saw Mike lose. Mike got up, and the thing he told Jake was crazy he said that one day I would become the world's best boxer and I would come back that day and beat you up, so badly everyone would see how bad you would lose. That day will come very soon, ok, we will see about that, said Jake. So Mike went to the boxing gym like always. At this point, Mike was about to give up when suddenly Mike changed his mind and said that he would keep on training and would never give up until he knocked out Jake so he kept on working and working. One day when it was graduation day he thought they would become friends but no Jake was the person he wanted to get punched in the face and he did. But then as Mike was about to win he knocked him out again he got so mad that after all that training he just beat him like he was easy, but Jake knew for a fact that he could become stronger if he just practiced a little, but Jake did not want that to happen so he was a lot of negative comments so he gives up. So as Mike was walking he was in deep thought of giving up, but he thought that he was getting better so he went ahead and gave up.

Everyone said don't give up, you almost won, then he went back to the gym and practiced 6 more months. Then after that he asked his friends that did you see him anywhere he then found out that he went in boxing so he decided to join and signed the contract, and then he started to practice and went he was practicing he kept on practicing and motivating himself that now is the day when everyone will see who loses and wins there were 5 days left for the day when people were about to see who will win he was practicing day and night getting ready for the day of revenge of all those days that he got beat he could not forget those days he stills remembers those days, and now he is going to show the world how dangerous he can become, now there was one day left he was prepared to fight when in the other hand Jake was chilling and practicing thinking this will be easy and the win go to him even though he skipped days made excuses he was posting videos about how he is always going to be stronger than mike, but this time everyone knew that Mike can win and that was true he looked more prepared than Jake. Now it was the day of revenge, the day of blood.

Jake was walking to the stage he was so confident he looked ready but in reality, he was not ready, but he did not want Mike to know because he would take advantage of that. Then the referee told the audience, so the fight was about to start the referee Jake was afraid that he might lose because he had not practiced that. So then the fight started and Mike punched him and knocked him out badly everyone was shocked that Mike just beat him like that they did not expect that though they expected a fun fight to watch but this was like one punch and done. The referee jumps and announces the winner who practiced years just to make this happen. That day Mike became so proud of himself that he went home and went back to put himself on the newsletter so he could be proud of himself. though all the kids thought it was funny. Ok, guys we got to talk about the theme now so basically the theme is never to give up when it feels like you can't do it. It's fine keep trying and you will get there. So yeah, that's it.

THE END

About the Author
Ayesha Rana

Ayesha Rana is a fourth grader who goes to MCC Academy . She has two brothers. Ayesha is a 10-year-old girl who loves to play basketball, paint, build legos, and spend time with her family and friends. Ayesha is the youngest girl of her family and she knows how to crochet. She recently made a small business called Delightful Decor. She is an amazing cook who also loves helping her mom make tasty food. Her favorite games are Skip Bo, UNO, Go Fish, Headbenz, Guess Who, and The Old Maid.

For my mom, who takes care of me every single day.
—A.R.

The Underwater Kindom of Gold

By Ayesha Rana

O nce upon a time, in the land of the Underwater Kingdom, lived a poor man named Adam and his wife named Afifa. They lived in a very old house where the bricks were broken and the garden was in a very bad condition. On the other side of town, lived Prince Yousuf and his wife Princess Zainab. Prince's family were the rulers of the Underwater Kingdom. They had a beautiful floating castle, which was surrounded by water. Their garden and the view was breathtaking and was very calm.

"Don't you feel very relaxed here?" said Princess Zainab.

"This is God's creation Zainab; indeed it's so beautiful." said Prince Yousuf.

Adam and Afifa were thieves of the town. They wanted to steal Princess Zainab's gold jewelry and Prince Yousuf's rings and money. The reason they want to steal it is because Adam and Afifa saw how expensive the gold jewelry was when they saw the prince and the princess wearing it at a party. The rings and jewelry are worth millions of dollars. They know that because the tag was still on when princess Zainab wore it. They are aware that the Prince and Princess only wear expensive jewelry, which is very rare and unique to purchase.

"Afifa, what do you think about stealing that necklace and the ring?" said Adam.

"We can, but it's nearly impossible to steal because of the guards," said Afifa.

Adam and Afifa were thinking about how to steal their gold jewelry so they could be rich. Afifa had an idea of going into their floating castle at night when no one was awake. They got the layout of the castle and made a plan. They knew they had to be very careful so that the guards wouldn't be able to see them sneaking in. Then, Adam got inside quietly and was able to enter the Prince's bedroom and found the key which was under his pillow. Afifa on the other hand, was waiting for Adam outside and kept checking that no guard was going inside. Adam opened their safe and stole all their jewelry and money.

"Adam, are you out? Someone is coming inside!" said Afifa.

"Oh no! I'm almost done packing the gold." said Adam.

"Hurry! Hurry!" said Afifa.

He was able to leave the castle secretly without the guards noticing. Afifa was relieved that her husband was out and they had a very successful steal. When Adam and Afifa came home, they were so happy to steal millions of dollars of jewelry and rings. Afifa had a thought and she shared it with her husband. Afifa told him that they should change their looks. They both worked on their looks and started sketching. Finally, they decided and went on to getting pink creepy eyes from an Evil Eye Doctor, pointy red hair by the Wicked Hair Salon, and sharp teeth by Vile Dentist. They made up a very evil and scary look to make themselves not noticeable. Nobody was able to identify who they were because of their changed looks.

On the other hand, the prince and princess made some changes to their floating castle to make it that emits a smell like the fragrance of flowers. The light looked like it was from the golden chandeliers, the artifacts were very expensive, the furniture was also very beautiful. The princess looked inside her closet and to her surprise, she found a special and dazzling treasure! In the castle, they were very happy to see the treasure that can make them more rich. The princess wanted to put the special and dazzling treasure in a safe but noticed that the key was missing. They looked for it everywhere but couldn't find it. At last, they found the key inside the safe, which they noticed was open and their jewelry and money were stolen.

Later, Prince Yousuf and Princess Zainab remembered Adam and Afifa who they met at a party. They were talking to the town couple Adam and Afifa about the robbery of their jewelry and money. Princess Zainab told them about the amazing treasure that had popped out of nowhere. The Prince and Princess did not know that Adam and Afifa were the thieves that stole their belongings. They unknowingly asked them to help find the thieves in town. Adam and Afifa were trying to be friends and acted like they were helping them but in reality, they were not. Therefore, the Prince started trusting them more. However, on the other side, the princess was suspicious that there's something fishy about this couple and did not want to blindly trust Adam and Afifa.

"Prince Yousuf, I hope you're not doing wrong by trusting Adam and Afifa," said Princess Zainab.

The prince later involved police and filed a police report. In the investigation, they searched all neighbors' houses and also searched Adam and Afifa's house too. The Prince and Princess found the jewelry at Adam's house. The robbers were headed to jail for stealing castle rulers' belongings. On the other hand, the Princess learned a hard lesson about not sharing personal information to strangers.

"Next time we should keep things to ourselves," said Prince Yousuf

"Yes, you're right! We should," said Princess Zainab.

With all their experiences, The prince and princess set traps around the treasure to make it nearly impossible to steal. They put pointy metal gates, they had special weapons, and they had so many security guards. They also had a red laser beam that no one can see but if they go by the treasure it will beep and everything will be locked. Not only that, they also had security cameras and alarm systems too. The prince and princess ruled over the floating castle with fairness. They were also thankful that they had friends who helped them make the floating castle. They serve the people of their country by being compassionate, caring and kind. The people also love to be there for the leaders of the country and their family. The Underwater Kingdom of Gold got saved!

About the Author
Mohammed Abdulbaseer

Abdulbaseer is a 10-year-old boy whose favorite color is red and blue. He has one sibling so total has a family of four.His hobbies are sports and playing video games. When he is around his family he gets happy. Abdulbaseer likes to make new friends. His friends are Saad, Anas , Zaid whom he loves playing basketball with . During his free time he helps his mother clean and organize the room. He is a super energetic and positive person.

For the only sister Allah has sent in our house! my best friend and my best sister Anum Fatima who has brought joy in our family. The reason I want to dedicate this story is that she is a good listener and always appreciates the things I do to her. She is an important person in my life and I would like to share my happiness with her.

—A.B.

THE POWER OF UNITY
BY MOHAMMED ABDULBASEER

Once upon a time, there was a small village in Russia. It had small houses with big farms next to one. The villagers lived there with love and care towards each other. The families were friendly, and it was a peaceful and fun village until a terrible incident happened.

That morning the cops came to the village. Everyone was so confused why the cops came to their village. Then one person got caught by the cops. Then they realized. Everyone kept from side to side while shouting, "Help! Help!" in a fearful way. But...it was too late, and the cops captured them all. This kept all the villagers in a thought of why the cops had captured them.

One old man saw a note on the floor which said which said, "We are going to put a dinosaur in the village and there is going to be a force field around the village so no one can escape". Reading the note left the old man in shock.

A few days later, the cops send the captured villagers back to the village and right when they stepped in the old man warned them about the dinosaurs and force field. Listening to the old man's words, all the villagers laughed and thought he was joking. He tried to make everyone believe him by showing the note, but no one did. Later at night, a man went outside for a walk with his kids. The man hears a loud ROOOAAARRR!

''Papa, what's that noise?" said the small boy being scared.

The man got furious but to keep the boy calm he said to his son.

"Nothing, it's just a wind blowing very fast, or it's some friend trying to scare us ".

But again they both heard the noise getting louder and got them more furious. When he looked behind, he saw a big mouth with big teeth, and big arms, and a big body with big legs. It had big eyes, and big sharp claws on its arms and legs, it also had a big tail. They were thinking if this is any kind of monster but coming closer they saw it to be a dinosaur. Seeing the big dinosaur, the father and the kid got very scared and tried to run away, but their luck was not with them. When the sun rose, all the villagers come out and see them dead. Everyone was in shock and all the family was crying. One man found a tooth the size of our hand.

"This looks like the teeth of the Dinosaurs ". Said the other man

They said to one another this might be the tooth of the dinosaurs which the old man was talking about the other day, which no one believed him. Everyone had their jaws dropped and was in fear if the dinosaur could come again in the village at night. The old man told everyone not to go out in the dark and be very careful. But some people didn't listen to him and went out at night and were killed by the dinosaurs.

So now all the villagers came for the meeting and decided to make a weapon which can fight and scare the dinosaur to leave the village. All the villagers got busy making the weapons and have made a lot of them. Everyone in the village was carrying one weapon with them whenever they went out for a walk. Again one night the dinosaurs followed up the other man, the man took his weapon out to kill him, but the dinosaurs killed him instead. The villagers started looking for him in the morning, but they couldn't find him. After a few hours, they looked around the bushes and saw him there. All the villagers seeing this got scared and more fearful. The villagers had tearful eyes and started crying. Not for long the dinosaurs came and killed the families slowly and almost destroyed their homes, the lands and the families. They were bursting into tears.

Now the villagers have decided to make sure the villagers are all safe and can create a big army to fight the dinosaurs and make more and more weapons. Villagers had decided to train more people and be strong and safe everyone. They started praying for them to be strong and live the lives before how they used to.

One fine day three new babies were born, they knew how to talk in less time, they knew how to walk, and also they knew how to fight and do things in no less time. So the triplets said," we all have to train ourselves so well that we will beat the dinosaurs and throw them away from the village and keep the village safe every one again "

Now the training for them had started for day and night. It was very tough for them, but they kept in mind to fight for it and make everyone happy. They made a gym area look so cool they can work out, they spent a lot of the time taking care and made their body super strong. The gym was full of new things and got better and better, and the triplets kept growing faster and faster. The people kept getting stronger and stronger, and at this point they were happy that they had someone who could fight and keep thcm safe. Now the army has gotten larger, and they started training more and more people from the village. As the days passed, they were confident to fight the dinosaurs. So all the villagers were ready and waiting for the dinosaurs to come and attack them at nighttime. The soldiers started fighting the dinosaurs. One by one they started hitting them with their sharp weapons which left them injured and couldn't move. During the fight, the soldiers gave them incredible punches and fought until they were killed completely. But sadly, some of the soldiers died and a lot of them got hurt. The triplets punched 20 times with weapons. When they got hurt, they still never gave up. And the triplets saw he was unharmed?

So the triplets punched so hard the dinosaur lost all of his teeth. And the triplets punched one more time, the dinosaur died.

My story was to inform people about the unity we have to keep with people and never give up to fight back. We all have to do team work.

THE END

About the Author
Zara Fatima

Zara Fatima is a young fourth grader who is a creative person. She loves to write stories. She spends hours putting her thoughts into words and creating new worlds with her imagination. Zara is always curious and eager to learn about new things, whether it's science, history, or anything else that catches her interest. When she's not writing or learning, Zara enjoys spending time outdoors, exploring nature and going for walks. She also values her relationships with friends and family, often organizing get-togethers or just enjoying each other's company. Despite life's challenges, Zara approaches each day with optimism and a determination to make the most of every opportunity.

For my mom and dad, who always believe in me and inspire me to follow my dreams.

—Z.F.

THE SECRET TUNNEL: KATRINA'S TALE OF BRAVERY

BY ZARA FATIMA

It was springtime. The weather was gradually warming up following the chilly winter. Everything around was covered with colorful flowers. Leaves were growing on the trees again. The air was filled with the fragrance of the blossoms. Birds were singing sweet songs and returning to their nests. Life was returning to the world after the winter.

The time had come for Katrina to emerge from her home and embrace the delights of spring. Katrina was a sweet little girl who lived in a town near a big forest. She was a fair girl with blonde hair and blue eyes. She was very smart and brave. Everyone in her neighborhood liked her. She had a lot of friends in school. She not only enjoyed reading books a lot,but also had a mini library in her house.

One day, as Katrina was wandering through the forest, she stumbled upon a hidden path she had never seen before. She was very curious to know where the secret hidden path actually went. She followed it.

The passage was very dark. As she walked, a thick fog rolled in, making it hard for her to see anything around her. Even though she was terrified, she still walked further. And suddenly, she fell into a big, dark tunnel. She screamed super loud, but there is no one who can hear her or help her. She thought she made a mistake going there alone. But then something strange happened.

As she was falling through the tunnel all at once, she started feeling lighter than a feather. She felt like she was flying instead of falling. The tunnel was so long that she thought there was no end to it. From far away, she could see a glimpse of light. As she got closer, the light got brighter. And then, with a sudden rush of air, she came out of the tunnel and saw a beautiful place with lots of pretty colors and a magical feeling. Katrina couldn't believe her eyes. Even though she was alone, she was ready to explore this amazing place and find out what secrets it had.

Katrina felt excited. She never thought such a magical place existed, and she wanted to look at every part. The air was filled with the sweet scent of flowers. She saw tiny animals moving around here and there. They had colorful feathers and fur, which made the place even more magical. Birds sang songs from the trees, and butterflies flew around, making the place look beautiful.

She then saw a sparkling stream. The water was very clear and had gems and diamond pebbles. The fish that were swimming in it were made of gold and silver. She picked a few gems for her treasure. Suddenly, she saw something moving in the water. She thought it could be another gemstone. As she reached for it, a pair of glowing eyes appeared on the top of the water. Katrina got scared and backed away.

A huge dragon emerged from the water, its shiny scales catching the sunlight. It roared loudly and spread its big wings, making a shadow on the ground. The dragon had fiery eyes and sharp claws. Katrina felt scared as she watched from behind some bushes. She saw its sharp teeth and felt the ground shake with each step the dragon took. She stayed silent, not wanting to be noticed. The dragon sniffed the air, searching for any signs of intruders. Sometimes the dragon turned away and went back into the water.

Katrina took a deep breath and came out of the bushes. She had a feeling that she was being watched. She looked behind her, but there was no one. Suddenly, the dragon jumped out of the water with a loud roar. Katrina got terrified and looked around, trying to run.

But before Katrina could move, the dragon blocked her way.

"Who is this intruder into my territory?" the Dragon demanded.

Please don't harm me; I wasn't meant to disturb you. I'll leave right away, said Katrina, fear clear in her voice.

But the dragon just laughed.

"Too late. You've trespassed in my place. Now, you shall face the consequences," the Dragon declared ominously.

The dragon roared and opened its huge claws to grab her.

"Please, just let me go," Katrina pleaded.

Katrina ran with all her strength. The dragon was getting closer and closer. She panicked, trying hard to find a way out. She then found a small space between two big rocks. Katrina dashed towards it and went inside the gap just in time. The dragon's big claws couldn't pass through the gap.

She was tired of running, so she stopped for a while. While resting, she looked around for help and discovered a gap between some rocks leading into a dark cave. She heard whispers coming from inside.

Katrina went into the cave slowly. She was shocked to see children who looked pale and weak.

Katrina inquired, "Who are you all?"

One child exclaimed, "the dragon has captured us."

Another child explained,"We were exploring this secret path when the dragon caught all of us."

Katrina stated, "I'm here to free all of you."

The child hesitated, "But... but the dragon is too powerful."

Katrina reassured, "Together, we can defeat him."

Katrina was thinking about how to free the children and defeat the dragon. She then thought about a story that she read in a book where a king saves his kingdom by defeating an evil dragon. She read in the books that a dragon's weakness is its wings. So if you hurt their wings, they will have no power left. She was aware of a special fruit that had the power to stop the dragon from breathing fire. While gathering gems from the stream, she stumbled upon the special fruit and tucked it safely into her pocket.

With the help of the other children, Katrina made a huge, big rope with the twigs and branches of the trees. She then tied two big rocks at the ends of the ropes. Slowly, she came out of the rocks to attract the dragon's attention. As soon as the dragon saw Katrina, it jumped over her. The children from behind aimed at the Dragon's wings and tied the surrounding rope. Katrina then threw the majestic fruit into the dragon's throat.

The dragon roared in pain. It felt useless and had no power. It fell to the ground with its wings tied. Not only that, but it could not breathe and was helpless. Seeing this opportunity, all the children with Katrina escaped the cave. They all ran towards the path from which they had entered. And soon they were out of the dark tunnel. After coming out, they all together closed the doors of the tunnel with rocks and stones so that no other children could go back again.

Katrina felt a rush of happiness swelling inside her. She understood that she had shown true bravery. Even when she felt scared, she didn't give in. Working together with the other children, they defeated the dragon and rescued their friends. All the people in the town were bursting with pride for Katrina, and the other kids admired her greatly. They all looked at her with respect and awe.

The End

ABOUT THE AUTHOR
ABDUL HAMEED SYED

Abdul Hameed Syed is a fourth grader at MCC Academy who likes basketball and likes reading. His favorite subject is math, and one day he dreams to be a hafiz.

My dedication is to my elder brother, because throughout the whole story he has helped me do lots of stuff in the story.
    —A.H.S.

THE DISAPPEARING KING
BY ABDUL HAMEED SYED

Long before time had a name, there were two kings. One of the kings was rich with massive armies, while the other king was poor with barely any soldiers. Before I tell you about the story, let me tell you a little about them. The rich king's name is King William, and he is a middle aged man with a lot of arrogance and a tiny mustache and long hair. The other King's name is King Charles, he is an old wise man, with a big gray beard and long hair. Since you now know a little about the Kings,I will tell you about the disappearing King.

It was a early morning, and King Charles woke up to the birds chirping, while he started freshening up he saw an army but he knew the banners were different than any banners he had seen, the army was King Williams so he ran outside and started yelling, "Evacuate the castle!!!"

But he already knew nobody would survive so he grabbed three soldiers and yelled, "Let's go quickly!"And as he stared down at the ground 15 feet below he closed his eyes and jumped. The second he started falling, he started screaming,"AAAAHHHHH!!!"

After King Charles fell down, there was a loud thum p.The soldiers looked at King Charles scanning him for any injuries they saw none except a few major bruis-es,then they asked if he was fine, King Charles respond-ed with, "I am okay but we cannot stop running we need to find somewhere to hide."

They replied with, "yes sir".

And so, they stared at a mountain range a few miles away and saw a little cave in the mountain. So they started making their way to the mountain halfway to the mountain range. King Charles says "stop right here"the soldiers all at once asked "why?" King Charles says "because there is a nest of tiger flies which could kill us right now we can't make a noise because they are attracted by noise"they all say "yes sir"all of them start walking around the nest and made it to the cave but a shiver went up all of their spines because there were skulls everywhere. But they kept walking,when they reached the end.

They saw somebody, then king Charles asked: "who are you!" but no answer again he asked but this time he yelled "WHO ARE YOU TELL ME!!!" in a slow voice he said "I am sir John milton the third" the king yelled in joy "ARE YOU ACTUALLY JOHN MAN I MISSED YOU!!!"John yelled right back at him "IS THAT YOU CHARLES"King Charles said " yup that sure is me"John said to King Charles " we need to talk about something" King Charles askes what? John says "about the ring we use to think the ring was a myth right but now I have found the location of the ring."

King Charles said "what myth and what ring? " John said "do I really have to explain it all over again?". King Charles said "yes, explain it again I forgot". John said, " now let me start, once upon a time there was a king named Finn he and was the richest man in the world. One day the workers in a mine found a very shiny piece of crystal. Finn called it crystaniam and he made a ring out of it. One day he said to his most loyal guard to bring a little bit of invisibility stone and then king Finn went to sir Danny in his blacksmith shop and after three grueling nights of combining the two ores, sir danny created the ring of invisibility. King Finn took the ring and kept it till he died. He hid the ring in the pyramids of Finn and inside of the pyramids there would be three deadly traps. Only people who were worthy would get the ring or else would die. "King Charles said "oh yes", where are the pyramids. John said, "it is located in the desert of Doom. This is the only desert where people went missing but we will get the ring and defeat King William's army and bring him to justice". King Charles said " that is a very good plan, let's start packing up and then we will start the journey". John said "okay then start preparing for the pyramids and get ready for the worst in the pyramids". King charles replied "okay I understood you do not have to remind me five times"

Seven days later...

King Charles said "are you ready". John said "yes, of course we literally had seven days to prepare. How would I not be ready when the ship is ready to go?" King Charles said "yeah we just need to get it into the water". King Charles said "start pushing harder, HARDER A LITTLE HARDER JUST A LITTLE MORE UGH FINALLY!!!get your stuff inside and let's start the journey."

John yelled, "DO WE NEED ANYTHING ELSE. LAST CALL OKAY OR WE START THE JOURNEY!!!"

Three hours later, King Charles said "hey John". John said "yes, what do you want and why are you holding my book? fine it does not matter". King Charles said "Look here John, in your book it says that the first test to see if you're worthy is being able to find the pyramid and make it to the door and then the book ends, so if we make it to the door, then we are worthy of having the ring?" John said "be quiet for a second do you hear that? That sounds like a killer whale, it could eat us all in one bite"

One of the soldiers yelled "LOOK BEHIND, JOHN PUT THE SAILS UP KING CHARLES STEER THE SHIP AND I WILL TRY AND DISTRACT IT GIVE ME A BIG PIECE OF MEAT THEN I CAN DISTRACT IT!" John threw the piece of meat as far as he could throw it then King Charles said" we have reached our destination, the pyramids of Finn. Bring some water and nothing else. Look there, I see the pyramids there. Only 100 meters away. Everybody walk carefully there might be traps". Slowly but surely they made it to the pyramids and they all yelled, "finally we have made it!". Everybody insisted that King Charles would open the door and King Charles said "let's go". As he started opening the door, he saw nobody had touched the place in hundreds of years. As they started walking they saw statues of Finn and his army. Finally they saw the second test. It was a maze filled with tiger flies. Then, King Charles started running through the whole maze and made it to the end of the maze without making a noise.

Two hours later they all made it to the end of test two they saw a pool filled with hundreds of killer whales and somehow they had to make it to the other side.

Then King Charles saw an opportunity to jump on a whale so he jumped on the whale. Then the other whales tried to bite King Charles but they bit the whale and that created the perfect distraction for them to swim to the other side. They all got to the other side and King Charles grabbed the ring and they were about to leave but King William's army appeared and King Charles said, "let me deal with him". King Charles swam all the way to King Williams and King Charles grabbed his sword and stabbed him in the neck there was blood everywhere. King Charles had blood all over and after King Williams died peace was restored and everybody lived happily ever after.

About the Author
Zakariya Khan

Zakariyya khan is a 10-year-old boy in fourth grade at MCC Academy. He has two sisters, and he loves the colors blue and green. He likes writing, reading, playing sports, games and making things. He recently thought of a business called Cube. Zakariyya wishes everyone will love his story.

For my parents, who introduced me and brought me to this world.

—Z.K.

A New World

By Zakariya Khan

New Beginnings

"Zaid" Zaid!" Zaid's mom called out as he woke up slowly.

"What happened?" Zaid asked, but there was no response. Zaid was puzzled for a second but then he remembered, he was moving to a new city today.

"Zaid!" Zaid's mom called out one more time. So he finally got up and walked slowly out of his room and into the bathroom. Zaid was a 10-year-old boy who lived in Houston, Texas. He loved new adventures and was so excited to start a new chapter in his life.

Zaid brushed his teeth, used the bathroom and took a shower, all within 5 minutes. "Wow, that was fast." He thought to himself. He had packed half of his stuff the day before, but the other half was still in the closet. Zaid remembered his soccer ball was in the closet and when he opened the door all of his stuff fell out.

"UH-OH'." Zaid said as his soccer ball hit him in the head.

He took one of the storage boxes that was under his bed and put his clothes inside. Then he ran downstairs as fast as he could and threw his stuff in the trunk of the car. His family was waiting for him and as soon as he sat in the car, they were off.

Zaid's family was moving from Houston to Chicago because his dad got a new job, and they were headed to George Bush International Airport. The flight from Houston to Chicago was a four-hour flight. He loved airplanes and flying so he looked up all the information about his flight online.

They arrived at the airport with extra time so they didn't have to rush. Security and check-in went by quickly, so they reached the gate with plenty of time to spare. Zaid was so excited, he couldn't wait to finally board and be in the air.

Zaid slept most of the flight because he had woken up very early that morning. When they reached O'hare International Airport he felt the wind and thought

"No wonder it's called the Windy City." They went in a shuttle to the rental car station and then headed to their new home. When they reached their new house, it looked different than it looked in the pictures he had seen on his parents' phone.

Zaid entered his bedroom and started imagining where all of his belongings would go. He looked out the window and then opened the closet door. After he took one step inside, the ground started creaking and in an instant the floor fell under him and everything was spinning around him. He closed his eyes to prevent him from getting dizzy.

When his feet reached solid ground he opened his eyes.

"Where am I?" Zaid thought. He was the most confused he had ever been in his life.The walls around him were old bricks that looked like they had been sitting there for thousands of years and scary torches lit up the dark and creepy hallway.

As soon as he turned around the corner he screamed, ''AAAAAHHHHH!''

"Is that a crocodile headed hamster? I didn't even know those were real creatures." Zaid mumbled to himself.

"Who are you? Or actually, what are you?" Zaid asks.

"I'm a furry crocodile." The creature says.

''Makes sense. Can I ask you a question?'' Zaid asks.

"Yes, sure."

"Where am I?"

"You're in Meyaan, a magical world with kingdoms. It's in the galaxy called Megaverse."

"So youre saying I ended up from Chicago to a whole other world?" Zaid asked.

"Yes, what's your name?" Asks the creature.

"Zaid, and what's yours?" Zaid asks.

"Yusuf."

"'Okay, good to know.'" Zaid said.

A minute later, "Uhh what's Chicago?" Yusuf asked.

Zaid didn't reply because he was still in shock. They started walking together through the hallway of dark bricks and torches. After a long walk, the new world finally appeared. Zaid was astonished.

"This is Meyaan." Yusuf said. "Come on, I'll show you my house."

On the way to Yusuf's house, Zaid noticed Meyaan wasn't that different from Earth. There were supermarkets, buildings and other familiar things. The only aspect that was different was that it was magical and also more natural than Earth. When they finally reached Yusuf's house, it was just like a regular normal house on Earth. When they went inside, Zaid realized he didn't have any of his belongings so he had to borrow clothes from Yusuf. The clothes were not that different from Earth, either.

''So tell me about Meyaan.'' said Zaid.

''You might want to get comfortable before I tell you.'' Yusuf said. So then Zaid did exactly that by settling on the bed.

''Our planet, Meyaan, has a bright side which we live on and a dark side. The dark side is inhabited by evil creatures like witches and villains. I work for a thing called S.C.O.M, Secret Codes of Meyaan. It's an organization that studies the secrets of the world. At S.C.O.M. we found out that the dark side of our planet is the home of Nebula. Nebula is the king of the dark side. An evil fire super wizard that is capable of doing anything in the boundary of the dark side. Recently our spy cams have captured him saying to his people 'I, Nebula, am going to take over the entire bright side.' So now we need to stop him before he does.''

''Do you have any idea of what they could be doing?'' Zaid asked.

''Not a single trace.'' Said Yusuf.

''That's interesting, but I really want to know how I can get back home.'' Zaid said.

''Hmmm, there are two ways you could go. Either you could say a magic spell and go to a different planet, but you don't know which planet you will end up in." Says Yusuf.

"And the other?" Asks Zaid.

"You would have to get the highest amount of magic in the history of magic in Meyaan." Said Yusuf.

"Where can I start off?" Asks Zaid.

"The easiest one to get right now is probably the rarest most dangerous plant: The Blue Neptune." Says Yusuf. "To find the Blue Neptune you have to go into the secret rainforest of Zooma. But it has a gate so you need to get the Lava Cube and put it in the square shaped keyhole." Yusuf continues.

"I know I can find it." Says Zaid.

"Yes, you can." Says Yusuf. Then they started on their quest.

"First, we need to get the Lava Cube, then we can go to the gate of Zooma." Says Yusuf. "In order to find the Lava Cube we need to go to Dragon Island. It is in the middle of a lake." Said Yusuf.

As they walked closer and closer, Zaid got more and more curious. When they finally reached the lake, it looked more beautiful than he imagined.

Now that they reached the lake, they had to find a way to get to Dragon Island. There were no boats or anything that could propel you in water.

"Don't worry, I have teleporting magic." Says Yusuf.

As soon as Yusuf said "Teleportis Quinta," they were on the island in the blink of an eye but they still had to reach the top of the mountain. The rugged landscape made it hard to reach a higher altitude.

"The Lava cube should be in The Rock of Emerald City." Said Yusuf. Then they started walking more inward rather than upward. Finally, they reached The Rock of Emerald City.

Yusuf explained that in order to get magic from something you have to say "Magicus Pocis." So that is exactly what he said. Then a red flamy object came out of the rock. It was the Lava Cube.

"How do you know all these spells?" Asks Zaid. "Everyone in Meyaan knows this magic. I'm actually less than average in magic. Now let's go to the gate of Zooma." Says Yusuf. "Teleportis Quinta." Yusuf said again and in a blink of an eye they were at the gate.

Zaid puts the Lava Cube in the gate and twists it but when he opens his eyes the gate was still closed.

"I don't understand why it's not opening." Yusuf said but he had a gut feeling that the evil Kraken was behind all of this. Kraken was Nebula's evil sorcerer. Then when he turned around, sure enough Kraken was standing there with his hand out stopping the door from opening and Yusuf angrily said "Kraken!"

The Dark Side

''Call in the royal sorcerer Kraken." Nebula says.

"Yes, your majesty." I am your sorcerer, what would you like me to do, your majesty?" Says the sorcerer.

Nebula says. "I don't think you can do it."

"Yes I can, your majesty." Said the sorcerer.

''Okay then, I want you to make a super villian to destroy the bright side." Said Nebula.

"Okay your majesty." Said the sorcerer.

On his way to the laboratory, the sorcerer thought about what to make. Maybe a robot, a human, or a monster he thought. When he got to the lab, he settled on an idea: A SHARK. When he got the right spell he took his wand and said, ''Alacocis supertella." The spell was so strong it knocked him into the pot. The pot took the sorcerer's evil magic and what emerged from the pot was more dangerous than it was supposed to be. A super killer shark appeared that was two times as evil as the sorcerer and he was off to destroy the bright side.

"Destroy the bright side!" Said the monster shark. The shark had an eye patch, a hook hand, and the most menacing look .

As he walked past Nebula, Nebula said "Good work sorcerer, good work."

They were inside a castle which was right beside the ocean, so the monster shark could just swim to the bright side. He swam twice as fast as a regular shark because he had magic in his blood. Anything near him would get shocked because it was as fast as a bullet in water.

Back at the castle, the news spread to the king about the sorcerer being part of the monster shark. Nebula was starting to regret telling the sorcerer to do that because now the monster shark was terrorizing the bright side. The shark was breaking down the roads, houses and shops. Kraken has less power than before because the pot took it away and fed it to the shark.

Zaid and Yusuf heard screaming and shouting from the town people. They quickly rushed to help the people and left Kraken where he was. Zaid bought a sword and struck the monster shark. It was not easy and it was a tough battle.

When Kraken saw this happen, he had to tell Nebula. So he used teleporting magic to get back to the dark side. He told Nebula how the monster shark was gone.

After Nebula heard this news, he stopped regretting telling the sorcerer to do that.

The Blue Neptune

After Kraken left, Zaid asked "'Who was that?" to Yusuf. "That is Kraken, the royal servant of Nebula. But anyway, let's go find the Blue Neptune." Says Yusuf. Finally the gate opened and on the way Yusuf said "The Blue Neptune is dangerous because it can give you strong magic like Aliform and Letrix, so you can get hurt. Be careful if you want to find it. You have to be quiet, slow, and sort of invisible."

After some time they finally found it, they found the Blue Neptune. It looked amazing and beautiful just to look at, but touching it and using the wrong magic words could hurt you.

"I hope this works. Croaces magicus." Says Yusuf. He turns to Zaid and gives it so it goes through him.

"Alacoaces Medacosa." Zaid said the teleportation spell and thinks of Chicago."

"Assalamualaikum." Says Yusuf.

"Assalamualaikum." Says Zaid.

As he floats slowly and disappears, he closes his eyes and then starts to spin again. When he opens his eyes he sees his bedroom and hears his mom calling him from the bottom of the stairs.

"Zaid! Zaid!" Says his mom. "Take one of the boxes that is yours."

"Okay." Says Zaid while thinking of the adventure he had just had.

"I wonder if I will ever go on an adventure as crazy as this one again. Or even more crazy than that." Zaid says out loud."Maybe." He says. "Just, maybe."

ABOUT THE AUTHOR

UMAIMAH KHORAJIYA

Umaimah is a reader and she likes soccer. She is in 4th grade. She's 9 years old. Umaimah's school is MCC Academy. Umaimah's favorite colors are pink, blue and white, and her favorite cars are Honda and Tesla.

At the Beach

By Umaimah Khorajiya

This is the best thing I like to do in summer time at the beach with my best friend, Fadilah. The sun cast its golden rays across the sandy shores as Fadilah and I stepped onto the beach, our toes sinking into the warm grains. The sound of crashing waves greeted us. We loved the beach because it made us feel happy and calm.

As we walked we saw an old man sitting on the beach. He looked friendly.

I like to get snow cones.

I like to swim at the beach in summer with my family because I like them and they also like to swim at the beach. I also like to play with sand at the beach.

My family likes to grill the bbq at the beach. We do a lot of fun activities and have fun. But my dad always worries that I might get sick. I wish they had jumping activities at the beach. I don't like the Chicago beach because they are too dirty. That's why I go to Indiana dunes beach. I like to relax on the sand with the sun's rays pouring on me. I wish I could go a lot in summer but I know I have to do my Hifz homework and other homework. This is my story. When I go to the beach I put on sunscreen and I also play in the sand with my family. I love to play ball at the beach. And I also like to make sandcastles at the beach. I love eating barbecue on the beach. I also eat ice cream, but they usually melt. And I also eat popsicles at the beach.

One day, I went to the beach and I had a lot of fun. The day when I went to the beach It was sunny and beautiful. When I went to the beach, I watched some tv. And I relaxed at the beach. And I like to play hot potato and catch as well. I play freeze tag with my friends too. I like to splash water with my family. My family and I play in the waves at the beach. The beach is usually crowded with happy people, some of them lying under brigtly colored umbrellas. I can see the blue sea filled with people splashing with glee. As soon as we stop, I hop right off. and sprint with my dad towards the sun kissed sand. Sticking and umbrella tall. I get out my beach ball. Throw and catch and run fast and have a great blast. and I also try to catch myself. And I also play tag. And I also love the feeling of putting my feet in the sand and covering them. And I also play the game

Red Light Green Light at the beach. I also play Ludo at the beach. I also play Zombies at the beach. I like to watch the crabs crawl and run. starfish bathing in the sun. Snails gliding on rocks. Tens of seagulls squawking in flocks. I get into the sea and puddle about the water feel's lovely without a doubt. As the sand beneath me twists and swirls I wonder if I could find some pearls the fast and frisky fishes swim some are as big as my shin. I hope you like my story and I hope everyone who goes to the beach will enjoy themself and their family and everyone will be safe. I can write my name in the sand at the beach. And I also draw in the sand at the beach. And I also play mafia at the beach. The blue sea was crowded at the beach. If you go to the beach you can see the gold sand. On a hot summer day when I went to the beach it was sunny.

When they arrived at the beach they kicked off their shoes and ran toward the water. The sand felt warm between their toes and the salty breeze made them giggle with delight.

"Let's build a sandcastle," exclaimed Fadilah, grabbing a bucket and shovel.

The three friends worked together piling up sand and shaping it into turrets and towers. They added seashells for decoration and dug a moat around their masterpiece. as they worked they heard a loud rumbling noise. Look out, shouted Fadila as a big wave came crashing toward them washing away their castle. But instead of feeling sad they laughed and started again, this time building an even building and bigger and better casle. After playing in the sand for a while they decided to explore the beach .They searched for seashells, chased seagulls and splashed in the shallow waves.

Suddenly Fadila spotted something shiny sticking out of the sand .It was a treasure chest. They dug it up and opened it to find it filled with colorful seashells, sparkling stones and even a shiny silver coin.

Were rich exclaimed Fadila his eyes wide with excite-ment . But Fadila had an idea: "Instead of keeping it all for ourselves, let's share it with everyone on the beach," she said. So they spent the rest of the day handing out seashells and stones to anyone who walked by. The smiles on peoples faces made them happier than any treasure could. As the sun began to set painting the sky in shades of pink and orange the friends sat together on the sand watching the waves roll in and as they walked home hand in hand they knew that he would always treasure the memories they had made together at the beach.

About the Author
Ibrahim Kothaala

Ibrahim Kothawala is a 4th grader attending the MCC Academy Hifdh program. He has an elder brother and a younger sister both attending the same school. He loves playing basketball and video games with his friends. He also likes playing Brawl Stars on his iPad with his brother and cousins. He does taekwondo and is 9 months away from getting his black belt. He enjoys teasing his little sister but also takes very good care of her. He likes being outdoors in summer and enjoys riding his bike and scooter. Ibrahim wanted to create a story based on fantasy and magical creatures, and wanted to keep the readers intrigued.

I would like to dedicate this story to my little sister who brings joy to my life. Having a sister has taught me to be kind and caring towards others. We love spending time with each other doing pretend play and sometimes even fighting but then patching up in a few minutes.

—I.K.

Magical Mayhem in the Closet

By Ibrahim Kothawala

It was a week before Blake's 8th grade graduation at Mccormick Middle School. Blake was sleeping soundly on a Saturday afternoon at his home. It was around 12 pm when he woke up. He was very tired from field day shenanigans. He was super hungry and went downstairs to grab some food from the kitchen. Right when he was done, he heard a knock on the main door.

His friend Louie, was outside with his bike.

Louie asked Blake, "Do you want to come with me to ride a bike on the hill?"

Blake replied, "Yeah sure, let me change and I will be back in 5 minutes."

At that moment he heard his mom calling him. Mom said, "Blake, can you go and clean up your room first, it's such a big mess. Then only you can go biking with your friend."

Blake was disgruntled and murmured in his breath but let his friend know that he will join him after some time.

He went to his room and started cleaning piece by piece. He went to put his clothes in his closet, but while he was doing that he saw a door that he had never seen before. He was scared and didn't know if he should go in. He went in and thought he had made the right choice. He was in a location he's never seen before. He was right by a very big mansion, which was by a lake. He heard some familiar noises that sounded like ghosts he'd seen on television.

Blake was shocked,it was an elf! At first he didn't believe his eyes. He thought he was dreaming. Then he felt a deep pinch and realized that this is real!! The elf's name was Freya, and she was a construction manager. She had to give instructions to her coworkers and tell them where to put the materials and what to build. Blake thought it was a bit boring but when he entered the city, it was like a whole new world. It was a colorful and garden-themed city.

Blake was following Freya while she gave him a tour of the city. There were a bunch of shops and cafés around them. While Freya was giving Blake a tour,they walked past one of the most supreme shops ever, which was by an electricity facility. They also saw a medicine store, which for some reason also had candy. While he was walking, his legs started to hurt, and he had a headache. Freya then took Blake back to her house. While Blake was in Freya's house, his mom was at home looking for him.

She was getting worried, but she told herself she would wait a bit or else call 911. Blake then remembered he had a graduation to go to. He asked Freya "how to get back home?", and it was simpler than he realized it would be. Freya replied, "First you have to drink a gallon of teleportation juice. Then you have to make a special mushroom with 5 ingredients. Last, you have to go to a secret cave and if you finish the steps, you will be back".

Blake followed the instructions with care and before he realized he was in his home He went straight to his mom's room. She was super happy to see Blake. Her mom asked "Blake where were you, I have been looking for you for such a long time". Blake lied and said, "I went biking with my friend without telling you since I knew you would get upset". He then hugged his mom and went to his room to get sleep.

The next day, he had an entire 2-foot pancake all to himself. He made it really early to his graduation and got ready for his speech. The teachers said he had a lot of knowledge and he was a good learner. At the end of the graduation,his friend gave him an invitation to a party. He still remembered his trip to the random place he went to. He went home, got ready, and went back to the closet but the door wasn't there.He was sad that he couldn't go back to see Freya but was also a bit tired. He went back to his room and went to sleep.

Suddenly he heard his name being called and when he opened his eyes, he saw Freya standing beside him. Blake realized that when he was drinking the teleportation juice some drops fell on Freya and she came with Blake to his house. He panicked and asked her to hide under the bed, as he didn't want her to be found by his mom. Blake again tried going to sleep but was also worried about Freya. He heard her sobbing and when asked she said she was hungry and wanted some food. Blake went to the kitchen to grab some leftovers for her so that she can eat and go to sleep. He was so tired that in no time he dozed off to sleep.

When the sun rays fell bright on Blake's face, he woke up and remembered that Freya was under the bed. But when he checked she was nowhere to be found. He searched his whole room looking for Freya everywhere. He checked in the closet, behind the curtains, in the washroom but there was no sight of Freya. Then he thought maybe she got back to her land and he was relieved. He heard his mom calling him for breakfast, so he took a bath and got ready to go down to eat. As soon as he took a first bite, he felt a tug on his pants and when he looked down to see what it was, he saw Freya staring at him from under the dinner table.

She was hungry again and was asking for food. He sneakily took some food and gave it to her so that she could eat as well. He then waited for his mom to leave so he could figure out how to get Freya back to her world. After his mom left, he took her up and tried to think of ideas with her. They were thinking for twenty minutes but couldn't think of anything. They thought they were wasting time so Blake and her went to the park to get some fresh air.

While they were walking, they heard a strange noise coming from the woods and decided to check it out. They found the spot and saw something tiny. It looked like a mini version of Freya so Blake asked her if it's an elf. She said yes. He thought that was a good sign but it started to grow. It was way bigger than Freya and was super buff. It made a very scary howling noise that sounded like a wolf but louder and rougher.

They tried running, but couldn't as they were too tired. The elf was too fast for them so it was able to catch them. Blake turned to look at Freya and saw her pulling something out of her pocket. It was a sword with a very weird blade. It was curved but very long. Her eyes started glowing and so did the sword. Blake was just staring when Freya told him to move out of the way. She slashed the sword once and the elf was gone.

Blake didn't even see what happened but was glad it was over. Freya asked Blake "Are you ok?" But he didn't respond as he was too shocked about the recent events. Then after a few seconds Blake replied "Thanks Freya for saving my life. You have been a savior". While he was talking to her, he saw a red shining door appear. Blake super excitedly said "Freya, look at the door behind you!!!" Freya turned around and was equally surprised to see the door just appear right in front of them.

She started smiling but was a little sad as well. She realized that she had to say bye to her best friend and return to her world. She told him she would miss him but Blake told her that they will meet again for sure. She gave him a big hug and went in the door with a promise to be back whenever he called her.

About the Author

Umar Khan Mohammed

Umar Khan Mohammed is a 10-year-old boy in 4th grade doing full-time Hifdh at MCC Academy. He also shows creativity and imagination in their writing. He may have a unique writing that sets them apart from other writers that are the same age as him. With guidance and practice the author has the potential to become a successful writer in the future. He has three cars but the one he loves to ride the most is his Tesla Model Y. One of his favorite sports is soccer. He was on a soccer team but later he stopped and now he is enrolled in martial arts. One person he dedicates to is his cousin. He appreciates his cousin because his cousin inspires him to write a lot of books in the future. His cousin is a great writer and always helps him to find ideas for books. His cousin is a kind person and always there for Umar when he needs it. Umar is someone who can be extroverted but he is always respectful and kind to the people around him.

For my cousin Maryam, who is always kind and is always there for me when I need it.

    —U.M.

EMPEROR FERON VS. EMPEROR UMAR

BY UMAR KHAN MOHAMMED

Boom! Boom! Boom! Bombs were falling from the building. Do you know the Power Ninja team has been dredging up who is doing this?

Let's look into the book, discover who is doing this, and get more input. Do you know this is a secret expedition for the Power Ninja Team? Just imagine being on Saturn. The skies were yellow and brown with swirling clouds and fierce storms. The cities were floating high in the air, surrounded by lightning and strong winds. It was too cold, and people needed special suits to go outside. Despite the harsh weather, the people of Saturn built beautiful floating cities with green parks and sparkling buildings. Families felt safe and happy because the Power Ninja Team protects them. Emperor Umar's planet was Saturn, a place where brave people lived in amazing floating cities, enjoying their advanced world.

Meanwhile, Mars had been Emperor Feron's planet, and it had been much worse. The ground had been covered in endless red deserts and dangerous volcanoes, with skies filled with choking dust and storms that had never seemed to end. The cities had been cramped and dark, built inside big glass domes or carved into cliffs to hide from the deadly environment. Kids had rarely played outside, and families had stayed indoors most of the time, scared of the harsh weather and constant danger. Mars had been a place where people had struggled to survive always on edge, and had hoped for a better life. Umar's goal had been to fight Feron and defeat him.

Emperor Umar was a person who was kind and always wanted to help and save people. He was selfless and always put others before himself. While Emperor Feron on the other hand, he was selfish, and always wanted to destroy everything and everyone. He wanted to control everyone and wanted everything for himself.

The birds were twittering. A popular shopping cart man named "Chai Wala" was making breakfast. The sweet aroma of freshly brewed coffee filled the air, a small luxury the shopkeeper allowed himself before the day began. He hummed softly to himself as he cracked eggs into a sizzling pan, the sound of chicken frying added to the symphony of morning noises.

People gathered to buy breakfast, men were working, children were coming from school, and babies were sleeping in their cribs. It was cold that day. Suddenly, The Ninja Power Team Robot live detector started beeping and the Ninja Power Team arrived.

"I will demolish your planet," said Emperor Feron to Umar.

Umar thought to himself that Feron would never demolish his planet and instead, he was thinking about how he would demolish and destroy Feron's planet. It was already depressing, he just needed to make it gone.

Umar said, "That will never happen."

Ashton used his power by using laser beams and bombs to destroy them. There were so many bombs falling at once, so everyone panicked and started running. Babies started crying out, bus drivers panicked and stroked the school bus into trees, men injured themselves as their hands came into the machines, and lastly, moms just left cooking and came out to see what was going on. They saw Paxton was releasing the bombs.

So, Ashton and Brighten decided to attack them first, so they shot them with their laser beams to pull all their powers, but Payton flew high above the clouds, and Payton went underwater to escape from the laser beams. Still, it was too late for them to escape within the time frame because of the meteorological conditions, and they could not escape faster. Brighten sealed the water so that Payton could not escape. He kept trying to come out of the water but could not. He tried to reach his planet's Emperor and his team with his device in his hand but the signals bounced back with the seal that Brighten had created. But Payton was injured badly so he left Saturn and went back to his home planet Mars to his Emperor Feron to explain all that happened.

Emperor Feron sat on his grand throne, feeling very angry. Payton had not only failed to demolish Saturn but had also gotten hurt. Feron thought long and hard about what to do. He believed that Payton's mistake needed a big punishment so everyone would understand the importance of following orders. Even though Payton might have had his reasons, Feron decided he had to freeze him to show that failing was not acceptable.

Emperor Feron said, "Freeze them."

At this palace, the Emperor will freeze all the losers who will lose the expedition and that place is called "Losers Stay Here". On his planet Mars, there was a rule that whoever failed their missions would be turned into statues. They would be screaming for help, but no one could help them. This punishment was given to motivate others not to be losers. So they would be able to work hard for their next mission and those who win will be awarded a region where they will be Emperor of that region.

Moreover, there was also one more place where losers fell into the fire. It's called "The Fire Loser Place." It was for a small mission failure in the fire loser team; they had to be in the volcano for two years and would be dipped 100 feet inside the volcano.

On the other hand, Emperor Umar was pleased and said, "Go and announce the celebration to everyone on Saturn,"

Everyone on Saturn was so happy, while everyone on Mars frowned. Saturn people celebrated their victory very proudly. They decorated the whole planet with lights, flowers, and helium balloons. Kites were flying in the air. There were many food kiosks, and each person could have it forever. They can also fly in the air and have a great trip in the fly horse buggy. This is an automatic buggy where people can drive with the moment of a hand.

Finally, The people of Saturn felt a moderate safeguard. The Power Ninja Team has a new mission to find the invention. They will create a layer to their planet so that no one from another planet can enter Saturn anymore.

One year later, it was a typical Monday morning in the small town of Maple Wood. The sun was just beginning to peek through the mountains of Elm Street, signaling the start of a new day. The Power Ninja Team is officially working on a new mission to find the invention in Neptune. Emperor Umar came to Neptune because, since Mars lost, Emperor Umar is now the Emperor of Neptune. Unlike Mars, Neptune was cold, ice blocks were falling, freezing, and shivering. They were feeling as if they were about to give up. But they knew they couldn't, they would have to continue their mission to find the WXY model robot they were looking for.

Emperor Umar, a young ruler with a big heart, sat feeling a bit puzzled. He was on a quest to find something called the WXY model, which everyone said could make things better for everyone in his kingdom. But Umar wasn't sure where to start looking. Maybe it was hidden in the royal garden behind the tall trees, or perhaps it was tucked away in the dusty old attic of the castle. Umar decided to ask his friends, who were also very clever, to help him search. With their imaginations fired up, they set out on an adventure, ready to solve the mystery of the WXY model and make their kingdom an even happier place to live.

Emperor Umar said, "Where could it be?"

Ashton and Brighten stood among the chaos bullets flying, and explosions erupting all around. Aliens swarmed the scene, their strange forms adding to the surreal atmosphere. It was a tumultuous sight, like being caught in the middle of a storm.

"Fight them!" roared Leon, his voice cutting through the chaos like a thunderclap.

Ashton's heart raced as he exchanged a determined glance with Brighten. "We need to fight back!" he urged, his voice barely audible over the noise of the battle.

The Power Ninja team sprang into action, their laser beams slicing through the air with a brilliant flash. It was a mesmerizing sight, the beams painting streaks of light against the dark backdrop of the battlefield.

Despite the aliens' feeble weapons, the Power Ninja team pressed on, their determination unwavering. They fought with the ferocity of warriors, each movement a testament to their resolve.

But the true test came when Emperor Umar faced off against the most formidable aliens. Their weapons were powerful, their presence intimidating. Yet Umar stood his ground, a beacon of strength amidst the chaos.

Ashton and Brighten joined the fray, their laser beams adding to the spectacle of light and sound. It was a dance of energy and motion, a clash of wills in the heat of battle.

In the end, victory belonged to the Power Ninja team. Their bravery and determination prevailed, their laser beams cutting through the darkness to illuminate a path to win. And as the dust settled and the echoes of battle faded, Ashton and Brighten stood tall, their courage shined bright.

Now, there were no obstacles, all they had to gaze at was the robot. The whole team searched to find the robot. They looked for it everywhere, behind and inside the ice caves and lakes, but found nowhere. They gazed and scouted out for a long time and were about to give up. They decided to go one more time before they gave up. Ashton was the most determined person, and he found the robot WXY model. Finally, they found the robot after so many attempts of hard work. At last, they realized that with effort they could accomplish any-thing just that they needed to set their minds.

About the Author

Adeena Muzammil

Adeena Muzammil is an aspiring author in fourth grade, who dreams to be an attorney someday as well as following her passion as a writer. She lives with three sisters, her parents, and two chirpy Australian Cockatiels. A dream car would have a 90's aesthetic, while actually being a modern vehicle. Her favorite pastime is definitely reading.

For Ms. Bradley, who always said I would be a famous writer one day.

—A.M

Eid Mubarak

By Adeena Muzammil

"B*eep! Beep! Beep!"*
I hear the sound and jump up from scrolling on Instagram and admiring other teenagers' happy lives, so fast my first thought was if I actually looked like a blur. I raced down the stairs like a horse galloping at full speed, jumping through the air and landing down on the soft grass gracefully. Except nothing about *my* landing was graceful in any way.

I toppled face-first over the creaky step at the end of the stairwell, and landed on the doormat that had been carelessly flung all the way here, instead of being twenty feet across the room sitting neatly in front of the door.

My cat, Hidaya, meaning guidance in Arabic, (not that my family can speak much of it) gets up from her sleep, disturbed. Yowling and meowing, she jumps onto my body and walks up the stairs to go find another place to stretch out her body and yawn and go to sleep, just like that! Oh, how I wish my life was as simple as hers.

I get up from the floor and reach down to touch my toes, remembering too late that it was no time for solo yoga. The timer goes off again, indicating I hurry up and scoot my tush or my strawberry cheesecake would burn.

As I dash to the kitchen, I pray that it hasn't burned already. But, as I bang open the glass doors leading into the kitchen – not even caring that a small piece of glass pops out from the top pane.-I realize I'm too late. Just like I always am.

I can smell the seemingly impossible, but very real, smell of strawberries burning.

I turn off the timer before it can do its annoying beep again – and succeed in making me irritable at every-thing today – then I turn the oven off before it can burn down our house, causing even more sadness and argu-ments. But I don't let it - there's already too many.

I open the oven door and carry out the glass tray, staring at the black, charcoal-colored mess.

I carry it over to the trash can, and after dumping out the burnt cake, I carry it over to the sink and fill it with soap and water as I take the kitchen steel wool and scrub the clinging burnt bits out. I place it on the drying mat and head into the family room, where our family *used* to make happy memories, before it got split into three pieces.

I sink down onto the cushioned recliner, and remember the words my mother had said to me with so much certainty just about a month ago. It seemed as if she had been disgusted by me too.

I had walked into her bedroom to talk to her about my feelings about our family situation lately. After I was done sharing about how I wished I could fix the rift between my parents, she looked at me as if I was abnormal, and told me like she *really* meant it: "Well, you were late Humaira, just like you always are to everything. Maybe if you *had* noticed sooner, our family wouldn't have been split right now, but you didn't, so it is."

Then she turned her back to me, signaling the end of the discussion. I stared at her, unsure of what to do, then walked out of the room devastated, thinking about how horrible Eid was going to be.

And now, it's coming true. Ramadan had already been terrible with everything going on. I was determined to make Eid better, that's why I had worked so hard yesterday *while fasting* to make a strawberry cheesecake from my grandmother's scrumptious recipe, *just* to make Eid better. But today's Sunday, and tomorrow's school, and the day after is Eid, which means: school, getting ready for Eid, Eid, and... No time to make another cake.

Yup, this year's gonna be a horrible Eid.

.....

I'm back at school, and already the kids are excitedly buzzing about the Eid field trip that's two weeks from now. I'm not even going. I probably won't even enjoy it; there's too much on my mind.

A hand reaches out to touch my shoulder and I reel back, only to see my annoying, yet popular cousin, Farah.

"Learn to chill, Red," she says, addressing me by the meaning of my name, a factor that works as part of her ultra-annoyingness.

"I will, thanks," I snap back.

Her whole gang of friends gather behind her, and she turns her attention from me to them in a flash.

As they trail behind me, I can hear them talking loudly about the 'incident' at my party last summer. You hear how snobby she is? *Last* summer! She's really done it this time, but I'm not gonna make a scene about it right now. I have a math class I need to be at, in exactly – I check my wristwatch – 4 minutes.

Let me tell you the kind of snobby that girl is. She's the kind of girl who: wears her hijab lopsided (so everybody can see her hair!) and she's *always* gossiping about me, *right* where I can hear her, and then she texts me asking for test answers.

But what she did last week topped it all off. During English class, before the bell rang, she was standing around gossiping with her friends, when she notices me walk in.

And the day before I had confronted her in front of her parents about how mean she is to me, (so she had it out for me) and right then she decides it's the perfect time to tell the entire 8th grade that the reason my dad wasn't at the class Iftar party is because he's living at my grandparent's house because he and my mom are fighting.

And then everybody shoots me their stink eyes, and I'm standing there embarrassed because I lied and told everybody he's just on a business trip. I ran out of the classroom, into the bathroom, and stayed there for around 5 periods.

It was absolutely mortifying.

Then when I finally came out, she happened to be right there. And when I told her to stop acting like she was better than me, she announced loftily "Popularity *rules*." and sashayed away.

She makes me *so* angry.

.....

It's *finally* the day before Eid, and Farah and her mom are over at our house today to help us clean, like cousin tradition, but it doesn't matter, I'm giving her the cold shoulder.

Her mom insisted on coming over, even though my mom said it was fine; reasoning that Farah had to study with me in such a manner it seemed as if she was a housewife haggling with an old, stubborn fish peddler.

We're just about finishing the last room me and Farah have to do before we have permission to go upstairs and "study" in my room.

Farah wipes up the last bit of grime of the former-ly-greasy kitchen counter just as she wraps up her hour-long story of how she got the lead role in the fall play the 8th graders are doing this year.

"Well, Farah, Humaira, I think it's about time you two go study." Says Izdihar Auntie, Farah's mom

Me and Farah both let out an inward groan, knowing perfectly well that even if we did manage to cram in some studying, this meet was *not* going to end well; *and* I was still giving her the cold shoulder.

We both trek up the stairs grudgingly, as Farah whips out her phone and starts exchanging texts with a mystery friend, giggling as she goes.

We've finally reached my room, and let me tell you, my room is dripping with the color pink, it has a white cushioned bed in the center of the room, and everything else revolves around it. I have a brown mahogany desk with a white lace cover, and I have my study essentials stacked neatly on top of it. I love my room.

When I've finally closed the door gently with a satisfying click, I can't resist anymore; I pop my head over her shoulder and take a peek at her phone.

Her conversation shatters me.

Mazia: hey farah where r u

Farah: cousins house

Mazia: ew humaira? u know she failed the math test

Farah: really? how bad

Mazia: like, failed it failed it, mr. smith gave her an f

Farah: sucks 2 suck I guessbut, like u know, she's so weird

Mazia: like yeah she's so dumb, nobody likes her

Farah: yeah and her clothes r sooo weird but she thinks she's sooo popular she thinks she's better than me

Mazia: yeah, u saw the fit she wore to kinzas house right?

Farah: and how do u get a f in mr. smiths class, he's so nice

Mazia: btw, she's so ugly

Farah: and she thinks makeup will fix it too she wore 2 kinzas house

Mazia: nothing can fix her face, she's too ugly

Farah: I heard she got a facial cuz some1 told 2 her face she's ugly but it didn't work out

Mazia: no wonder, she's 2 ugly

Farah: stp txt ing s he saw my phone

Startled, Farah elbows me in my mouth HARD just as I pull my lip in. I fall back onto the ground and pull my lip out to see a bleeding little bump. I lift myself off the ground and try talking without having my tongue bump into my lip while trying to make normal speech.

"Why are you so mean to me?" I ask softly, deeply hurt that she would spread rumors about me as well.

"First of all, why were you peeking at my phone? These conversations can be private, you know!" she responds, shaking her phone vigorously in front of my face.

"Those "private" conversations aren't all good. Backbiting is not even allowed in Islam," I retort, half-fuming-half-hurt.

"Then why do *you* do it all the time with Ms. Aziza, about *me*?" she asks. She's talking about the school counselor; a kindly lady who never yells at a student, even if a student is not doing their work, she finds other ways to get them to do it; I used to suspect bribes, but it's not even that.

I started seeing her about 8 months back, to talk to her about my math teacher who used to verbally abuse students, including me and my friends. Then, one time, when Farah had hurt me particularly badly, I complained about her to Ms. Aziza, who listened and nodded, and even offered help.

But, for some reason, Farah had business with Ms. Aziza that day, to drop off books that the wondrous woman was going to donate. So then, she barges in right when I'm ranting about how she spilled puttanesca sauce all over my lovely apron when she and I were assigned partners in home ec, (and didn't even say sorry!)

So till this day, whenever I head out of Algebra to go see Ms. Aziza, Farah assumes I'm going to go gossip about her, and shoots me daggers.

"You *know* I would never do that, why do you hate me anyway?" I inquire, my voice wobbly, and my eyes filling.

"You're such a liar," she says, bending slightly away from me, and breaking eye contact.

"I'm not lying," I whisper gently. " You and I used to be *best* friends, but you hurt me, and you never said sorry, if you can fix it right now, we can be friends again."

I say it like I mean it, and I do. I know I can always accept Farah as my friend; I'm just worried she won't.

She turns to me, a look in her eyes I can't interpret, then she says, "You hurt me too."

I stumble back a little, surprised. "Well, I'm sorry."

"You're lying," She responds, and turns away from me, a wild look in her eyes. I almost don't believe her; but then I think that's probably what she thinks of every word that comes out of my mouth. I decide to change the topic.

"You still didn't answer my question, why are you always so mean to me?"

"Because I'm jealous!" She explodes, her voice rising with every word. "I'm jealous of *you*. *You* always get good grades, and *you* have a natural talent for all things literature, *you* are the only child so *you* get all the attention, *you* are memorizing the Qur'an and *you* don't have fake friends. This girl," she says, shaking her phone in front of my face, "only hangs out with me because I'm wealthy, and cause I know everyone she does, so she can gossip about them with me, do you think I *like* talking about how her autistic sister acts, she's got a neurological disorder for God's sake!" the words rush out of her mouth quickly, like she can't hold them in, and it feels so good to get them out of her mind.

"Why are *you* jealous of *me*?" I ask, I need to know this.

"I just told you," she responds, "you have the perfect life."

"Hell-o," I spit out disbelievingly, "do you even *see* what's going on in my family?"

"Yes, I do," she answers, a little calmer, "I'm a little bit jealous of that bit too, believe it or not."

"What!?" I exclaim, "Why, for what reason?"

"You know how my dad is," she responds.

Yes, I do know how her dad is; he's just like my math teacher.

"But, but, that's wrong," I stutter, "Why would you, just-" I stop short.

"I don't have the energy for you right now Farah," I say, exhausted. "Please just, leave my room." My words set her off.

She looks at me, a look of fire in her eyes, her mouth curls up in a U-shape and she clenches her fists. The skin on her forehead goes taut as she pulls the ends of her eyebrows as back as they can go, and the muscle beside her left nostril twitches. Then, she runs at me.

She runs until she knocks into me and uses her arms to push me back against the wall opposite of my bed, and my head knocks into the wall, *hard*.

Blood rushes to my head and I feel dizzy. I lean back against the wall and slowly drop down, crumpling like a paper.

I am *so* tired, or at least that's how I feel right now. I just want to put my hands down at my sides and lay still like that forever; but when Farah approaches me, I don't let that stop me; I swing my fist at her face and hit her nose; I immediately see two little dots of dark red pop up and drip slowly down her face.

She falls back and pops herself on her arms, crying softly, but I don't. My expression stays blank.

I don't know if this makes sense, but it feels like I have too many feelings to feel anything, like my two options are to feel all the anger, and confusion, and sadness, arrogance, and ignorance, and pain, or, to just not feel any of it, and of course, I choose to ignore it all.

Soon, I hear Farah get up and leave my room, running across the hall as quick as she can to get to the bathroom, but in the flash of a second when she opens the door and runs out, I hear something my mom and Izdihar Auntie are talking about. And despite where I am lying, and why I am lying here, it makes my day and brings a small smile to my face: dad's coming back.

·····

When I wake up, I have this cozy feeling all throughout my body. I smile, remembering what my mom told me this morning-and the fact that it's *finally* Eid.

When I woke up this morning to pray *fajr* prayer at around 5 o'clock, I moved myself from the ground to my bed, before I remembered it's not time to go to sleep. I got up, then dragged myself to the bathroom to perform abolition.

When I finally arrived in the praying area me and my mom styled and set two years ago, I saw mom was already up, moving swiftly up and down on *my* prayer mat. I sighed and went over to the straw basket with scarves folded and piled neatly and carefully extracted a pink scarf and wrapped it over my head, securing it with a pin. I wanted to pray on my prayer mat, so I sat down on a nearby couch, tapping my foot impatiently, waiting for my mother to finish, so *I* could pray on it.

When my mother finally finished praying, she looked at me with a wide smile and happily crinkled eyes.

"Yes mama?" I said uncertainly, she looked so joyful; I don't know how she can be this way what with everything going on.

"First pray darling, then I'll tell you," she answered in a sweet voice.

My mother instinctively moved off my prayer mat, seeing my gaze repeatedly flitting to my name embossed at the top. I prayed, going up and down in identical movements as my mother, begging to god that the news was good in both me and my mothers perspective.

When I finished, I took off the pin and pulled the scarf off my head and re-folded it into a triangle shape, then I put it away into the straw basket. I joined my mother on the long couch and looked her in the eyes, expecting her to start saying something about the country's well-being or something. But no.

"You might already know this," she began, "But when Izdihar and Farah were over yesterday, I got a call. When I looked down at my phone, a whole lot of insults were running at the top of the screen, where either the number or the name of the caller is usually supposed to be. It was your father."

I opened my mouth to say something in protest of *why* she renamed him with a bunch of insults, but she held out a hand and shushed me, continuing with her story.

"I excused myself to the other room, and picked up the call, I sat down on the sofa, and he began by saying that he was sorry. I said I was sorry, we talked for another half hour, and we both agreed that our fight was dumb and stupid, and did neither of us good, your father's coming back home. But since he's in Missouri with his parents, and were all the way here in Miami, and he's driving, he'll be back *tomorrow,* not today."

It feels like I *really* believe it now that my mom told me, I was skeptical before because they could've been talking about anything; it didn't necessarily mean what I thought.

"Sounds good to me," I responded, smiling, and then I dragged myself back to my room and went back to sleep; we were hosting the Eid party at our house this year, and it is gonna be *packed* in our house. I had to get up and help mama for that in a few hours, I drifted off to sleep, and I just woke up right now; all that happened at Fajr time, it's around 8 o'clock right now.

I drag myself off the bed and walk to the bathroom, where I wash my face with my strawberry-scented face wash, and brush my teeth with my coconut-flavored toothpaste.

It's a sunny morning I think to myself as birds chirp loudly outside, *Perfect for Eid weather.*

All the housework we finished yesterday, and the Afghani restaurant we ordered the food from refused to make and deliver the food today, so everything is sitting in our ultra-large fridge down in the basement, rotting and freezing to death. So all I have to do is warm it up, set it out on the table, wake up mom, and get ready; so that's what I do.

.....

By the time I've warmed up all the seems-like-one-million pounds of food, my legs are aching from walking the distance between the kitchen and the *massive* dining area, so I decide to just take the electric chair; I figure I have a good enough excuse.

But the electric chair is so loud, mom comes out and starts yelling while covering her ears to turn it down, and I yell back that I can't stop it since I already pressed the button. Once I finally reach the top of the ugly back stairs we had the chair installed on since mom insisted it looked far too ugly on our polished front stairs mom says under her breath "We should never had had that wretched chair installed, it makes a cartload of noise."

I laugh out loud and say"It's okay mom, don't get yourself all worked up, it's Eid."

"Your right," she says, laughing now too, "Let's go get ready, we have to be at the masjid for Eid prayers in a short while, we better hurry."

An hour and a half later, me and my mother present ourselves to each other, both of us looking gorgeous in our new abayas and dazzling makeup. She's wearing a sparkly green abaya with a white slip underneath embroidered with shiny gold string and fastened with a matching belt that has golden tassels hanging from it. To go with it, she chose a deep green hijab decorated with golden sparkles all over, and her makeup compliments her skin tone in such a way it make her face look like it is glowing.

I chose a plain, satin, light pink abaya that is all the same color. It's long, and flowy, and makes a *swish* sound when I spin, which is incredible fun in this. It's so soft, and also has a belt, which also has tassels hanging off of it, which are also the same color as my abaya. I chose a cream colored chiffon hijab that matches perfectly with my abaya. I did the best makeup that I can do, and if I do say so myself, It turned out pretty good.

"You look gorgeous," I say in awe. "You're like, shining.

"So do you-" she stops and glances down at her watch. "We're late!" she exclaims, and we haughtily run out to the Lexus, tripping over the ends of our dresses and giggling.

By the time we arrive at the masjid, the Eid prayer is about to start, so we quickly find spots where we can accommodate others, and surprise ourselves by finding Izdihar Auntie, Farah, and her two little daughters Noora and Najma; they're twins. She has two sons downstairs named Ayyub and Aqeel; also twins.

But mama and Izdihar Auntie don't get much time to chat, since the Imam calls out "Allahu Akbar," declaring the start of the prayer. Throughout prayer, I try my best to focus, but my mind keeps wandering, eventually I take care of that problem by ordering my brain to stay in one place by telling it that I only get to pray Eid *salah* once a year; that seems to do the trick.

.....

After prayer ends, we exchange 'Eid Mubaraks' and greet old aunties and say salam to anyone else we see that we know. We tease one another by telling them we got them amazing gifts and refusing to tell them, saying they'll get to see at the party.

Usually, the three days of Eid are the annual don't-hate-on-each-other days for me and Farah, and we have sleepovers, and play board games and hang out with our other girl cousins; in conclusion, we have tons of fun; but that's obviously not happening this year.

Our mass of cousins and family friends leave the masjid, the girls carpooling and cracking jokes, and the men stuck with the boomers in an old suv, while the girls take our lexus, somebody's tesla, another person's Rolls Royce, or Izdihar Auntie's Porsche; my favorite.

We arrive at the Annual Miami Eid Fair and get out of the cars. I warn my mom and run off to find my friends, I see Farah do the same. When I find my friends, I think about how it must take every ounce of Farah's willpower not to tell her buddies what happened last night, it doesn't for me though; I never tell unless it's something positive.

I have *so much fun* with my friends, we play games and eat cotton candy and just sit down and talk; it's awesome.

When we leave the Eid Fair 3 hours later, me and mama head back to our house, and change into Indian clothes for our party, my dress is light green and I leave my makeup on and do my hair up, and put on some jewelry, when I look in the mirror, I catwalk across the room, showing me myself.

Half an hour later, the guests arrive, and so do my friends and their families. I greet their mothers, and fathers, and sisters, but avoid their brothers. I'm not wearing my hijab.

Again, me and my friends have a blast, but are brought down to earth when my mother calls me to serve the sweets, I don't even like any of them.

I swerve through metal chairs in the women's side and say Eid Mubarak to all the people I didn't meet at the masjid. They all ask me how my studies are going and what juz I'm on, and I'm so happy that I don't even have to fake a smile; it comes naturally. I laugh and joke with all the adults, and when my favorite auntie of all time, Asma Auntie sees my straight, white teeth and says "You better be glad you don't have braces," to me, I burst into laughter, talking more about related and also non-related stuff, but when I reach the end of the line and am talking informally with another one of my many, many aunts, I see Farah sitting at a table, fake smiling and laughing with a group of women she hates because they spread rumors about her mom, I know she was speaking the truth yesterday and her friends ditched.

So when she stands up and is talking with the women while they are all on their feet, I put the empty plate down and I go up to her tap her shoulder, and when she turns around, startled, I take a deep breath, smile my biggest, most happiest smile and say, with the most joy in my heart, "Eid Mubarak."

The End

020d77bc-9f28-48ce-b43c-f55a4a9f589cR02